BLOOD BROTHER

Also by Frank Palmer

Testimony
Unfit to Plead
Bent Grasses

BLOOD BROTHER

Frank Palmer

St. Martin's Press ⚆ New York

Library of Congress Cataloging-in-Publication Data

Palmer, Frank
    Blood brother : an inspector / by Frank Palmer.
        p.   cm.
    " 'Jacko' Jackson mystery."
    ISBN 0-312-13435-5
    1. Jackson, Jacko (Fictitious character)—Fiction.   2. British—France—Paris—Fiction.   3. Police—England—Fiction.   4. Paris (France)—Fiction.   5. England—Fiction.   I. Title.
PR6066.A438B57   1995
823'.914—dc20
                                                    95-34244
                                                    CIP

First published in Great Britain by Constable & Company, Ltd

First U.S. Edition: December 1995

10   9   8   7   6   5   4   3   2   1

For Rebecca

1

The vision came to him on a flat, straight, deserted stretch. Always did.

The glint of cat's eyes, the swish of tyres. No longer a road, but a runway. The steering wheel felt smaller, a gap where the top third used to be.

Behind him passengers, faces tense, were strapped in their seats, eyes on the back of his head, willing him on and up.

Difficult – no, impossible – for him to know just how or when this recurring daydream entered his subconscious and stayed there.

Public men, men of power, don't analyse their fantasies too closely and never discuss them. Too many other, more important things to think and talk about. Looking up as a boy, maybe, seeing those Vulcans, delta-winged like massive moths; in formation, a formidable sight.

The vision always came to him when he was alone in his car, feeling good. Tonight he'd never been so high. He was on his way. Up. Soon he'd be helping to pilot his party to power. The people who depended on him, his people, had a safe pair of hands at the controls.

He glanced at the panel. Nearly ninety. Wouldn't do to be pulled for speeding. A man in a hurry, the headline might say, but he needed his name on the political pages, not in the court reports.

He slackened his foot and his speed, cruising at a steady seventy.

2

Even by his slow standard of driving, he was making poor progress on a road choked with caravans in tow and boats on trailers.

No hurry.

She – whoever she was – was dead. A shooting. That's all he'd been told.

Getting himself killed on an arrow-straight road with hidden hollows wasn't going to bring her back.

He drove in the way he worked – with caution.

The traffic whined to a halt at a country crossroads where white figures flitted behind a thickening hawthorn hedge in the season's first game of cricket.

He glanced at the mirror. A bespectacled left eye glanced back through blue-grey cigarette smoke. A healthy tan accentuated the creases spoking out around it.

He flicked buttons on his car radio until he found the local news. Nothing on the 5 p.m. headlines. He listened to the results from soccer's last league Saturday as the vehicles ahead stuttered forward.

On the outskirts of the town, he switched off as he stopped again at traffic lights. On green he drove carefully into a narrow street packed with laden shoppers.

Outside the police station, ancient and overadorned at the front, modern and plain at the back, he reversed into a line of parked vehicles that included a yellow British Telecom wagon.

He got out, hitched up his blue lightweight trousers and reached back inside to collect his thicker, darker blue jacket.

'About bloody time, Jacko.' The man who greeted him was

shortish, stoutish, smartish in a clean white shirt and navy-blue slacks, both newly pressed.

Detective Chief Superintendent Richard Scott had an urchin's face as an urchin would draw it – very round, dark dots for eyes and a triangle for a nose.

It was his lips Jacko always read first. Saucer-shaped meant happiness. A straight line indicated indecision. The reverse U meant trouble. They were spelling double trouble.

He was surrounded by high-flyers, including an assistant chief constable, all holding several conversations at once.

'Want me, sir?' Jacko only called his chief 'sir' when there were big bosses about.

'Soon,' said Scott, not looking at him. 'Just read in.'

Jacko nodded and walked on.

The atmosphere of a major incident room never failed to give him a charge. A high-tech beehive was being built before his eyes. Phones, wires running haphazardly from the ceiling, sat on trestle tables. Offices throughout the station had been ransacked for desks and filing cabinets, some still being carried in.

You never knew where you might end up on jobs like these, he told himself. Abroad? Nar, not with his luck. He'd never been sent abroad. But people you meet; interesting people. Unless, of course, it turned out to be a domestic. In which case he'd probably be home in time for a late supper.

In one corner half a dozen computers, their screens still blank, stood on a heavy table. In the opposite corner was a bigger table, surrounded by swivel chairs, all empty apart from one. In it, head down, reading, was a man in his early forties whose totally black suit gave him the melancholy air of a funeral director.

Jacko stopped alongside him. 'Hallo, Happy.' Everyone in the Major Crime Squad called their collator Happy, a name he accepted with mournful resignation. 'Wot we got?'

Without looking up, Happy nodded at his in-tray. Jacko hung his coat on the back of the next chair and picked up the top sheet as he sat down.

'Urgent. Immediate action,' he read. 'Attn: Chief Constable, ACC i/c AT3, DCS i/c CID:

'Female body was found at Southview Cottage, Far Lane, Hutton-on-Trent, soon after 3 p.m. this afternoon. Doctor called to the scene certifies death from a bullet wound to head.

Discovery made by cleaner who noticed uncollected milk. She informs beat officer PC Peacock at the scene that the victim was Penelope Browne, single, in her thirties. She runs an independent TV production company in Nottingham.'

Not exactly your average council estate pissed-up on a Friday night battering to death this, Jacko thought, interest mounting.

He reached the last line. 'Next of kin is Mr Russell Browne, MP for Trent Valley and newly appointed Minister at the Home Office (Police Affairs).'

His mouth dropped into a reverse U far deeper than his chief's. He was the squad's background specialist, the officer in charge of poking and prodding into private lives where the key to most murders is to be found. Exhuming skeletons from the vaults of a family whose head was the political boss of the entire British police service held no appeal, no future.

'Christ,' he groaned. 'Hope this isn't a domestic.'

'If so,' Happy said in a hushed tone, 'why's Silent here?' This was the nickname for Assistant Chief Constable Knight, in charge of AT3 (the Anti-Terrorist Task Team), a policeman so secretive he wouldn't tell a beat bobby the time.

'Does he suspect a terrorist attack?' Jacko asked quietly but urgently.

A shrug, non-committal.

'Has he got a lead?'

'Well . . .' Happy sighed unhappily. 'If he has, he wouldn't tell a couple of foot soldiers like us, would he?'

There's no such thing as love at first sight, Jacko was telling himself. Lust certainly. But that, for him, was usually accompanied by a well-filled sweater. More often than not it evaporated the moment he got to know her. If she had no sense of humour, if she was self-regarding or condescending, if she disliked simple things he held dear to his heart (like, say, dogs, detective novels, smoke-filled pubs, Bogart films, sad songs and rude jokes), he switched off immediately.

So why, in this idle moment, am I studying this complete stranger, he was asking himself, and thinking about love and lust? Her baggy striped sweatshirt seemed only half-full.

It was the tilt of her chin, he decided. She was surrounded by top brass, nothing under chief inspector. Yet she held it high, unafraid, and was making the occasional contribution to the debate. He liked people who didn't cow-tow to rank, wished he could be more like that himself.

She looked as though she had dressed to dance the hornpipe. Her blue and white sweater was pulled down over black tight slacks which rode at half-mast above small flat blue canvas shoes. Dark, glossy brown hair was held into a pony tail at the back by an elastic band, but several wisps hung loose over her ears and her forehead.

Scott nodded her in the direction of Happy's table. Her approach was so graceful that she appeared to be drifting on broad hips and strong shoulders – a swimmer's shoulders, Jacko guessed. Her chin remained high, very proud.

'Are you Detective Inspector Jackson?' She spoke in a southern accent, not quite cockney. Happy tossed his head sideways without looking up.

'That's me,' said Jacko, smiling cautiously.

'I'm WPC Floyd-Moore.'

'Hallo, Floyd.'

'Floyd-Moore. It's hyphenated. The Little Fat Man told me to report to you.' She flicked her head back in the direction of Scott.

Christ, he thought. A posh bird with a double-barrelled name as a sidekick. A WPC who openly calls a chief super by his nickname. He said nothing, sizing her up.

'What's our assignment?' she asked.

'Dunno yet.' He motioned her to the chair with his jacket hanging on the back of it. 'Background, usually.' He pointed to the tray. 'Have a read.'

. She put a black leather shoulder bag on the desk and felt inside for a packet of Bensons which she offered to Jacko, who took one. Her rummaging left a paperback with a plain cover and black and green lettering – Joseph Wambaugh's *The Black Marble* – poking out of the bag.

She sat, smoking, reading, missing nothing. 'Do they think it's the IRA?'

As if following a cue in stage direction, Silent Knight strutted out, his team of a dozen heavyweights following. He was a man in his late forties, Jacko's age, but the resemblance ended there.

11

Grey-suited, immaculately coiffured, he looked a commanding figure, fit and smart.

The crowd around Scott melted away. He walked towards them, mouth still down-turned.

Jacko knew now why his chief seemed so irritated. As head of CID, he'd lead the investigation but Knight, who outranked him, would take charge of the security end that came with any crime involving the family of a government minister. There'd be political infighting. It was not going to be a smooth job.

The phone rang as he reached them. Happy picked it up, listened, then handed it to Scott who said, 'Mmmmm' several times, then, 'Yes. Fine.' Finally: 'Certainly, if the pathologist says so. Seal the cottage when the Scenes team leave but post a guard.' Without a goodbye to the caller or a thank you to Happy, he handed the phone back.

He looked down at them. 'You two are with me on Russell Browne. Now we are moving his sister to the morgue we can get him to do the formal ID.' He walked away.

Jacko and WPC Floyd-Moore filled in time with idle chatter. 'What's it like, working for the Little Fat Man?' she asked.

'Terrific,' he answered, enthusiastically. 'He chases you but he'll never let you down.' And he shared with her the secret of Scott's meter-mouth, mimicking the three shapes to look for.

Her brown eyes lit with laughter. She had a wistful sort of beauty, her mouth inclined to turn downwards and stay that way, even when she smiled. Her eyes, not her lips, were her mood barometer, Jacko decided.

Another cigarette, Jacko's lob this time, and they talked about what they were doing when Control bleeped them away from a day off. 'Unloading the car after a fortnight pottering round Ireland,' he said.

'I was seeing a fella,' she said, brown eyes mischievous.

'Messing about in a boat, were you?' Her eyes registered incredulity. He nodded at her sweater and she laughed again.

When the buzz went round the incident room that the Minister for Police had arrived and was talking privately to Silent Knight and Scott, everyone feigned industry, apart from her. She gazed about her, studying the senior officers without a trace of awe.

Jacko did what he always did in the army when there was

12

brass about – walk round with a bit of paper in his hand, looking busy. When he returned, she still sat there, soaking it all up.

A cool one, he thought. He wished he could be like that, wished he didn't flap sometimes. She's got class. Maybe some of it will rub off on me. He began to wonder if she'd fancy a bit of rough like him.

Soon Scott reappeared. 'OK, you two.'

A uniformed constable opened the passenger door of a big blue Volvo. Russell Browne, Minister for Police, stepped out without acknowledgement. The man who had driven him stayed at the wheel, gripping it, looking straight ahead through the windscreen, not wanting to witness the pain of the scene.

Browne was two or three inches taller than the six-foot constable; much, much slimmer in his lime green slacks and sage-green lamb's-wool sweater. The news, Jacko supposed, had been broken in the middle of a game of golf. The sun had bronzed his severe, angular face and lightened his fair hair.

Scott, who had travelled from the police station in the Volvo, let himself out of the back.

Jacko and WPC Floyd-Moore walked swiftly from his once white, now filthy Montego to catch up. She was wearing a stylish grey check jacket over her sweater and clutched her shoulder bag to her chest.

He felt the evening breeze chasing away the warmth of the day. Or maybe it was just his imagination. He wondered, worried really, how many of the cars parked around the hospital contained Silent Knight's undercover men, all tooled up, ready for armed action.

He knew the constable was not among them. PC Peacock was fifty, florid and flabby from after-hours drinking and free game from local poachers, the perks of a village bobby. They'd been good pals in Jacko's days here, in this busy, agreeable market town of Newark-on-Trent, before promotion and transfer to the Major Crime Squad of the East Midlands Combined Constabulary. They winked at each other as Jacko walked by.

They went inside a flat-roofed building set apart from the town's hospital, a familiar fusion of old original and new extensions. A sergeant gave Browne a stiff salute, opened a door. 'This way, sir.'

It was a subduedly lit room with three tables. One was covered with a purple cloth. On it stood a small silver cross. The second had a vase of artificial flowers and a plastic bag containing something Jacko couldn't make out.

On the third she lay. Her small body was outlined beneath a pall which blended with the altar cloth. Her head was covered with a crepe bandage. She looked like a beauty salon client awaiting a facial. Only her face was visible, white as candle wax, eyes shut.

'Oh, my God,' Browne whispered. Then, hardly any louder, 'Yes, I'm afraid so.'

'Absolutely no doubts?' Scott spoke with equal softness.

'None, I regret.'

'Just look at this, please.' Scott led him to the table with the flowers. He picked up the plastic bag, untwisted the paper-covered wire and poured a ring into Browne's palm. It was the size of a pound coin. On a coral background was the face of a lady, as white as the one they had just viewed.

Browne squeezed his face and his hand in unison. 'It belonged to our mother.'

Scott picked it out of his palm, rebagged it and guided him out. At the Volvo, he said, 'Inspector Jackson here and his partner will take your statement tomorrow. Not tonight.' He paused. 'Unless you can think of anyone, anyone at all, we should be talking to tonight.'

Cleverly put, Jacko acknowledged. An invitation to tell them if he thought it was a domestic and who might have done it. All it drew was a long, slow headshake.

'At my home then,' said Browne to no one in particular. 'Ten would be a good time.'

She'd been moved into a white-tiled room, much brighter than the chapel, and now lay, looking even smaller, on a large stainless steel table which had been slotted on to four poles fixed to the tiled floor.

The pathologist, in green plastic smock and white calf-length

14

boots, was attaching a tube beneath the table to a rubber pipe which ran into the floor. Scott, Jacko and WPC Floyd-Moore put on white smocks. Her chin was down, eyes grave. She still looked far calmer than Jacko felt. His heart pounded wildly. His stomach was stirring up a rebellion.

The doctor stood, pulled on black surgical gloves, bent forward under a bank of stark lights hanging from the ceiling. 'There's no tape here, so who's taking the notes?'

Jacko fiddled for his book. Floyd-Moore crouched quickly, opened the black bag at her feet and took out a secretarial-style pad and an old-fashioned ink-pen. 'I'll do this, sir.'

'Right,' said the doctor, back to them, 'the time is . . .'

Scott checked and called out, '19.50.'

The doctor went on: 'The subject is a white female . . .' Floyd-Moore seemed to be able to write as fast as she'd read through the messages in the incident room.

'I'm cutting away a blouse, white, bloodstained, and handing it to the exhibits officer.' The video whirred. Jacko took the blouse and saw that the shoulders were covered in dark, dried blood. He put it into a transparent bag and wrote out a label. The rest of her clothing soon followed.

'I am now removing the bandages applied for cosmetic purposes during formal identification,' said the doctor.

Jacko saw the sight that her brother had been spared. A neat round hole, purple-edged, was two inches above her closed right eye. The blood had flowed down one side of her face into her wavy, mid-brown hair. The other half, high-cheekboned, very attractive, was untouched, so she looked a female Phantom of the Opera with no mask. Jacko groaned inwardly. The camera clicked.

Gently, the doctor turned over the body by raising her left shoulder. The back of her head seemed to have vanished. Jacko clamped his jaws, looked away.

In detailed medical phraseology the doctor described the wound, using tiny tweezers to tease away fragments of bone. Floyd-Moore's pen kept pace.

'My conclusion is a single shot from a hand gun. It was fired from above, probably as she sat. The point of entry indicates her head half-turned when the shot was discharged.'

For almost three hours, the pathologist chiselled, cut and

occasionally sawed and kept up his commentary. 'No bruising or fluids to indicate sexual assault ... a partly digested meal consumed some two to three hours before death and containing egg.'

All the time blood trickled away through rib-shaped channels in the stainless steel table and down the plughole.

It was no use Jacko telling himself it wasn't hurting her. It was harming him.

He thought of the Kerry mountains and lakes – anything to shut out these sights, smells and sounds – and it was working, really working. No middle-class WPC with a double-barrelled name is going to see this lad from the back streets bottle it, he kept telling himself.

Then the doctor spoke of 'the faint but distinctive smell of the early stages of decomposition'. He started to remove her fingernails; routine, really, to see if she had put up a fight and clawed away any of her attacker's skin.

Jacko felt his stomach balloon, about to burst. He breathed in heavily, tightening it. A hot spring shot upwards.

He walked through a reception room, his fast footsteps making a hollow, faraway echo. He pushed open a door marked 'Men', which slammed back on its spring. He shouldered open the cubicle door, which hit the dividing wall. He had moved so quickly that the bang sounded like the shot Penelope Browne heard in the last split second of her life.

Shivering, he was sick. Groaning, he was sick. Sweating, he was sick. 'Shouting for Hughie down the great white telephone,' the squad boys call it on wild nights out and they'd laugh. He wasn't laughing now.

He took off his smock, rinsed his face and seemed to wash away his holiday tan. He hung around in the reception room, feeling weary and weak.

The party joined him, Scott in deep conversation with the doctor, Floyd-Moore bringing up the rear, stowing her notebook in her bag which hung from her shoulder, extracting her cigarettes.

Her brown eyes appraised him anxiously but she said nothing patronizing, to make him feel foolish.

'Did I miss anything?' he asked, taking one, feeling foolish anyway.

'Well,' she said, slowly, 'the doc reckons any time between Thursday noon and Friday noon. Can't be more positive without further tests.'

She paused. Then, so softly he had to strain to hear, 'She had an abortion within the last twelve months.'

3

Bombs in Belfast. Bombs in Beirut. But the Browne bombshell had not yet hit local radio. He switched off the 9 a.m. news.

He recognized the little terraced house where he had dropped off Floyd-Moore in the dark eight hours earlier by an estate agent's sign screwed on a square pole flush to the deep red brickwork beside the street door. 'Sold – subject to contract,' it said.

He drew up, bang on time, and pipped. She opened the door and beckoned, making him feel like a chauffeur. He got out, annoyed, and took a few quick steps towards her.

'Come in while I slap on some make-up.' Her face was healthy, just slighty tanned, and didn't need any, but her hair was like a nest built by a drunken crow.

She left the door open. He followed her in and watched her run almost noiselessly up a set of uncarpeted stairs that led out of the lounge. She was wearing a sober dark suit with a pleated skirt that ended just above her knees. He got a breathtaking view of lovely legs.

The room was small with waxed floorboards. A grandfather clock, walnut, brass-faced, was the focal point and caught his eye long before the small TV. Next to the video machine was a neat pile of films. Among them: *Casablanca* and *The African Queen*. His annoyance evaporated.

The walls and ceilings were white with just a hint of lime. There were lots of books about. Two posh papers, already flipped through, were in a pile on one of a pair of chesterfields, two-seaters, low-backed with floral print. He caught sight of the kitchen, small, spotless, and a tidy garden through a back window and he guessed, with an inexplicable pang of disappointment, that there was a man-about-the-house.

17

On a small bureau stood two silver-framed photos. One was of a couple. The man wore studious horn-rims. He looked around Jacko's age. The other was of a dog, a black Labrador, in a garden. He picked it up and was holding it when she ran downstairs.

Her hair was in a neat bun now. Her only make-up was a trace of pale pink lipstick, as understated as the room which had been planned with unfussy attention to detail.

She nodded at the dog's photo. 'My best chum. Sometimes, when I'm home, if I see a black dustbin liner when I open the back door, I want to call his name. Even after all this time.' She looked very sad.

'What was his name?'

'Fred.'

His own father's name, very working-class, out of fashion. Just hearing it without a middle-class 'y' added stopped his heart for a second. 'Mine's a mongrel.'

'You do surprise me,' she said, absently.

Smiling, he put the photo down and she moved to the chair, gathering up her newspapers. He went out first. She slammed and tested the door behind them.

As she climbed into his car, she tossed the bundle of papers into the back where they fell apart, adding to the debris of his family's holiday – grains of sand, screwed-up paper bags, some still containing the crust from sandwiches, black and tan dog hairs, lollipop sticks, creased road maps.

'Nothing much in them,' she said. 'A few pars here and there. No name or anything.'

'Same on the radio.'

His seemed to be the only car on the move in Newark. Down a short side street he glimpsed the cobbled market square surrounded by beautifully restored medieval buildings; a serene, deserted scene. The ripe smell of yesterday's fruit seemed to hang in the air.

There was plenty of room to park at the police station. They walked into the incident room, as quiet as the streets outside, and up to Happy's desk. 'Where's everybody?' asked Jacko.

'The brass are preparing a press release.' Happy didn't look up from his reading. 'The Little Fat Man wants you to bounce that off Browne.' He flicked his head towards his in-tray.

It was a photocopy of a note which Scenes of Crime reported

18

finding among two days' unopened letters and newspapers on the doormat at Southview Cottage. It had been written in a small neat hand on blue paper and read:

'Hi Duck – Sorry to have missed you. Will call mid-June after storming Europe. Love, Gramps. PS Don't leave the gate open!'

Floyd-Moore read it over his shoulder. 'Could be a grandfather who popped round when she wasn't in.'

'Found the gun?' Jacko asked Happy.

'No, but Fingerprints have found a couple of foreigners. Records are checking them.' Happy finally looked up, his face funereal. 'And House to House have come up with a strange car in the village. No index number but a dark red plate.'

'Republic of Ireland?' Jacko had seen them all over the southern counties.

Happy gave him a neutral shrug and returned to his reading.

On a Sunday morning, even by Jacko's standards, it was less than a twenty-minute drive to Lincoln where Russell Browne lived, near enough to be regarded as local by his Tory supporters, far enough away to stop the great unwashed traipsing to his door with their endless gripes.

It was the city where Jacko had been born and served until his transfer to Newark after his first marriage broke up. He told Floyd-Moore this, as he drove, dawdling, Irish style.

She was twenty-eight, she said; twenty years younger than Jacko. She talked of her parents with deep fondness. Mum had taught her shorthand, she said. Floyd-Moore had been a journalist for a short spell. 'Couldn't stand the tit and bum.' Dad worked for a council on the south coast. She didn't say at what but, with a double-barrelled name, Jacko reasoned that he wasn't a dustman. She'd been a policewoman for six years, being shunted between departments. 'But not for much longer. I'm off next month.'

'Where?'

'Round the world. On my own. Been saving for years. Don't say, 'How courageous.' Everybody says that. It's something I just have to do.'

He felt a warm glow followed by a cold, sharp shaft of envy. She was about to achieve an ambition he'd never had the guts to go for. Just for a moment, he longed to go with her. Impossible, of course, he told himself. While she'd be youth hostelling, he'd be old folks homing.

He decided to be rather rude – to test her. 'I've always fancied that. I'd probably end up begging on the streets of Calcutta among the amputees. They cut off the least used bits of their anatomy to evoke sympathy, you know.' He put on a sad face. 'And, with my luck, you know what bit that would be.'

She threw her head back against the rest with joyful laughter. The warm glow returned. She'll do for me, he decided.

She'd answered the all-hands-on-deck bleep when the murder broke because, yes, she was messing about on a boat moored on the Trent with a date. 'God, he was boring.' She pulled a contemptuous face. 'I was glad of the excuse to ditch him.'

Every other field shone fluorescent yellow with oil seed rape, giving off a heavy, sickly smell. The harshness of its colouring was softened by drifts of bluebells in spinneys and blue Conservative posters on wooden stakes in hedgerows from the local government election three days earlier and the European Parliamentary campaign to come next month.

'Which way did you vote?' she asked in a teasing sort of voice.

'I was away.'

'Which way will you vote next month then?'

'Green,' lied Jacko, without any thought.

'Green?' A low chuckle, sexy. 'The owner of a car that looks like a travelling dustbin and hasn't been converted to lead-free fuel voting Green?'

He laughed. He liked women whose humour was without malice, who were independent, who expected to be treated as equals. 'When you travel with Jackson, you travel first-class. My workmates call me Jacko, by the way. And you?'

'Patricia,' she said, 'but my family calls me Tricia. My lovers seem to call me Trish.'

'Lovers?' Another sidelong look, shocked this time.

'Only one at a time. With long spaces in between, leading a very chaste and worthy life; all hanging baskets and night-school. None at the moment. I was shacking up but, well, we said goodbye. No point in involvements, is there? I'll be gone in five weeks.'

He allowed a smile to spread slowly over his face. 'Welcome to the squad, Tttt . . .' He let it hang there and they laughed again.

On a hilltop ahead stood the triple-towered Minster, not the best view of it, and it reminded him of the difficult interview to come, but he felt not the slightest trace of anxiety about it – not with her at his side.

Just beyond the city boundary he turned left and within half a mile left again at a white gate which had the name 'Beck Manor' on the top bar.

Two patrolmen inspected their warrant cards and let them in. From a plain car two more men in plain clothes, Silent Knight's officers, eyed them as their tyres cruched on a pea-gravel driveway which ran between tall bushes, most in yellow flower, until the house came in sight.

It was narrow at the front with windows that grew smaller with each of four floors until they were tiny in the attic. Five stone steps led to a white door with stone pots, packed with tired-out tulips, on each side.

Spot on ten, he parked his travelling dustbin behind the big blue Volvo. He turned on the radio and heard the opening few bars of 'The Lincolnshire Poacher' which announced the local news.

Boom. The bomb had dropped. 'Police have just named a woman found dead in the Trentside village of Hutton as Miss Penny Browne, thirty-three-year-old sister of Trent Valley MP Russell Browne. They have confirmed they are treating the case as murder. She was discovered with a head wound but the cause of death has not yet been disclosed. Frogmen are searching the nearby river for the murder weapon.

'Senior officers will not comment on the possibility of IRA links but it is known that the crack Anti-Terrorist Task Team has been called in. Mr Browne has just been appointed a minister at the Home Office with special responsibilities for the police service. Before that he was under-secretary for aviation and is strongly tipped for Cabinet rank soon. More details on his sister's murder are expected from a press conference later today.'

No time for a rerun of Belfast and Beirut. A woman opened the white door and stood at the top of the steps, waiting for them.

The cosy study had the smell of cigars which always reminded Jacko of Christmas.

He glanced at books on two walls. Nothing on the police. Not even Roger Graef's *Talking Blues* – a new and riveting read. Nothing much on aviation either, except, perhaps, for J.G. Ballard's *Empire of the Sun* about a schoolboy growing up in Jap-held China and his passion for planes, a book which Jacko had loved. Maybe he keeps his professional reading in Whitehall, he thought.

He turned. Tricia was looking out of a long window on to a garden with a large lawn, lime and sage green stripes neatly alternating.

They were still standing when a woman, full-bosomed and broad-hipped, a bit horsey, in a brown knitted dress, carried in a silver tray stacked with pots, cups and saucers.

Behind her came the towering figure of Russell Browne, casually dressed again, this time in a horizonally striped shirt, green, red and yellow, short-sleeved with a white collar; old rugger colours, Jacko assumed. 'Sit down, please.' His face was thin and grey.

Tricia sat at the corner of a leather-topped antique desk, window in front of her. She took her notebook and pen from her shoulder bag. Jacko sank into an easy chair. Browne sat behind the desk. On it was a neat pile of fat newspapers, a battered red dispatch box, closed, and a box-file, flip top open. He picked it up and placed it on a white blotting paper pad in front of him.

With some effort, he raised his eyelids, heavy from lack of sleep. Jacko accepted the unspoken invitation to speak. 'It's basic facts we're after at this stage. Biographical details, acquaintances . . .'

The horsey woman, Mrs Browne, Jacko presumed, handed round china coffee cups.

'No positive leads?' There was a hint of surprise in Browne's solemn voice.

'It's early days,' Jacko answered, evasively.

The white phone on the desk rang. Browne lifted the receiver.

He listened, irritation mounting. 'Sorry. No. It's a matter for . . . No . . . You must get in touch with them.' Firmer now. 'Sorry. I must go.'

He put the phone down and said to the woman perched on the arm of another easy chair, 'The *Daily Mirror*.' She put on a disgusted face.

Immediately the phone rang again and she rose swiftly, picked it up, glowered and said, 'Will you please, p-l-e-a-s-e, get in touch with the police at Newark.' She slammed it down violently.

Browne dug into the box-file. From a folder he extracted a birth certificate, the shortened version. He slid it across the desk. 'Take that. I have spares.'

Jacko studied the details. Name: Penelope Mary Browne. Sex: Girl. Date of Birth: 4 February 1956. Place of Birth: Zurich. Registration District: Lincoln.

Browne waited until Jacko looked up, then began to speak fast. 'Youngest of three children. Our father was Edward, a professional soldier, killed on active service in Cyprus in '55, so he never lived to see her, I'm afraid. Mother spent some time in Switzerland afterwards and she had Penelope there, as you see. Mother was Marjorie. She died in December. My elder sister Caroline, too. Same accident. A car crash on the A1.'

The phone rang to give Tricia's speedy hand a break. The woman rose. 'I'll take this.' She strode purposefully out of the study.

Browne, eyes shut, waited until the phone stopped ringing and began again. 'A very normal family.'

'Education and so on?'

'Boarding school, university at York with a degree in social and economic history. Then the BBC. Just under a year ago, she left to set up her own TV production company. Seemed a sound move. A quarter of all programmes on all channels are soon going out on commission to independent companies, you know.'

Jacko didn't.

'She floated about a bit with the Beeb, training and so on. Short spells here and there. A longer spell in Belfast. A few foreign trips on research. Her base then was London.'

'How long's she had Southview Cottage?'

23

'Three or four years. Originally, just for weekends from London. Convenient to Mother. They were very close.'

'And a flat in Nottingham?'

'New, that. To live above the shop, I expect.' Browne sensed a question coming. 'I don't know whether she planned to keep on both places. I didn't see all that much of her. There's almost ten years between us. With schools and careers . . .' He tailed off, shrugging very slightly.

'When did you last see her?'

'Last week. She's – was – doing a programme on the decline of trade union power under our administration.' He didn't look displeased about it. 'We did some filming. At Browne and Green's, the bottlers, you know.'

Jacko knew. Who from Lincoln didn't? Once they'd been one of the city's biggest employers, a firm with a troubled record of industrial relations. 'I was on the board until I became a minister.'

Tricia had caught up. 'What day was this?'

'Bank holiday Monday. In the afternoon. The filming went on for an hour. They'll probably use a couple of minutes.' A frigid smile, soon gone. 'If they go ahead with it now.'

Several times the phone rang and he stopped until it was silenced. Each time he started where he'd left off, train of thought intact.

Once or twice the woman put her head round the door to announce a name – a relative or a close friend, Jacko guessed – and these calls he took at his desk. 'Most kind . . . Thank you. We'll certainly let you know the arrangements.'

Each time he picked up the threads. 'She had no professional enemies she had talked about, no financial worries . . .'

The woman stood at the door again, agitated. 'The PM.' A startled Browne stood suddenly at his desk. 'I'll take it through there.' He'd walked half-way out of the room before adding, 'Excuse me.'

Ah, well, thought Jacko, lounging back, in his world PM stands for other things apart from post-mortem.

Soon Browne returned to his chair but the threads had snapped. Jacko prompted him. 'We were talking money matters, sir. You had to give up your interest in the family firm when you became a minister. Did she still have an interest?'

'No. No.' Hurried. 'Sold out some time ago.'

With stiff fingers, he fumbled to open the transparent wrapping of a small cigar. His hand shook as he lit it. Jacko watched him closely, unsure whether he was beginning to surrender to grief or whether the distasteful subject of money or the PM's phone call had unnerved him.

Tricia ended the short silence. 'Ever visited her cottage?'

'Only once before. To drop off some personal things after our mother and sister died.'

'Before?'

'Before bank holiday Monday.' That frigid smile again. 'Didn't I tell you? Sorry. *En route* to London I followed her to her place after we'd finished filming at the factory. We had a cup of tea. I stayed about half an hour.'

'What did you discuss?'

'Her programme.'

'Have you seen or spoken to her since Monday?'

'No.'

Jacko carefully framed his next question, with the pathologist's finding in mind. 'When you did see her, socially, I mean, did she have an escort?' A good safe word that, he'd decided, but before he could congratulate himself Browne's cold smile was back.

'Lovers, you mean. I'm sure she had some. She was very intelligent and attractive.'

'Anyone special?'

He looked down in thought. 'A financial correspondent in Fleet Street, I gather.' He gave his name. 'Married, I think. So you will be discreet.' He made it sound like an order.

'Any other hobbies?' Jacko wished he had not said 'other' but Browne didn't appear to notice.

'She was excellent at music. Played the oboe at school and university but not lately. She didn't want to make a career out of it.' A more's the pity shrug. 'She went into television instead. Her radicalizing university experience, I expect.' A rueful look, faintly disapproving.

Mention of her career brought Jacko round to a question he had kept to near the end. 'You said she did quite a long spell in Belfast. Was she subjected to any threats there?'

Browne leant back in his chair. 'Not that she mentioned.

25

One piece on Sinn Fein caused a bit of an uproar.' A pause, pondering. 'But no. I'm certain I would have been told. Special Branch would have turned up anything like that.'

'How about you? Have you been threatened, in view of your position?'

He dealt with it sharply. 'You'll have to take that up with your assistant chief constable, Mr Knight.'

'But you see our point. It's possible that . . .'

Browne cut him short. 'They were after me but got her. That is something you must take up with Mr Knight. I've already had a long conversation with him.' He nodded to the white phone.

Jacko tried again, mainly because he was irked at Knight muscling in. 'Let's double check some of it.'

'Speak to Mr Knight.' A definite order, slowly delivered.

Jacko was silenced.

Tricia stopped writing and slipped a copy of the note found on the doorstep from her book and handed to him. 'Does this mean anything to you?'

Browne put his elbow on the desk, forking two fingers which he pressed to a trimmed fair eyebrow as he read it. He shook his head.

'Let's think about it,' she said coolly. 'What about her grand-fathers?'

'Both long dead.'

'Any close friends who gave her the nickname of Duck?'

It was a local term of endearment, very plebeian, unlikely in this stately setting, thought Jacko moodily.

'I would doubt that, wouldn't you?' Browne gave her a corrosive look.

'Do you have a photo of her we might borrow? You see, it's normal to release one to the media.'

'I'm not sure I want that.'

'It's possible that locals who knew her by sight but not name might come forward with information on her movements before . . .' Tricia paused for a fraction of a second, then added rather lamely, 'Hand.'

Browne sat perfectly still and silent. Tricia talked fearlessly on. 'As a member of the media herself, I'm sure she'd understand.'

Browne still looked unconvinced so Tricia nodded at the phone. 'It will save you being pestered.'

He looked down into the box-file, stirring the papers inside with his fingers for several moments. 'This was taken about a year ago.' He pushed a photo across the desk.

Jacko picked it up and looked at a family group of four in colour in a leafy garden. His eyes went straight to Penelope Browne on the left. She was wearing a blue denim suit, the jacket unbuttoned, and a super smile. If she had been pregnant when the photo was taken it certainly didn't show. On the right stood Browne, whose smile and dark suit were much more formal. Between them were two women in summery dresses, taller and fairer than Penelope, who looked to be the runts of the litter, an afterthought, much younger than her sister, probably unplanned.

'It was taken at mother's place,' Browne was explaining.

Jacko's eyes settled on the oldest of the three women, the colonel's widow, a thin, handsome woman. Then his gaze shifted to Penny's sister Caroline, equally elegant and self-possessed. Within a few months both were to die together in a car crash and now Russell Browne was the sole survivor of this family group.

Jacko gave his head a slow, sad shake.

Browne nodded at the photo. 'You can crop Penelope but don't issue the rest of us.'

Jacko slipped the photo into an inside pocket along with the birth certificate.

'Now.' Browne pushed himself back in his chair towards the window, about to stand.

'One more thing,' said Jacko, spurred by Tricia's persistence. He wanted to match it, to shine for her. 'Your fingerprints.'

The minister's face sharpened.

'We've found two at the cottage we can't account for. You were there on Monday. Yours could explain one set. We'll need to eliminate them. Just press your fingers on the blotting paper.'

Browne did as he was told.

'We will, of course, destroy them at the end of the case, in accordance with Home Office policy.'

'Naturally,' said Browne, a touch sardonically.

*　*　*

27

A line of press cars, drivers talking into mobile phones, stretched each side of the white gates as they drove out.

'What do you think?' asked Jacko.

'I don't like him.' Tricia squeezed her chin. 'Look how composed he was apart from on the topic of the family firm's finances.'

So she'd spotted it, too, thought Jacko, impressed.

'See his sneer when he talked about her radicalizing experience at university. They were in different political camps.'

Hadn't noticed that, thought Jacko, guiltily.

Her brown eyes shone enthusiastically. 'You don't think we're on one of those Agatha Christie feuding families in country house cases, do you?'

Jacko groaned. He hated the bloody things. 'Hope not.'

4

'You did *what?*'

Alarmed eyes swivelled from screens and rested on Chief Superintendent Scott. The sight, the sound, the fury of a bollocking from the Little Fat Man was never to be missed, provided you weren't on the receiving end. They would tell I-was-there stories for days afterwards in the Old King's Arms, a real-ale pub close to the cobbled market square which the squad was using for its local. Even the Happy Reader looked up.

Scott was wearing his saucer smile. Disappointed eyes went back to their screens.

He sat, leaning back, hands clasped across his ample midriff. His shoulders stopped shaking as his laughter subsided. Jacko stood above him, beaming. In Tricia's hand was a folder which contained the fingerprints of the Minister of Police.

'You've got to be the first two dicks ever to do that,' Scott said, in genuine admiration.

Tricia departed, to decant her notebook.

'Lovely legs,' said Scott, watching her go. Jacko had detected that already but took another look.

Lovely altogether, he acknowledged privately.

He had easy-going, sometimes flirtatious, working relationships with several women. But this time this woman was different. She was so, so placid, assured but never arrogant. If her class wasn't rubbing off on him, her calmness was. He'd never felt such confidence, so relaxed in a colleague's company.

On the way back from Russell Browne's she'd rifled uninvited through his tapes and put on Sinatra singing 'I've got you under my skin'.

Eyes happy, she'd conducted Nelson Riddle's orchestra through the slow build-up to the rousing central passage with her left hand, which she often used when talking.

He'd told her a story he'd picked up on his holiday. This big-time American record producer was touring Ireland, see, looking for new material – sad songs, mainly, about partings and poverty which they do so well because they know so much about both.

Miles from anywhere, he'd stopped at a pub where a toothless old man in welly-bobs put down his pint of porter and sat at a battered upright piano. He began to play a tune so beautiful that it brought tears to everyone's eyes.

'Excuse me,' he said, wiping them away, 'but who wrote that?'

''Twas all my own work,' said the pianist proudly.

'Tell me, does it have words?'

'Indeed yes.'

'What's it called?'

'I have entitled it after the opening line.'

'Sing it to me, please.'

'I love you so much,' he sang to his own accompaniment, 'that I could shit meself.'

Her laughter seemed to last more than a mile.

That lunchtime they'd dropped into the Old King's Arms for a drink and a bite to eat. She'd studied the snacks menu. 'Cobs?' she'd queried. 'Do they mean rolls?' And she'd put on a superior voice and expression, having gentle fun, and he found himself thinking: Of all the real-ale joints in all the towns in all the world, she walks into mine.

He told Scott of Penny Browne's married lover on Fleet Street, passing on the warning to proceed with caution.

His chief updated him. 'A shopkeeper reports Penny bought groceries including eggs on Thursday afternoon. That's the last sighting so far. No break-in but her briefcase had been turned out. We need to find out what, if anything, is missing.' His mouth was registering neutral, his undecided mode.

Soon green letters dancing on a computer screen's black background sent it saucer-shaped again. They stood round Happy reading them. The staff at the fingerprint bureau had identified a thumb print taken from a used coffee mug in a dishwasher at Southview Cottage. 'Subject: Richard John Richardson. Born 1.8.58. 67 Green Street, Lincoln. Convicted by local magistrates of a public order offence on 10.3.79.'

Jacko addressed the back of Happy's head. 'Who's in charge of Scenes?'

His head flicked sideways to a man with a mop of red hair, a sergeant whose workmates reckoned he could smell out clues with his bulbous nose. He'd once reached into a vat of pigswill and fished out a gun which had dispatched the smallholder. They called him the Ginger Pig.

On the desk in front of him were the fruits of his scavenging at the cottage. Jacko strolled up. 'Did you find a contacts book, Ginger?'

'Yeah.' A grunt as he handed over a book with a black plastic cover and the letters of the alphabet running vertically down the right-hand side.

Jacko thumbed it open at R. Near the bottom of the page was Rich with a six-figure number and the code for Lincoln.

He borrowed his phone, dialled 100 and asked for the Lincoln operator. Then he noted down: Union of Bottlemaking Allied Trades and an address in the main street.

'Could be a contact,' said Scott when he reported to him.

'Could be a lover,' said Tricia, perkily.

'Nice and easy does it,' said Scott. 'We've already had the Home Secretary on to the chief constable asking if we have all the logistical support we need. It's Whitehall's way of saying "Get your finger out." We don't want Transport House on, too.'

The travelling dustbin came to a stop outside premises in downtown Lincoln.

It had been a corner cobbler's shop in Jacko's days on the beat here twenty years ago. Now the signboard was telling him it was the Bottlemakers' Union's district office. Posters in the windows were demanding, 'Reinstate the 38.' Above the door with a sign that said 'Office Closed' was a rusting burglar alarm.

Next stop was Green Street, half a dozen terraced streets away. Cars were parked nose to tail on a single yellow line, some getting their Sunday shampoo. They found a place just before the street rose over a river bridge with the Browne and Green bottling factory beyond.

They walked back to No. 67 which had a brown bay window. The front door opened into a cool, tiled passage. Half-way down Jacko knocked at a side door.

The man who opened it was too old, too tubby, to be their quarry. 'We're looking for Mr Richardson,' Jacko told him.

'You've found him.' A tired tone.

'From the BATS office?'

'Ah, that's my lad these days. Who wants him?'

'Police.' They showed their warrant cards which identified them as officers of the East Midlands Combined Constabulary.

His eyes were bleary and his creased face suggested he had been awoken from a nap. The word 'police' seemed to throw cold water over it. 'What do you want?'

'It's just a security thing.'

The face looked as though it had been hit by iced water, wide-awake, unwelcoming. 'Security?'

'Crime prevention, really. The alarm's on the blink,' Jacko lied, hurriedly.

Mr Richardson senior gave his son's address, shut the side door on them.

They drove over the bridge and turned left at the factory. A long platform ran the whole of its length at ground level. Above that, the deep red brick building rose up like a Victorian warehouse. Written in large white capitals on the top floor above a line of small windows and below the purple slate roof were the words: BROWNE AND GREEN BOTTLES.

Tricia looked up. 'If they'd taken on Mr White as a partner they could have grabbed all the franchises for bottle banks.'

Within a few minutes they were outside a bungalow on an

estate in the southern outskirts of the city, only a walk away from Russell Browne's manor house.

The grass on the small square front lawn, encouraged by the warm weather, cried out for a cut. Unpruned roses stood in a bed clogged by weeds. In the driveway was a grey Cavalier, its hood up. He's in, thought Jacko.

A thin, harassed-looking woman opened the door. She had a baby cradled in her arms and a girl, about three years old, half hiding behind her pink skirt. They asked to speak to Mr Richardson.

'Away all day.' She seemed set to cry.

'It's only the office alarm,' Jacko repeated, anxious not to frighten her. 'Will he be late?'

'Quite late. Union meeting in London.'

Tricia reached forward and gently touched the baby's nose with the tip of her little finger. It didn't stir. 'He's good.'

'She. Not normally. I hardly get a minute's peace.'

'Let your husband take his turn, then. I would.'

'He's never here.' She had dark, close-cropped hair and no make-up on a face that, Jacko judged, had seen happier times. Her very pale blue eyes had a vacant, distant look.

Tricia turned her attention to the car. 'Trouble?'

'He couldn't get it to start this morning. Had to beg a lift in his branch chairman's old banger.'

Jacko walked unhurriedly towards it and stood staring into the exposed engine.

Mrs Richardson followed, toddler girl still behind her. 'It had a full service on Thursday. It was all right when I ran round to the dry cleaner's yesterday.'

'Can't you call out the garage?'

'Burton's aren't open on a Sunday.'

Jacko could tell that she was happy to talk, keen on adult company on what must have been a long, lonely Sunday. 'Maybe it's just flooded. Shall I give it a turn?' She nodded consent.

He opened the door and got in, not really knowing what to do, a mechanical illiterate. The key was in the ignition. Documents and books were scattered on the back seat. Union headed notepaper peeked out of a torn wrapper. Columns of figures showed through a plastic folder which had fallen on the floor. A travelling dustbin, like mine, Jacko thought. An on-the-road man's vehicle.

The petrol gauge registered three-quarters full when he turned the key once. He looked at the mileometer: 18120. He started humming dum-dum-dum-dar-dee-dum. He turned the key again. Nothing.

He got out, still humming, and stood looking into the engine, baffled. Tricia moved alongside. She leant forward and fitted a black coil to a brass slot. 'Try now,' she said.

Jacko got back into the driver's seat. It started first go. He let it run while Tricia, smiling a superior smile, lowered the bonnet. He switched off.

Driving away, Tricia said, 'The Lucar connection was loose.' Jacko had never heard of it. 'Just a case of connecting male to female.' A saucy laugh.

'Where did you learn that?'

'Did a spell on Traffic.' Pause. 'She's on drugs – Valium, I bet.'

'Let me guess. You did a spell on Drugs, too.'

She ignored him. 'Not surprising, really. Home all day with two screaming kids. And he's never there.'

Jacko felt a guilty impulse to go home and was delighted but surprised when he spoke to the Little Fat Man on an office-issued portable phone attached to the cigarette lighter on the dashboard.

'Checking in on the BAT phone,' he said, breezily, and he quickly briefed him.

'See him in the morning,' said Scott.

'Sure?'

'Why not stay over?' Scott sounded ebullient. 'Book into a hotel and give one to that chic sidekick of yours.'

Jacko switched the phone from left to right ear, hoping that Tricia hadn't heard. 'I'm so knackered I'd need a nap first.'

'So long as you don't sleep on the job.' Scott hung up. Jacko clipped back his receiver.

'What did he say?' asked Tricia, brown eyes mischievous.

'It's what he didn't say that's interesting. He's full of himself.' Jacko had seen this mood before. 'I reckon he's had a breakthrough.'

'Didn't he tell you what?'

'He will when he's ready. One thing's for sure, though. It can't be at this end of the inquiry or he would have had us sitting on that doorstep all night.'

He dropped her off at her home. 'A quick coffee?' she asked.

Suddenly, shocking himself, he thought of Lucar connections. Well, not so much connecting as hugging and holding, but you never know where these things might lead, he cautioned himself. Nowhere most probably, he added with realism that calmed him. 'I ought to be getting home.'

'Yes.' She wore a distant expression he couldn't fathom. 'You have that look about you.'

5

A different vision tonight. Entirely new. No escapist daydream. A frightening nightmare.

He was at the controls again, wrestling with them, fingers gripping them, sweating all over.

Behind him, his family. Their faces pleaded. Their hands reached out towards him in terror; abject terror.

'Do something,' they begged. 'We're crashing.'

He seemed to be flying dangerously low through a narrow lane of trees, the moon glinting on a river to his left, street lights ahead, getting closer.

'I'm trying.'

He sobbed it out loud, alone in his speeding car.

6

Sorry, said a middle-aged receptionist at the BATS office next morning, Mr Richardson wasn't available or contactable. 'He's phoned to say he has some urgent business. I expect him back mid-afternoon.'

'Just poke around,' said Scott, with a dirty laugh, when Jacko check-called.

He drove up the High Street. The majestic Minster on its hilltop seemed to follow their progress, its three huge towers changing from grey to pink as the sun came out, a great Gothic grannie watching over her family. Tricia kept looking up at it and missed the drabness of the terraced streets leading down to waterside factories.

They parked by a big marina, once an inland port, on which white cabin cruisers and swans bobbed in time to her graceful walk.

Inside the modern *Echo* offices, all deep red brickwork and tinted windows, he said, 'We're on the Browne case and need a bit of family and business background. Routine, really.'

In a second-floor alcove, shielded from the newsroom by tall cabinets, they glanced at Monday's dailies. It was front-page in them all. POLICE MINISTER'S SISTER MURDERED, said the most sedate headline. TORY GIRL SHOT IN LOVE NEST, screamed a tabloid over a photo of Southview Cottage with a policeman standing guard. All carried Penny's picture cropped from the family group. All had different photos of her big brother Russell taken from their files. He had spoken to none of them. Instead a two-line statement via his solicitor recorded 'the family's deep shock'. Assistant Chief Constable Knight, not Scott, had handled the press conference. He hadn't ruled out a terrorist connection, he'd said, but made no mention of the car with red number plates.

'That's odd,' mused Tricia

'Unless he already knows who he's looking for,' Jacko ventured. That and Scott's easygoing manner, couldn't care less about what he was up to, convinced him he was on a duff end of the inquiry. 'Still, we'll go through the motions.'

For four hours they studied microfilms, bound back issues and thick cuttings files in brown envelopes, exchanging thoughts and ideas and cigarettes as they read.

In its first eighty years, Browne and Green Ltd had been a paternalistic sort of company, undemanding to work for. Trouble only came in the seventies with the appointment, at the age of thirty, of Russell Browne as managing director.

A new broom, he swept away old-fashioned practices and introduced new bottle-making technology which the union saw as a threat to jobs.

They staged an all-out strike to the backdrop of the Winter of Discontent, that season of disruption a decade earlier which Jacko sometimes credited (and at other times blamed, depending on his mood) for killing off the last Labour government.

The strike was led by Dick Richardson, their quarry's father. In those days, he was the BATS' district chairman and the factory convener, the big man in a big closed shop. His had been the most powerful voice on the union's national executive and at the annual conference where policy was decided by the number of card votes the delegate held – and Dick Richardson always held the most.

'Stacks of bellicose quotes from him,' said a disapproving Tricia, flicking through the cuttings.

'A creature of the seventies,' said Jacko dismissively.

To him it was a decade when trade union leaders, elected by the ten per cent of activists in an otherwise apathetic membership, used to drop in at No. 10 for beer and sandwiches and thought they, not politicians elected on eighty per cent of the votes of the entire population, ran the country. Like some showbiz and sports stars, they had made the fatal mistake of believing in their own invincibility. They'd even made the pop charts for a while and Jacko sang Tricia a snatch:

'*Oh, you won't get me, I'm part of the union.*'

She looked up, face pained. 'What's that?'

'The Strawbs song. Seventies.'

She smiled thinly. 'Where are they now, I ask myself?'

'Still around. More than you can say for the TUC.'

Her head went down, shaking, but she was smiling broadly.

The dispute ended in chaos, half the workers breaking ranks. The other half went back weeks later, hungry, tired and whipped. In the sweeping redundancies that followed, Richardson was among the first to get his P45.

In the Thatcherite eighties, like so many trade union figures, he had all but vanished from the public prints. There was just one short reference to him taking over as Labour Party agent in Riverside ward, an unpaid job, very part-time.

With a slimmed-down payroll and new tech, Browne and Green ploughed profits into expansion. Among its acquisitions was Lindum Crystal, a high-class cut-glass manufacturer.

Over the last few years profits had dipped. More redundancies followed and there'd been rumblings at shareholders' meetings of missed opportunities. No longer able to blame their poor performance on inflationary wage demands from the union, a toothless staff association these days, its directors moaned about high interest rates.

To add to the parent company's woes, its subsidiary Lindum Crystal was in the middle of a current dispute. Thirty-eight glass blowers had answered the union's call to strike in support of a national pay claim. All were sacked and they'd been photographed picketing the works with 'Reinstate the 38' posters like the one they'd seen in the union office window.

In Russell Browne's file, there were cuttings by the column foot to sum up his philosophy: 'Our policy is that of modern missionary management; theirs is a throwback to the Luddites of the lunatic left.'

Tricia sighed theatrically. 'No wonder Downing Street promoted him. I'll bet this sod disbands the Police Federation. I don't like the sounds of him at all.'

'Oh, come on. Browne and old man Richardson are just mirror images of each other. Both as bad as each other.' Between them and the likes of them, he'd convinced himself, the politics of consensus, his sort of politics, had been squeezed and strangled.

'Look at this,' said Tricia soon afterwards.

Jacko found himself looking at a black and white photograph of Browne, a fair, slim woman, not at all horsy, and two teenagers, both girls. Mr Browne and family, said the caption.

'I thought the woman who served us coffee yesterday morning was his wife.'

'Why?' asked Jacko, not admitting he'd made the same mistake.

'Well.' A shrug. 'It was just, well, the way she watched over him, took control sort of thing.'

'Maybe she's some kind of PA.'

'Or his lover.'

Jacko shook his head. 'Secretary.'

'Can't people who work together be lovers?' she said with a vague kind of look he took to be provocative.

Mind wandering, brain wondering, deeply distracted, he turned to the file of Penny Browne. Just a thin one. The media, he'd noted, don't like reporting on their own. To do so, they claim, is house magazine-ish, incestuous, but really it's because dog doesn't eat dog. Journalists gleefully expose other people's misconduct while lots of them live out the last days of Sodom and Gomorrah; the lucky sods. He wouldn't mind a piece of it himself.

Still disturbed, he had to concentrate on the main clipping about a row over the piece from Belfast on Sinn Fein her brother had mentioned. They had accused her of misrepresenting them. Right-wing MPs had accused her of acting as their mouthpiece. It was hard to work out who was the more angry – which meant, Jacko hazarded, she'd probably got it about right. In any case, security was down to Silent Knight and his AT3 tossers. He chucked it to one side.

The cuttings on Richard John Richardson, son of Dick, known as Rich to avoid confusion, dated back to his early teens when he won the top trophy at the local speech and drama festival three years running.

'Rum, that,' said Tricia. 'Elocution lessons have to be paid for. Fancy a socialist like Dick spending hard-earned cash on private tuition for his son. The old humbug.'

Jacko wasn't sure about that and explained why. His own father, for all his socialist principles, had worked overtime to

38

pay for his sister to go to ballet school when she muffed a free scholarship. 'Ballet? I ask you. She couldn't even clog dance.'

Tricia laughed.

Rich gained a double polytechnic degree in law and industrial relations. In '79, he'd taken a day off his studies to support his father at a mass demo outside Browne and Green at the height of the big strike and got himself arrested and fined for abusing strike breakers going through the picket lines in language he couldn't have learned at his elocution lessons.

He'd married young and followed his father into the union as a full-time official. Now he had a far fatter file of news clips than his old man. If Dick was a union baron of the right, young Rich was new left, a pacifist almost, against the Falklands, for pulling the troops out of Ireland, a vocal campaigner for the release of the Guildford Four and the Birmingham Six.

He had fought the general election two years earlier in a no-hope Tory seat and done badly. With nothing to lose he had campaigned on some controversial issues.

Since then, his extremism had been toned down as a wave of realism swept through his party, seeking to present themselves as electable again. These days he stuck to safe, sensible topics like government spending on the health and education services.

It was easy to see why.

Rich Richardson had recently been selected as a Labour candidate to fight the next general election.

'Guess where?' Jacko asked Tricia.

'Trent Valley?' She guessed right.

The marginal constituency where the sitting Tory was Russell Browne.

'He looks bloody ugly to me,' said Tricia.

'Sshh,' sshhed Jacko. 'You aren't supposed to swear in a cathedral.'

They were standing, necks craned, looking up at the Lincoln Imp, a small half-human, half-animal figure carved near the top of a tall column. Viewed from this position, the legs came first, right crossing left and held vertical. 'He looks as though he's dying for a pee.'

39

'Sshh, for christsake, woman.' Jacko was fussily conscious of reverential groups of tourists about them.

They had phoned the BATS office before they left the old pub where they had lunched. 'Not in still,' said the receptionist. To kill time, he was taking her on the grand tour of the uphill city.

He had whizzed her round the Norman castle with its ivy-covered courthouse. He pointed out where a year earlier he had come under fire as he and his team foiled a jailbreak, trying to sound casual, man of the world about it. She appeared totally unimpressed until he finally admitted, 'I was shit scared.' Her brown eyes softened.

Now they were doing the Minster. 'His face looks like a young devil's,' said Tricia, still gawping up at the figure on the stone column.

'In a way, he was. He played pranks on the builders so they slapped cement on him and left him stuck up there.' Doubt clouded his face. 'Or something like that.'

Tricia lowered her chin and smiled at him. His face saddened. 'Time to do a bit.'

Their footsteps echoed through the ice-cold nave. A slow easy walk down a cobbled steep hill was often interrupted to browse in book and gift shop windows.

As a medieval archway with a big clock loomed into view, Jacko said, 'We had a north-south divide here long before the Tories came to power, you know. All olde-worldy and money uphill. All factories and terraced streets downhill.'

'What were you?'

'A downhill boy.' A firm reply, no doubts.

They used the portable phone but Richardson was still out and Jacko grew restive. 'How will it look to the Home Office if he is our man and he's done a runner?'

'Perhaps they'll find him on some sun-kissed faraway island and send us to collect him. How would you fancy that, Jacko?'

Don't even think about it, he ordered himself. His reply was a weak smile.

They drove to the Richardson bungalow: deserted, windows shut, car gone. He phoned the BATS office again and relief flowed through his face when he was told to hold. 'Rich Richardson,' a local voice finally said.

Jacko introduced himself, said he was sorry to bother him but gathered he knew Penny Browne. 'Professionally,' he answered, guardedly. They fixed a meeting for six.

Jacko reported to Scott who listened without much interest.

'At least', Tricia sighed when the phone conversation ended, 'he knows we haven't been sleeping on the job.'

Richardson opened a drawer and placed a small, silver tape-recorder on the desk between them. He replaced the cassette and pressed Record and Play. Beneath its glass cover the spool stirred into life. 'You don't object?'

'No.' Jacko shrugged, easygoing.

'May I see your warrant cards?'

Jacko had only ever been asked for his card by barrack-room lawyer dealers on drugs inquiries in inner cities. He fished it from an inside pocket. Tricia delved in her bag and produced hers, along with notebook and pen. 'Mind if I take a note?'

Richardson gave a terse nod. He wore a soiled cream shirt, no tie. The creased jacket of a biscuit-brown suit hung over the back of his chair. His face was pale and lined and had that intense, nervy look that Jacko associated with busybodies like welfare workers who'd taken on more than they could cope with.

He was Jacko's size, three inches taller and two stones lighter than his father, but he looked just as washed-out as when they'd disturbed the old man's nap.

They sat across a desk littered with files, clips, bands and pens. That day's papers were in a bundle, folded, unread. Around them, books leant unevenly on shelves. A noticeboard was packed to overflowing with pinned posters and typed lists. Boxes on the elderly blue carpet spewed out documents. The waste-paper bin was empty. A word processor stood on a separate table, screen blank. Little work had been done in that office that day.

Tricia cleared room on the desk for her book. Unscrewing her pen, she asked, very friendly, 'How's your wife?'

He hesitated, frowning. 'Why do you ask?'

'She seemed a bit off colour last night, that's all.'

Rich looked rebukingly at Jacko. 'Not surprised. Not much fun having the law on your doorstep. That business you gave

41

her and my father about the burglar alarm was total crap. It hasn't worked for months.'

Jacko spoke just as sharply. 'What would you have us say? We want to interview your husband about a murder?'

A stand-off. They glared at each other.

Jacko got down to business. 'You said on the phone you knew her professionally. When did you last see her?'

He looked through his papers, retrieved a blue desk diary, opened it. 'Last Tuesday.'

'How did you get to know her?'

Tricia started to write.

Rich gave his statement in a flat local accent that had lost all the polish of prize-winning elocution – deliberately so, Jacko guessed. He told it fluently, the practised public speaker.

At the last general election he'd been Labour candidate in a rural Tory seat, a hopeless quest, but necessary experience. The only island of red in a sea of blue was a pit village where he set up his headquarters in the miners' welfare.

The yellow Liberal battle bus came to the village on David Steele's nationwide tour. Off the bus and into his life stepped Penelope Browne, then a political researcher for the BBC.

When the bus left, she stayed to jack up an item on how the split among miners after their strike three years earlier was affecting the Labour vote in the coalfields. 'We had a drink together when she'd got my interview in the can.'

The previous Easter, thirteen months earlier, he was at the national conference of his union. In a seaside hotel, he spotted Penelope. (Not once did he refer to her as Penny.) More drinks and this time they made the connection that both came from Lincoln. She revealed she was the sister of Russell Browne. He told her of his arrest in his student days for a picketing offence outside her family's works. Water under the bridge, both agreed. They finished up having a pleasant evening meal together.

He didn't hear from her again until autumn. She phoned out of the blue. She had her own production company now. She was working on an idea for a Channel Four programme on how the union movement was coping under Mrs Thatcher, her laws restricting them, their failure to recruit among the young.

'She wanted to home in on just one union and one strike from the Winter of Discontent.'

Rich was cautious. After all, it had been a defeat and it was an open secret that membership of the BATS branch had been more than halved in a decade. On the other hand it would give him exposure to balance the vast publicity his rival Browne was getting in his new government post. He promised co-operation. Finally he'd reached the events of the week of Penny Browne's death.

'She was here on the Monday, a week ago today, filming our May Day rally in support of the sacked thirty-eight at Lindum Crystal. A good up-to-date peg. Lindum and Browne and Green's have the same holding company. It was almost '79 revisited. She told me that she was also filming her brother at the factory that afternoon.' A sly smile. 'I take it you're also pestering him?'

Jacko merely nodded.

'Next day, the Tuesday, her crew took a few shots of me walking round Grantham. You know, the union man who's taking on Thatcher in her own backyard-sort-of-thing. When we wrapped up, she invited me back to her cottage up the A1 to discuss the script.'

He flopped lazily but threateningly across the desk, getting as close to Jacko as he could. 'When I left she was alive and very well.'

Tricia broke in. 'Did you have a drink?'

'Coffee.' A thought hit him. 'Why?'

Jacko knew that all trade union leaders suffer paranoid delusions that their phones are tapped. He decided on an explanation. 'Your prints were on a cup in the dishwasher.'

A vicious look. 'A piddling picketing offence ten years ago and I'm still on your records?'

Jacko, rebuffed and unhappy, curtly asked him to run through the rest of his week.

He looked back at his diary and said at dictation speed which Tricia took down with ease, 'Wednesday, industrial tribunal; Thursday, day off to help Dad in the local elections; Friday, admin day here; Saturday, picket at Lindum Crystal, Sunday . . .'

'We know about Sunday,' Jacko interrupted, all pretence at

civility gone. 'We have to check these movements, specially Thursday and Friday. We'll need to see your wife and father.'

'She's away for a few days.' He looked at Tricia. 'You're right. She's had it a bit rough. The doctor suspects post-natal depression.' He wrote down her sister's address not far from Newark. 'Go easy.'

Jacko had saved the trickiest question till last. 'You said you knew her professionally. Was it at any time closer than that?'

Rich shot forward again. 'Now, look here. It was never between the sheets, if that's what you mean. Got that?' He glared at Tricia.

Tricia had.

They drove back in silence for a mile or two. Then Tricia suddenly said, 'Do you think we've found her lover?'

Astonishing that, thought Jacko. At that precise moment he'd been asking himself the same question. OK, it was an unlikely relationship – the old boss's granddaughter and the shop steward's son. But Penny Browne had clearly moved much further to the political left than her brother. And look at the way he had those TV phrases off pat – jack-up, wrap-up, up-to-date peg, in the can, home in. He'd spent a lot of time in her company. Maybe they'd fizzed for each other over dinner at that seaside conference and he'd started thinking of her as Penny, instead of Penelope.

'Yes,' he said.

7

At the bridge, Jacko stopped. Phew, it was muggy for May.

He spread his elbows on the top ledge of a pebble-dash wall. At their knees, his check trousers brushed a weathered metal plaque: 'Opened by Col. Henry Browne, RHA, DSO, 1899.'

Below him the khaki waters of the river flowed past a thick clump of weeds where a family of swans rested.

His right elbow pointed to Browne and Green's works. In

44

such a factory he had spent two years after grammar school in a mundane admin job until three years in Paris in the army rescued him.

His left elbow pointed to Green Street. In such a street he'd been born. It was badly named, he reflected, gazing down it.

On each side, matt red houses with low concrete-topped walls in front of them ran in straight lines. From this view they looked like railway tracks stretching away into the distance across High Street to the floodlights of Sincil Bank where his beloved Lincoln City played.

As the plaque said, the bridge and the street had been built just before the turn of the century. On the west bank, the factory. On the east bank, the houses for its workers.

He looked to his right, down to the factory and, Christ, he thought, it had been so different on that cold day. He still found it hard to believe. Men he'd grown up with, men he'd gone to school with, hurling themselves at police lines, fighting, screaming in the snow. And spitting. Above all, spitting. At him. Ten years on and he could feel the revulsion that sickened him when he took off his uniform coat and saw the spittle sliding down the back.

In the general election that followed soon afterwards he didn't vote Labour. For the first time he rejected the party of his father. No party, he decided, funded by trade unionists who acted worse than soccer hooligans could be trusted to run a country. And since he could never vote Conservative he didn't vote at all, hadn't since and didn't intend to, not even Green.

Now he was going to see the man who'd organized those pickets that had turned him into an apolitical animal. And why? To seek his co-operation in trying to find out if his son had murdered his lover, the boss's sister. Funny old job, he mused. Interesting, though.

He looked down the river to where the outdoor swimming baths used to be, where he'd tried and failed to learn to swim. And to the banks beyond where he'd tried and failed in his first sexual encounter.

He'd been set up, no doubt about it. 'The biggest pair of knockers you'll ever see,' said his great schoolmate. 'She's crazy about you. Wants to meet you.'

She was there all right. A body thinner than Olive Oyl's.

45

'Don't mind a bit of petting,' she decreed, businesslike. Like two beans on a bread board, they were.

Sometimes he wondered if that embarrassing, disappointing experience had, well, affected his relationship with women. He liked to chat them up, flirt, but never got too close. He was, he knew, afraid of failure. He looked down at the river. Water under the bridge, he told himself.

The street door was open and he entered the cool passage. A cycle, a woman's without crossbar, wicker basket on the handlebars, leaned on the wall near the side door.

Dickie Richardson, crumpled green shirt rolled up to the elbows, was crouched, sowing seeds from a packet on to a minuscule patch of bare, raked earth. 'You again?'

Jacko felt as though he had stepped into his own backyard. 'Sorry about the misunderstanding over the burglar alarm. I didn't want to worry you.'

'Huh.' Dickie grunted as he continued sprinkling seed into drills drawn in the sour, sad-looking soil.

Yes, he muttered, without looking up, Rich had told him to expect the police round to check on his movements on election day. And, yes, his lad had been with him on Thursday, all day, nine-to-nine. They used his front room here as Labour's committee room for Riverside ward. As he walked in Jacko had glimpsed lists of printed names, cut from the voters' register and pasted on white paper, piled on a flower stand in the bay window.

'Been the agent for five years. My lad always helps on council election day. I help him in parliamentary campaigns.'

'Was he here all day?'

'Well, not all the time.' A grudging concession followed that Rich had to pop out now and then to pick up old ladies or the disabled who had promised their votes in return for a lift to the booths. 'He was never away for more than an hour at a time.'

Time enough, Jacko reckoned, to nip to Southview Cottage and shoot a lover who, maybe, had become a problem to an ambitious married man. 'Did he use your car for those trips to the polling station?'

'Don't have one.'

'His own vehicle was being serviced that day so how did he get about?'

Dickie gave the name of a ward committee member who had loaned his car for the day. 'At nine, Rich walked up to the Drill Hall to witness the count.'

'With you?'

Still crouching and concentrating on pinching the seeds into the rows he'd drawn, he shook his head and mumbled something about seeing countless counts in his time.

Jacko understood. As a uniformed constable he had stood guard at the Drill Hall on many election nights. They were like dog-racing or royal visits – seen one, seen 'em all.

Dickie nodded up the passage towards the bike. 'Went for a ride myself down the towpath by the river to see where the rings are rising, where the fish are feeding, to suss out the best spots. Season starts soon. Got home about . . .'

He stopped, studied the soil, then looked up and called out sideways, 'What time did I get in on election night?'

'After ten,' said a female voice out of view behind the curtain of an open kitchen window.

'Nearer ten thirty,' said Dickie, addressing the soil.

'Do you reckon I could have the names of the people Rich ran to the polls?'

'No.' He was burying the seeds by brushing the soil gently with his fingers. 'That's confidential.'

'Come on, Mr Richardson. My old mum promises her vote to anyone who knocks provided it's not during 'Coronation Street'. Once she's inside the booth no one knows where she puts her cross and I won't ask them.'

'No, I said.' He looked up, face as sour as the soil. 'You're bloody security police. You'll have their names on your bloody computers in no time.'

'We could always get a search warrant,' said Jacko, a little doubtfully.

'What! Raid a Labour Party committee room?' He began to rise from his haunches, hands on the knees of his baggy brown trousers, pushing himself up. 'We're not quite a police state yet. Piss off.'

'Mr Richardson . . .' Jacko was so shocked he almost cried out his name.

'Piss off, I said.' Dickie pointed to the passage like a referee directing a sent-off player to the dressing room. 'I've no time for the police. If you've no warrant, piss off. Go on. Piss off.'

It was drizzling, the first rain for a week, when Jacko reached Burton's, a small garage with two concrete islands for petrol pumps in the forecourt. He walked into the service bay, humming dum-dum-dum-dee-dum-dum.

'We've got a hit and run,' he told the service foreman. 'Nobody dead, just damage, but a dangerous bit of driving. We're looking for a grey-blue Cavalier about a year old. It happened on the Newark road late Wednesday. Any of that type come in since then?'

The foreman wiped his oily hands and led him into a grimy office. He searched through a file on rings. 'Only this.'

He took out a sheet: 'R. Richardson, BATS a/c. Date and time booked in: May 4, 08.00. Date and time booked out: May 4, 17.45. Delivered to home. Mileage: 18052.'

'No damage to the front, I see,' Jacko said, reading it again, wearing a tight smile. 'Can't be this one. Thanks.'

Tricia had driven a pool car west out of Newark, the opposite way to Lincoln, six miles or so, to a village on the north bank of the Trent and the address Richardson had given them the night before.

She was already back in the incident room and did not look up from examining a box of exhibits when Jacko sat beside her. 'How did you get on?'

'Eh?' She seemed to be many miles away.

'With Mrs Richardson.' Pause. No response. 'At her sister's.'

'Oh.' Reluctantly, she lifted her head, opened her notebook.

Not reading from it, she told him that Mrs Richardson had been sitting in a garden lounger, stiff-backed as though a disc had given way.

'I asked if she was feeling better and said we were sorry if we alarmed her when we called on Sunday.'

Her eyes finally went down over her book. 'Her actual reply was, "Rich was very cross about it."'

Tricia looked up again. 'She spoke slowly and with effort, like a drunk.' A sad headshake. 'I'm sure she's on drugs. I told her we'd had a long chat last night with Rich and thought we'd cleared up any misunderstanding.'

Jacko nodded.

She went back to the notebook, reading verbatim from it:

'Me: "Has Rich explained to you why I'm here?"'

'Her: "He phoned here after you and that inspector left his office to say you would be calling."'

'Me: "Then you'll know we have to establish the whereabouts of several people, your husband included, on Thursday. That was election day. What time did he leave in the morning?"'

'Her: "The usual time. No, I tell a lie. A bit earlier. About eight. He had to drop off his car for a service at Burton's garage and he caught a bus from there up to his parents' place in Green Street."'

Tricia seemed to sense, accurately as it turned out, that Jacko was picturing the scene now and suddenly dropped the pronouns.

'"When did he come home?"'

'"When it was finished."'

'"What time was that?"'

'"I don't know."'

'"Were you asleep?"'

'"Of course not. I always wait up. Let me see. About eleven thirty. He got a lift home after the results were declared. He was very pleased. They'd made two gains. The election programme hadn't started on TV when he came in. When it did come on, we watched for about half an hour and then went to bed. That's right."'

Tricia broke off reading. 'She spoke triumphantly as though she had just passed some kind of test.'

She went back to her notes, again letting the questions and answers identify who had been doing the talking.

'"The polls closed at nine, didn't they?"'

'"Rich went to see the votes counted and once you're signed in it's impossible to get out."'

'"Your husband tells us he knew Miss Penny Browne professionally. Did you ever meet her?"'

'"Not personally. Answered the phone to her a couple of

49

times. They were working together on some TV programme. I don't know much about it, though."'

Tricia closed her book, talking from memory. 'We chatted for a while, no notes being taken. She met and married when Rich was at the poly in Nottingham. She's clearly town, not gown. She worked in a shop until the babies arrived. Her mother in Nottingham is looking after them for a few days, just to give her the break the doctor ordered. Rich drove her across to her sister's yesterday, which explains why he was late in the office. I've checked with neighbours and looked up the TV programmes. Her story stands up.'

'That all?' asked Jacko, feeling disappointed, not really knowing why.

'Not quite,' said Tricia, mysteriously. 'Look what the Scenes team found in the flat over Penny's office.'

She dug into the exhibits box and came out with a small square transparent bag. In it was a silver charm on a pin. It had the face of a little devil and its legs were crossed. A silver Lincoln Imp. 'It was on a jacket in her wardrobe.'

'So?' said Jacko.

'That', said Tricia, very positively, 'is not the sort of thing a woman would buy herself. It's a memento. An admirer's gift.'

He gave her a smile, part in admiration, part in self-congratulation. 'If it's the man you're thinking of, his mileage doesn't add up. At 8 a.m. on Thursday his car was booked into Burton's garage for its service. Their records show 18052. He didn't use it on Thursday or Sunday. He claims he only did local mileage on Friday and Saturday. I've clocked the trips he told us about. They come to twenty, give or take a mile. He left his car behind when he went to London on Sunday. The meter registered 18120 when I saw it that night.'

Tricia frowned. 'You never mentioned that before. Did you make a note?'

Jacko knew some officers who would have said yes to that. It would have been easy to have slipped it in somewhere in his fast-filling notebook. It was a short cut to perjury and prison. He shook his head.

'Then how can you be sure?'

'Easy. 1812 times ten.'

Her brown eyes were baffled.

'You know, the 1812 Overture by Tchaikovsky.' He hummed her a snatch: Dum, dum, dum, dee, dum, dum. 'Apart from a bit of Mozart it's about the only classical music I know. It just registered with me, that's all.'

She wrinkled her nose, sniffing. 'Let's hope it doesn't become a vital bit of evidence. You've got a voice like a corncrake's. A quick burst of that from you in the witness box and the jury will acquit.'

She laughed but he didn't.

'It could be,' he said, very seriously.

'Why?'

'I've also clocked the distance from Rich's place to Penny's cottage. The round trip is forty-eight miles.'

Tricia jotted figures on a scrap of paper: 18052 at garage plus twenty miles since came to 18072. She took that away from 18120.

'Forty-eight miles.' She whistled softly. 'So he could have done it. He could have killed Penny Browne.'

8

LOVE NEST SHOOTING: IRISHMAN HELD, said the banner headline in the tabloid paper Tricia was reading next morning in the incident room.

Jacko had scanned versions in a broadsheet and a tabloid at home. Both quoted Assistant Chief Constable Knight as saying, 'A man, aged forty-six, has been detained under the Prevention of Terrorism Act.'

Part of him was pleased, part disappointed. He wanted the case solved, certainly, but he wanted to be the one who solved it.

He'd been sure they had found a scent on Rich Richardson. He'd taken a fancy to the case with its undertones of high-powered politics, wanted to be in on the end of it, but that was not just professionalism.

When he retired, he planned to write books about a few cases. His latest rough draft was on a supergrass's jailbreak from the castle cellblock at Lincoln which his team had uncovered a year earlier. He had told Tricia about it on their tour of the uphill city and she'd volunteered to give the script a quick read. He dropped 260 pages on her desk.

'It will give me something to do today.' She spoke with an enthusiasm he no longer shared. Being on the wrong end of this inquiry had given him nothing to write, no follow-up. Three days' hard graft for nothing. He suddenly felt tired and bored.

Soon Scott joined them, pulling up a chair. 'Sorry, I couldn't cut you in on that.' He nodded at Tricia's paper. 'Silent Knight put a need-to-know on it.'

'What's it all about?' Jacko asked, only half interested.

Scott nodded again, this time at Jacko's blank screen. 'There's an outline in there. Catch up with your reading.'

Tricia was already doing just that on Jacko's dog-eared, ill-typed script.

He switched on, laboriously tapping away until he found the right file. He draped his legs on the desk top, leant back and started reading . . .

Michael Riordan came to England from Donegal in the sixties. Knight's report hinted at him being an IRA sleeper.

He lived with a woman, not his wife, in a village near Penny Browne's home. He had no visible means of support but was not on social security.

Locals interviewed in the house-to-house had reported seeing him hovering about Southview Cottage three days before the shooting. There was nothing to tie him in with the car seen on the Thursday night with red Republic of Ireland number plates.

His was the second fingerprint found by Scenes of Crime specialists and identified by the bureau from his record which contained a string of convictions, mainly for assaults. The print was on a latch to a greenhouse.

Knight had let loose his scrapyard alsatians about the same time Scott had dispatched Jacko and Tricia to find young Richardson.

Last night, Riordan had returned home from a long lost weekend and the alsatians pounced. In the car bringing him to the station he said, 'You've caught me. Now prove it.' Marginally incriminating, Jacko conceded, but he didn't trust car

52

seat confessions. It was not unknown for a desperate detective to slip in a quote that had never been spoken. At the station, with the tapes on, when it really mattered, Riordan refused to say a word.

Jacko was not over-impressed until he got to the last two paragraphs. Swab testing had detected traces of explosives on Riordan's hands indicating he had recently fired a gun. And he had been interned at the Curragh in a round-up of Republican activists after a spate of shootings and burnings in the late fifties border campaign.

Jacko couldn't even recall it. He thought the latest troubles began with civil rights marches a decade later. He took Silent Knight's word for it. Not a bad lead, he had to admit gloomily.

Nothing better to do, he tapped into all the new files. The pathologist, he read, had narrowed the time of death to between 6 p.m. and midnight on Thursday. Ballistics had identified the bullet as coming from an obsolete revolver, probably Russian-made. Frogmen had failed to find it in the river. Worrying, that. Jacko worried. He loathed guns.

They were no further forward on the 'Hi Duck . . . Love, Gramps' note or the car with the red Republic of Ireland number plate.

A Scotland Yard team had filed an account of an interview with Penny Browne's married lover, the London financial correspondent. She had, he said, asked him how to get information about a company registered in Switzerland. 'I assumed it was research for a programme.'

They'd been having extra-marital sex for five years, mostly at her place in Notting Hill, but not since she'd moved from London, though they'd remained in friendly contact. She'd never told him she was pregnant and he certainly wasn't claiming responsibility.

He'd been in Brussels at a Common Market briefing at the time of the killing and a roomful of people confirmed it.

He'd kept the affair hidden from his wife but Penny seemed to have made no secret of it with her widowed mother and sister Caroline. On several trips north he had dropped in on them and Penny, and once he had stayed the night sharing her bedroom.

Christ, thought Jacko. My old mum would never have allowed that, not even between my marriages. Sex between singles was a sin in her eyes, adultery a passport to hell.

The moneyed middle class, he brooded, had always been privileged when it came to screwing. No river banks with stinging nettles for them. They could afford hotel suites, rent cottages and jet off to weekends in Paris. Unlike his old mum, they didn't give a shit about what the nosy neighbours might think.

Not that the Browne family had neighbours peering with runny noses over the backyard wall. Until their deaths in that AI crash, the colonel's widow and Caroline had lived in what sounded like a semi-stately home with tree-surrounded grounds to protect their privacy.

The Yard team had also spoken to several of Penny's friends from London who had spent weekends with her at what she skittishly called The Big House.

Mrs Browne, a sprightly seventy-year-old, occupied herself either working in the garden or reading in it. Caroline, a spinster in her late forties, kept busy working for charities. 'They both indulged Penny terribly,' said one visitor.

In her BBC days, Penny had done a spell as mother of the chapel which, a Yard inspector helpfully explained, was the chairwoman of an office branch of her union. She was much further to the left than brother Russell ever realized, Jacko concluded.

He read on to the best bit. Mrs Browne's estate, estimated at more than a million, had still to be settled. A development company wanted to turn her old home into a hotel but wouldn't put a price on it until planning permission was guaranteed.

Caroline had left half of everything to Penny, the rest to her charities. The amount that Penny would have received had been in dispute.

After a few bequests Mrs Browne had split her money between the three children. Lawyers for Penny had argued that a would-be rescuer had testified at the inquest that Caroline had outlived her mother, albeit by a few minutes, in the wreckage of the crashed car. So Caroline technically inherited her third of a million for a few grisly minutes, considerably boosting the fortune that passed on almost immediately to Penny.

Russell's solicitor claimed the crash witness was medically

incompetent to judge and that mother and Caroline should be deemed as having died instantaneously, so he ought to cop for a full half.

The legal dispute had been due to go to court: a sordid family squabble. In other circumstances, Jacko mused, a major motive for murder.

Penny was killed before she'd made a will and Russell Browne, as her next of kin, would eventually get the lot.

Fucking inherited wealth and power, thought Jacko angrily; obscene.

The phone rang. Tricia, he was aghast to see, was busy with a red pencil and made no move to answer it. He picked it up and really didn't have to be told the caller's name.

'Hallo, me old cock,' he chirped, always happy to hear from an old mate on a slack day.

A lovely stroll on a lovely day in a lovely town full of history.

Jacko had grown fond of Newark in his years here on divisional CID between his marriages.

He walked in the shade beside a long church with a tall spire that could be seen for miles. Down little alleys to his left came brief views of the cobbled square with its ancient pubs and the market with neatly laid out fruit and flower stalls, all the colours of a painter's palette.

A great little place for sights. His favourite was the ruined castle on the banks of the Trent. It was there that King John fatally OD-ed on rough cider after losing his jewels in the Wash and trying to tear up the Magna Carta, the silly old fart. Sometimes Jacko speculated – pointlessly but happily – on how many of the castle's walls had been blown down on the winds of royal flatulence.

More to his taste, much more, it was a great place for pubs. Once it had been one of Britain's biggest malting and brewing centres. Then the big combines moved in and closed down the independents. The drinkers revolted against their gassy beers, campaigned for the retention of traditional ales and made a kind of boozers' Mecca of the place that was coming into view.

The Old King's Arms was a small, simple building, painted

in black and white which set off the gold and green on its coat of arms.

Inside Jack Peacock was drinking incognito which, to an on-duty village bobby, means he had a dirty mac over his tunic top and he wasn't wearing his helmet. Only his black trousers and huge shiny boots blew his cover.

He was standing at the bar, nose over a pint glass of beer that looked too dark and too heavy for Jacko whose request for a Coke, his usual lunchtime order, was met with amused politeness by a small black-bearded barman.

Peacock went through the real-ale drinker's ritual, the whole repertoire. A sniff, hold the glass up to the light, a sip, then a contented sigh. 'Like nectar.' Finally, a wipe with the back of the hand across the mouth.

'What's up, Cock?'

Peacock silenced him with heavy, conspiratorial eyes. He was only a couple of inches taller than Jacko but four stones heavier, most of it hiding under his mac at his midriff. His tan-coloured, almost blond eyebrows were bushier than his hair, of which there wasn't much. His bald pate was weather-beaten, his open face pitted. He was a rough and ready old-time cop, a smashing man, very sound. He had been the first officer at the scene of the Penny Browne shooting, had handled it immaculately, as always. He supped and droned in a low local voice to the barman about gravity and texture.

Jacko gazed idly around – stained skirting board wood for ceilings, terracotta squares for floors, trowel marks left on the wall plaster. Cottage wobbling, old farm-hands used to call it. Old English plastering, trendy stylists call it these days. The only plastic was the white brackets which held up shelves lined with dusty beer bottles from around the world.

A place with a nice feeling, Jacko thought; pity about the conversation. Beer was to be drunk, to get on a glow that loosened tongues and inhibitions; not to be endlessly talked about.

On his second pint, Peacock led him to a wall table in the downstairs bar, quiet before noon. He sat down clumsily, looking about him, the conspirator again. 'Riordan's the wrong man.' He spoke out of the corner of his mouth.

'Why?'

'I've known him for years. He's been on the patch longer than me.'

'Silent Knight reckons he could be a sleeper.'

'He's slept longer than Rip Van Winkle then. The only kipping he does is to get rid of a hangover.'

Jacko mentioned his internment and a cloud crossed Peacock's face but only for as long as it took him to work out that Michael Riordan would have been a teenager then. 'If you can't be a rebel at that age, when can you be?'

'What about his record?'

'Mainly for punching publicans and gamekeepers. He's a poacher but straight. Never out of season.'

'Pheasants are out of season but he recently fired a gun.'

'At duck or a hare, I'll bet.'

'Why did he do a runner?'

'He didn't. He's always disappearing for days on end.'

'Doing what?'

'Wheeling and dealing. I don't ask. We have an understanding. Nothing on my patch and, if he strays, he holds his hands straight up. Nobody makes a move without me knowing.' His face had become very serious. 'Look, I take my pension soon but I do care about our reputation.'

This Jacko knew to be true. The vast majority of cops care. There are no more bent bobbies per head of professional population than quack doctors, shady lawyers and certainly dodgy journalists who write reams about police misconduct while ignoring their own.

'I'm telling you, you've got the wrong man,' Peacock went on. 'I'll stake that pension on it. He doesn't match the, er . . .' He'd lost the phrase through disuse.

'The profile,' Jacko suggested.

'He's no idealist.'

'He was in his teens.'

'I didn't know about that. But I do know he sounds off against the Provos every time the subject comes up in any local boozer.'

'Well, if he's a sleeper, he would, wouldn't he?'

A derisive snort. 'He never hides his Irishness. He waves the tricolour every time they play rugger against England. Would a terrorist do that?'

57

A shrug, uncertain. 'A double-bluff?'

'It's more than a gut feeling, Jacko. I know; just know, that's all.'

'What do you want me to do about it?'

'Let me have a go at him. He's been up to something, for certain, but not that.'

'Did you tell Silent Knight all this?'

'I told a couple of AT3 officers. Worse than Albanian secret police, they are. They didn't want to know.'

What's the point of having community policemen if no one listens to them? Jacko asked himself. 'Come on, Cock. Drink up. We're off to see my chief.'

'One for the road first, eh?' Peacock emptied his glass with one long swallow and held it out for Jacko to take.

'Come in. Come in.' Michael Riordan was big, burly and bald and could have been Peacock's brother apart from his accent which didn't have a West Cork lilt nor a Belfast harshness, so it was melodious to Jacko's ears. This time last week such sounds had surrounded him. It seemed a long time ago.

Riordan, in grey slacks and a too-tight black sweatshirt that displayed a massive belly, rose on one elbow on his cell bunk when they walked in. He made no effort to get up.

His eyes switched off their welcome when they travelled over Peacock's broad shoulder and rested on Jacko. 'Who's he?'

'Jimmy Jackson. A good mate of mine.'

Peacock slumped down on to the grey blanket at Riordan's stockinged feet, one big toe-nail beginning to peep through a hole. 'Tatoes, they call such holes in stockings round here, because they look round and white like new potatoes.

Jacko stood, hands in pockets, no place to sit in a tiny cell that was brightly lit but windowless and smelt badly of BO.

'What the bloody hell's going on, Michael?' asked Peacock, straight in, aggressive, somehow not threatening.

'You tell me.' Riordan sounded offended. 'I was walking home, happy with the world, minding my own, when two of your Garda hijacked me.'

Peacock did all the early questioning, very bluntly, often obscenely, and Riordan said, yes, he knew why he was inside, and, yes, he knew about Miss Browne's death. 'Sad business, so it is.'

'Why aren't you talking to the detectives?' asked Peacock.

'Because I've nothing to say. Ignorant bastards. That's why.'

'Tell me then.'

Riordan fell silent, crooking his sturdy legs, looking down, picking roughly at the blanket. Peacock shot Jacko an anxious look.

Jacko began to speak very quietly. 'Old Cock here says you didn't do it.' No one smiled at his nickname because everyone for miles around called Peacock that, even children in pushchairs. 'That's good enough for me. So will you help us find out who did?'

He gave a glum nod, hardly noticeable, and added just as glumly, 'So long as you don't ask me to drop anyone in it.'

'We've witnesses who say you called at Southview Cottage on bank holiday Monday. Right?'

Another nod. 'Right, sir.'

'Was she in?'

A third nod.

'Did you speak to her?'

A headshake.

'Why did you call?'

Nothing.

Peacock repeated the question twice, adding his Christian name the second time.

Riordan finally broke his silence. 'On my rounds.'

'If she was in, why didn't you speak to her?' asked Jacko.

'She had company.'

'Have you been back to Southview Cottage since bank holiday Monday – the following Thursday, for instance?'

'On my mother's life, no, sir.'

Jacko paused in thought; then, 'So since that Monday, where have you been?'

'On my rounds.'

'What rounds?'

Silence again.

'Come on, Michael. Tell us.' Peacock spoke very crossly but the only reply was a very troubled look.

'Where do these rounds take you?'

'All over.' A shrug with one shoulder. 'Lincs. South Yorks.'

Jacko again, brightly: 'If you can tell us where you were between 6 p.m. and midnight on Thursday, you can go home.'

Riordan wore a pained face, trapped.

'Let me understand this,' said Jacko, slowly, patiently. 'Obviously, you know where you were but for some reason you can't tell us. Is that it?'

A nod, looking away.

'Were you at Southview Cottage?'

A headshake.

Peacock took over again, belligerently accusing him of 'having a bit of fluff on the side', which was strongly denied.

Jacko shuffled in a very small circle, head down. He was up to something illegal. Can't have been game dealing. Out of season. What else could he be up to? What else?

He saw them then. That crowd of happy Irishmen he'd met on their fishing holiday. They'd asked him from the pub with a three-piece band to their rented cottage. They got out the unmarked bottle filled with a colourless liquid. Furtive, sniggering, sniffing, sipping, tasting, and nectar it wasn't. More like paraffin.

Jacko turned to face Riordan, smiling, looking down at him, still curled on his side, a cupped fist propping up the side of his face. 'How much do you charge, Michael?' Riordan had an alarmed look. 'For your poteen?'

'Ah, Jesus.' A resigned sigh as he uncurled and swung his feet on to the floor.

'What?' Peacock's stomach wobbled in rage.

'Ah, Jesus, Mr Peacock.' It was the first time Riordan had addressed him so formally; an appeasing voice.

'A still? On my beat?'

'Ah, Jesus, sir. It's not, it's, it's not . . .' He stammered, panicky, spat it out. '. . . a big one. Not too big anyway.'

He'd been brewing hooch for years, he eventually admitted. Right under Old Cock's nose. In a rented barn. His customers were widely scattered and Jacko guessed there'd be a few doctors, farmers and businessmen, magistrates even, among them. He didn't push for names.

Penny Browne had been a regular client for a couple of years. 'Loved it, she did. Mind you, it's lovely stuff.'

Peacock glowered.

'I thought you were a real-ale man, Jack.' An apologetic face. 'Or I'd have given you a little taste.'

He went round to Southview Cottage on the Monday with her monthly bottle. 'She had company. I popped her order in the greenhouse. The usual place when she was out or busy.'

'Our search team never found it,' said Jacko.

'Have they looked in the peat under the pink azalea?'

Then he'd set out in his battered old van on his long-distance rounds. On the Thursday of the murder he was in Norfolk but he refused to say where. He returned to Silent Knight's reception party.

He didn't deny telling the AT3 man, 'You've caught me. Now prove it.' He was taking about his bootlegging operation, not any shooting.

On his travels, sleeping in the back of the van among his bottles, he'd popped off a rabbit here and a pigeon there, just to keep his eye in. 'Got some nice duck on the Wash.' Very proud.

True, he'd been caught in a Garda round-up when he was living back at home because his old man ran a safe house. 'Had no truck with them since. The Provos are murdering bastards,' he added with a vehemence shared by most Irish people Jacko had met on his holiday.

'Why didn't you knock on Miss Browne's door to make the delivery and collect your money?' asked Jacko.

'Ah, she'd pay me in God's good time. Good as gold. Besides, I've told you, she had company.'

'How did you know?'

'I could hear them.'

'Hear what?'

'Her and a man, barneying. Fierce, it was.'

'See him?'

'Only his car. Parked outside.'

'What sort?'

'A big Volvo. Blue it was.'

Russell Browne's, Jacko thought, so startled he swallowed noisily.

9

'Detectives hunting the gunman who murdered the Police Minister's sister will today apply to magistrates for permission to continuing holding in custody a forty-six-year-old Irishman they are questioning.'

The radio newsreader's words seemed to be followed over headphones he wasn't wearing by an inner voice at the controls of his conscience. 'Divert. You must create a diversion.'

Why? How? he asked himself, feeling very lonely, completely lost in clouds that crowded in on him.

He answered himself slowly.

Why? Simple. You, you of all people, can't sit back and do nothing while a blameless man rots in jail. You can't salvage this scandal, save your family, at his expense.

How? Not so simple; took much longer.

10

Tricia dropped the red-pencilled draft in its creased covers with a thump on Jacko's desk.

'Well?' he asked, tentatively. An awful moment this, for a budding author. Like a mother showing off her new-born, not knowing if it's pretty or plain.

'I liked it a hell of a lot,' she said, eyes bright. 'The basics are good. Original.'

'And?' He put on his hopeful smile.

'But.' Slower, down a note. 'Complicated and a mite static. Overlong interviews. Lacks a bit of tension.'

He scooped the file up and slammed it into his top drawer, not looking at her.

'You wanted an honest opinion, didn't you?' Concern in her eyes.

'Yes.' Untruthful, thinking: How else can a detective get to the truth without a lot of talking and listening, you smart-arse?

He looked up, relieved to see the Little Fat Man approaching, bringing, he hoped, a bit of constructive conversation.

'Silent Knight won't release him,' Scott said, mouth horizontal, undecided. 'Not unless he comes up with the names of people who bought his hooch on Thursday.'

'He won't do that. It's against the bootlegger's code.'

Scott nodded. 'Knight wants to know if he ties in to the car with the red number plate. Take a look at that, will you?'

'Bloody hell, boss. I'm busy.'

'So busy that she . . .' Scott flicked his head towards Tricia. '. . . spent all day yesterday reading your penny dreadful.'

She coloured slightly, said nothing. People, even foot-sure people like her, backed off from confrontation with Scott.

Jacko, in a bad mood, wasn't about to. 'We've got to chase this lead on Russell Browne and the blue Volvo. About the barney Riordan heard him and Penny having and . . .'

Scott interrupted. 'Don't you row with your sister now and then?'

'Yes, but not about the difference between half a million and a third of a million quid. It's a strong motive.'

'He was dining with the PM on the night of the shooting. Some alibi witness, wouldn't you say?'

Jacko met his glare. Eyeball to eyeball stuff, this. 'I'm not saying he actually fired the gun. But he could have arranged it. And we're also sure young Richardson and Penny were closer than he makes out. They could have been lovers. We've unearthed two bloody good suspects. We've got a lot on.'

Scott's mouth went into the reverse U. 'Your first priority is to eliminate Riordan as a suspect. You and your mate PC Plod stuck your oars in. You sort it out.'

'Isn't the car down to Knight's team?'

'They're making a cottage industry out of it and I need to know if I can recommend Riordan's release.'

'Won't Silent object?'

Scott gave him a thin smile. 'I seem to remember you bellyaching to me that he'd got to Russell Browne on Sunday before you. Get your own back.'

Jacko knew that Scott was setting up one team against another, internecine warfare, a boss's weapon. 'But . . .'

'But nothing.' His mouth went into a reverse U. 'Fucking well get on with it.' He walked away, huffily, then turned sharply. 'Now.'

Ah, well, thought Jacko, that interview was short enough and tense enough. Piss off, he mouthed at Scott's departing back.

He made a few phone calls only to discover that eight ferries a day crossed the Irish Sea to Liverpool or the Welsh ports, bringing 1,600 cars with them, a fifth registered in the Republic.

'You'll be round the world and back again before I'm off this job,' he said as Tricia played on the keyboard.

'Maybe I won't come back. Maybe I'll meet Mr Right who'll storm my barricades and I'll live the life of an expat, pink gins and sunsets.'

And you can piss off, too, he thought, bitterly. Jacko could be like this. If his head wasn't patted now and then, if he felt that people didn't return affection he held for them, he was inclined to sulk.

Tricia was reading an extract from the Scenes of Crime report. (Jacko had gone through them all before and couldn't be bothered.)

'The following items were found in the porch of Southview Cottage – *Guardian, Times, Newark Advertiser*, dated 5 May; *Guardian* and *Times*, dated 6 May. Four letters addressed to Ms P. Browne. One note without envelope. All were lying on or near the doormat. They were in haphazard fashion and it is not possible to conclude in what order they were put through the letterbox.'

Each item had a code. She tapped out the last one. The note appeared on the screen. 'Hi Duck – Sorry to have missed you. Will call mid-June after storming Europe. Love, Gramps. PS Don't leave the gate open!'

She scrolled up the specialists' verdicts. The handwriting

experts were convinced it was female writing. The bureau found right-handed finger and thumb prints that did not appear in their records. They were unable to decide whether they were left by a man with small fingers or a woman with big fingers.

Forensics said the note had been written on a page from a blue Basildon Bond pad available at just about every stationery counter in Britain.

She returned to the index and fed in another number. The cleaner had stated that the garden gate had been on its latch when she entered on seeing two days' uncollected milk on the doorstep. PC Peacock reported that the porch door was on its Yale lock but the inside bolt was not in position.

A final figure was entered but it only disclosed what she and Jacko already knew. Penny Browne had no surviving grandparents.

She leant back in her chair. 'You don't think, do you, that the occupant of the Irish car had anything to do with the note?'

'It's a bloody long way to travel to hand deliver a letter,' said Jacko, gruffly. 'And you don't leave a note like that if you're just about to shoot somebody through the head. It's from some potty girl, probably public school.' He added for good measure, 'Probably with a double-barrelled name.'

God, he'd gone off her this morning, still wasn't looking at her and didn't see her exasperated eyes turn heavenwards.

Her fingers were soon busy again. Into the index, out with a number. The publicity file revealed that, though the sighting of the Irish car had been kept secret, there had been appeals in all branches of the media for the letter writer to come forward.

'Odd that no one responded.' She was talking at the screen. 'Maybe an Irish motorist did drop it off, went home and hasn't seen the English papers.'

'Balls.' Jacko now regarded himself as an expert on Irish affairs. 'English papers sell over there.'

'Let's take it from the top.' She flashed up the note again. 'Hi Duck,' she read. She looked at him. 'That's a Lincoln term of endearment. Right?'

Jacko nodded, just, not interested.

'Let's get her contacts book and go through all the Lincoln numbers first.'

Tricia rose without waiting for his approval and went to Ginger Pig's desk, ran off two copies at a flashing machine and returned.

They began to dial, she working from the front, he from the back. Jacko was certain they were wasting time but, as Scott kept glancing over in his direction, he thought he ought to look busy.

One woman, a contact at County Hall Penny Browne sometimes tapped, told him, 'I've never heard her use such an expression and I would certainly not dream of using it myself.'

'Oh, well,' he said, mischievously. 'Sorry to have bothered you, duck.'

A quip, any quip, always brightened him and he made his first positive contribution. 'It's a nickname. Something from a kids' play or panto perhaps.'

'You could be right,' said Tricia. 'There are still some girls in Sussex who call me Chopsticks.'

'I didn't know you were musical.'

'I'm not. I was a poor loser on the hockey pitch.'

He forgave her then, warmed to her again and rewarded her with his first smile of the day. 'So where are nicknames used?'

They walked to a green cabinet where a whole drawer had been marked: Penny Browne, Background. They returned to their desks with three files.

Jacko took the top one: BBC. A place, he reasoned, where they always used nicknames. Look how Jonners and Blowers drone their way through every Test Match.

It was a thick dossier beginning with her application form filled in during her university days and contained internal memos and assessment reports. There were several references to her spell as a militant-sounding mother of the National Union of Journalists' chapel. Names that cropped up frequently he cross-checked with her contacts book and, if they appeared, he phoned them. When he asked if Penny had ever been given the nickname of Duck, he got stunned silences or chuckles.

Tricia had worked her way through a thin file from Penny's boarding school. No friendship made there had stood the test of time through to her current contacts book. Old teachers whose names appeared on end-of-term reports were similarly shocked or amused.

She moved on to a file they extracted from the rear of the drawer: York University. In it were her application forms, medical report and degree results and a programme from a concert given in the Great Hall by the university orchestra in May eleven years earlier.

The second item was W.A. Mozart's Sinfonia Concertante for four wind instruments and orchestra in E flat major. The soloists were listed as Penny Browne (oboe), Lisa Hazlehurst (clarinet), Siobhan Riley (bassoon) and Matthew Stoate (horn).

'Browne's right,' said Jacko, impressed. 'She must have been a talented musician.'

He studied the programme notes, with their usual pretentious drivel, while Tricia checked the names with the contacts book. The horn player's musical acquaintanceship had not lasted the passage of a decade but the two girls had. One had a Berkshire number. The other Jacko immediately recognized as Republic of Ireland.

It turned out to be a guesthouse in Ballinasloe, Co. Galway. 'She's in no trouble now, is she?' said the woman who answered.

Jacko said no.

'You're sure now?'

Jacko closed his eyes, letting the accent wash over him, said he was sure.

Mrs Riley had read about the shooting. 'Tragic, isn't it just?' She immediately answered her own question, the way of the Irish. 'So it is. Siobhan will be mortified when she finds out. I can't get in touch with her until tomorrow. She's touring, you see.'

'Where will we find her tomorrow?' Jacko took the details. A secret smile changed into a silly grin.

Mrs Hazlehurst told Tricia that her daughter was a music teacher and gave her the name and number of the school.

Jacko, brimming with enthusiasm now, made the call. He caught Lisa as she was about to walk out of the staff room to give a lesson.

Yes, she said, she had read about Penny and had written a letter of condolence to her brother. Yes, they kept in touch with exchanges of Christmas and holiday cards. And, yes, she said, with a self-conscious giggle, they still used the nicknames they gave each other when they played together at a concert in York for schoolchildren.

'What are they?'

'I'm Pussy Cat, Siobhan's Gramps and Penny was Duck.'

'Why?'

'Well, the clarinet is the cat, the bassoon's the grandfather and the oboe plays the duck.'

Jacko wondered what nickname the girls had given the chap with the big round horn but decided not to ask. 'In what piece of music was this?'

'Oh, Inspector,' she said sorrowfully. 'You did have a deprived childhood. Have you never heard "Peter and the Wolf"?'

He stood at his desk and bowed repeatedly and gravely to Tricia, a conductor taking his applause. 'I'm off to tell the Little Fat Man that the Irish driver is a bassoonist, not a terrorist, and that we're going to see her.'

'Where?'

'Paris.'

Jacko was first off the airport bus when it drew up at the Etoile. He pirouetted in slow motion.

The awe-inspiring sight of the Arc. The sound of the endless traffic encircling it anti-clockwise. The hot musty smell, like chestnuts roasting, rising from the Métro. All drifted over him.

'Oh, my God.' His eyes shone behind his bifocals. Tricia's brown eyes understood.

They pulled their overnight bags higher on to their shoulders. In steady even step, they walked down the sloping Avenue Wagram past cafés with canopies on the wide pavement shaded by plane trees which didn't seem to have grown much in his long absence.

He could have told her of his teenage years here in the army and the seventeen-year-old with green eyes and red hair he'd loved so deeply that he never suggested bed because he feared sex would change what was romantic perfection. Instead he opted to lose his virginity to a prostitute, an expensive disaster, an act of unfaithfulness that filled him with guilt. He said

68

nothing, just looked around for a glimpse of the Eiffel Tower between low-slung, stylish buildings, listened to the hum of tyres on cobblestones.

They turned off at flower stalls on a traffic island. They crossed into a narrow street with more piano shops than piano bars, a musical centre of some sort. They quickly found a modernish building with oatmeal-coloured brickwork, where, Mrs Riley had told him, the European Ensemble of Ancient Music was rehearsing and recording.

Tricia talked in fluent French to a uniformed doorman while Jacko, in his light grey court appearance suit, stood around, feeling useless.

They were directed across a tiled, pillared foyer to an old-fashioned lift with iron gates and on to a first-floor room with control panels and a big glass window. Behind it five men and three women, all casually dressed to the point of scruffiness, were standing in a semicircle, playing four different types of instrument, reading music from stands in front of them. He didn't know what they were playing but he liked the restful sound he was hearing.

When they stopped they laid their instruments on chairs behind them and filed into the control room in earnest conversation.

One of the women spoke. 'I'm still not getting the tenderness into that Andante. I know it.' She had an Irish accent but wasn't what he thought of as Irish-looking. No raven or red hair but three colours – blonde, copper blonde and brown, which seemed the most natural.

She wore tight black trousers that ended at mid-calf. Her black T-shirt displayed a bust all the more prominent because of the small size of the rest of her. The result, Jacko concluded, of filling her lungs and blowing into a reed as narrow as a milk straw all day and every day. She was not much bigger than the bassoon she'd been playing.

Tricia introduced herself and asked for a private word. They walked down stone stairs and out of the building, Jacko following, dawdling, head down, depressed at the news he was about to break.

Tricia, in black pleated skirt, cream linen jacket and pink cabled top, was four inches taller than Siobhan. They talked as they walked ahead of him. Their heads grew closer together. Suddenly Siobhan stopped and looked up into Tricia's so sad face. Jacko knew the job had been done for him. Tricia turned, nodding across the street to a café with musical notes on scarlet awnings.

Woman's work, she was telling him.

He sat at a round cane chair at a black marble-topped table and ordered *une bière*. His years in Paris had left him with the ability to order drinks and get a bet on at Longchamps but little else.

He looked about him. At a pigeon on the road that seemed too fat to fly and cars, more patient, less noisy these days, that stopped until it waddled out of their way. At women, sitting alone behind him, reading, a sight seldom seen in British bars.

Paris was cool and pale today, like its women. All but one, he corrected himself. Françoise. And he thought of her then, about the sunset they had seen sitting hand-in-hand on the steps of the Sacré Coeur and he wondered where she was and hoped that she was happy.

The bar seemed familiar, though he couldn't be sure. He'd drunk in most bars within ten minutes' walk of the Arc but, in all his time here, he'd never been to the Louvre or the Opéra, never been up the Tower and had visited Notre Dame only once. He wondered whether there'd be time to pull in a sight or two but decided that, on the whole, he'd prefer a bistro on the Left Bank.

And then what?

And the woman he was thinking of now had brown eyes, not green.

Tricia made the introductions. Siobhan's blue eyes, bluer than the south seas, had shed tears. Her unmade-up face was very pale. Long firm fingers curled round his as they shook hands.

He ordered *deux cafés et une autre bière* while Tricia took her notebook and pen out of her blue travelling bag. They began at the beginning, the easy way.

Siobhan Riley was a year younger than her great, late friend

Penny Browne. She'd been playing bassoon since her schooldays in Galway City. 'It's a grand sound, is it not?'

She'd opted for York University, a long way from home, because of the quality of their woodwind tutors.

'Penny was a lovely, lovely oboe player, but never wanted to make a career out of it.'

In their final year, she continued, both graduated to the principles' stands in the university orchestra and took starring roles in the 'Peter and the Wolf' piece by Prokofiev which gave them their nicknames.

'I made many friends there but she was the closest and remained so. She took me home for weekends to Lincolnshire. Her mother and sister made me very welcome. They really spoilt her. She was the baby of the family, right enough.'

For ten years they'd kept in close touch, spent holidays together in Ballinasloe during Penny's Belfast days on the BBC and lunched whenever they could in London. 'I knew about her married Fleet Street fella. Met him once. A nice chap.'

'Did you know that romance was virtually over?' Romance was not a word Jacko would have normally used but it came out quite naturally here.

'It was never going anywhere,' said Siobhan, not quite answering the question. 'It was a pity but there you are.' A little helpless shrug. 'She was just happy to spend time with him.' She twiddled with her long fingers. 'She would have been even happier if he'd have given her a child.'

It was such an astonishing statement that Jacko said, 'Sorry?' and Tricia said, 'Pardon?' almost simultaneously.

'Oh yes.' An instant reply. 'She wanted children, a child certainly. She regarded it as a woman's God-given right to be a mother, wasn't all that bothered whether she was married or not. I told her not to mention such modern ideas when I took her home to Ballinasloe.' A light sad laugh.

So what, Jacko was asking himself, was she doing having an abortion within the last year?

He dwelt on this for some little while but all he could establish was that Penny Browne held a view that she could combine a career with motherhood without the constant company of a man.

'She loved her Fleet Street fella but she wasn't a marriage

71

breaker,' Siobhan explained, musician's shoulders shrugging expressively.

Jacko was still trying to puzzle it through. If her Fleet Street fella hadn't made her pregnant, who did? 'Did she ever mention anyone by the name of Richardson or Rich?'

Deep thought delayed her answer. 'Not that I recall.' Then, more certain: 'No. Not to me.'

'Did you ever meet her brother Russell?'

'Only once. Only for a few minutes.'

'How did they appear to get on?'

'All right, I suppose.' A doubtful, almost dishonest, reply and she was immediately more forthcoming. 'They were not close, you know. It's sometimes the way with the English middle class, don't you think?' She blushed, fearing she had been impolite.

Jacko smiled sagely. 'Know what you mean.'

Encouraged, she became devastatingly frank. 'I think she hated him, really.'

'Why?' No response, in her shell again, so he asked, 'Was it a political difference?'

'I don't begin to understand your politics. I think she was a bit of a red or a radical. She objected to her brother's politics but it was deeper than that.'

'Did she explain why?'

'She had this theory – I think it came from her study of economic and social history – that families like hers, wealthy families, had a responsibility to the workers who had made them rich. She thought her brother had treated the workers badly. She thought he was greedy for power and money and he had mismanaged the company. She was determined to put matters right, if she could.'

'How?'

'She was going to make a programme about it.'

'Saying what?'

'Sympathetic to trade unions. She was very left wing, you know.'

Siobhan had heard from Penny about the death of her mother and sister in the car crash. She couldn't make the funerals but sent flowers and spoke to her at length several times on the phone.

She knew about the legal dispute between Penny and Russell

72

Browne over the wills but only vaguely. 'She said he had benefited enough out of the company and she wanted the money for training bursaries, a trust of some kind. She had this bee in her bonnet that working-class kids, blacks especially, weren't going into the media because it had become over-qualified. She thought it was losing its back-street flavour or something. I cannot claim to have understood everything she stood for.'

She grew restive, agitated almost, tears welling. Jacko moved her on to safer ground, unconsciously slipping into her lingo. 'Well, now, let's be getting on to Thursday, 4 May.'

The ensemble had the day off between concerts in Edinburgh and London, she said, calming herself again. She and the lead oboist, her steady fella called Declan, took their time travelling together down the A1. A musician friend had promised them a bed at his home in north London but he had a concert himself that night and wouldn't be in until midnight.

They dropped in on York, saw her old tutor and wandered round the ancient city. They still had time on their hands so decided to call on Penny Browne. She had never visited Southview Cottage, always her Notting Hill flat, but she knew the address.

'We found the village right enough. It would be ten.' She stopped. 'No. Before. Quarter to. We spied this chap at his garden gate with a dog and he gave us directions to Far Lane. Dec stayed in the car and I went to the door. I rang the bell and knocked a lot but there was no reply.'

'Were the lights on?'

'Oh, no. Or I'd have known she was in.'

Tricia pulled a copy of a note from the back of her book. 'And you popped this through the letterbox?'

She read it, smiling sorrowfully. Yes, she said. She returned to the car. Dec gave her the pad. She wrote it on the car roof.

Tricia asked her to explain the postscript.

'It's just a joke, you see. Peter's duck got gobbled up by the wolf because he left the gate open.'

'And she or someone had left her garden gate open?'

'Yes.'

'And you?'

'I shut the gate behind me.'

73

'Apart from the man at his own garden gate who pointed the way, was the village deserted?'

She thought deeply and spoke slowly. 'There was one other car.' They let her take her own time. 'Coming down the lane away from Southview Cottage as we got near Penny's place.'

'Anything special about it?'

'It was definitely a Cavalier,' said Siobhan, definitely.

Jacko sat forward. 'How can you be so sure?'

'We often tour in hired cars. I've driven one.'

He sat back, satisfied. 'What colour?'

'It wasn't dark or white but lightish. Light blue or grey, perhaps.'

Richardson's, thought Jacko, his stomach revolving. 'Did you see who was in it?'

'A family.'

'A family?'

'A couple in the front and a child in the back. A girl, I think. She was the one I noticed. She waved at us. I waved back.'

'How old was she?'

'Not much more than a toddler. Three or four. It's unusual in England to see children out that late. That's why I noticed her.'

Dec, her fella, joined them for an omelette lunch (Jacko ordered *jambon*, showing off) in a restaurant encased by smoked glass. Dec had been concentrating on his driving down a lane that was unlit. He hadn't noticed the girl in the back. There had been two people in the front, both men, he thought, the driver the younger of the two, but Siobhan stuck to the opinion that the couple were a man and woman.

Dawdling over coffee after Siobhan and her fella had left, Tricia said, 'You don't think, do you, that Rich took his family on the outing to kill her?'

Unlikely, both eventually agreed, but they'd need to check his alibi at the election night count.

Jacko used the café phone, certain Scott would sanction a night in Paris, prepared to fend off his suggestive barbs. He wasn't in so he briefed Happy, the collator.

Tricia waited outside the booth. 'Come on,' she said as he slid back the door, 'show me your old haunts.'

* * *

74

* * *

Strolling down the Champs, tawdry these days with its fast food shops, she slipped her arm in his. Outside his two marriages, he'd never felt this close to any woman and he knew that the people they passed would not bother to ask themselves if they were a father with devoted daughter or a tired man with young lover. In Paris no one would care whether he was thinking of her as Tricia or Trish. He couldn't make up his mind himself.

They walked up towards the Place de la Concorde, she spelling out for the first time her criticisms of his jailbreak draft and suggesting ways of simplifying it to inject more pace, and he listened, learning.

They took an underpass, headed for the river, leaning on the high white wall for a clear view of the Tower, watching the wide flat-bottomed sightseeing boats go by.

'If we get the go-ahead to stay the night,' he said, looking across the slow, brown water beyond a church with a spire weathered green, 'we'll have a meal and a couple of bottles of wine over there, on the Left Bank.'

'Sounds lovely.' She spoke in a cuddly sort of voice he'd never heard her use before.

And afterwards, he decided, they'd head north to the Sacré Coeur and watch dusk casting pastel shadows over the crowded roof-tops and maybe hold hands.

And then what? he was asking himself. She was smart, spirited and supportive, intelligent and independent; just being with her made him happy, and she was lovely.

Suddenly, she was Trish to him. He wanted, so desperately wanted, to hold her and kiss her.

And then what? Oh, Christ. Adultery. Such an ugly word. He felt a pang of fear, the sort he'd experienced with that trusting girl with green eyes. Would lovemaking damage a relationship that was wonderful as it was? Could he handle the guilt that was bound to follow?

They walked arm-in-arm past two bridges, talking, laughing, and he told her all about the green-eyed girl then. She tugged down on his arm so that their shoulders touched. 'There's much more to love than hopping between the sheets, you know.'

75

The Tower at their backs, they walked past golden fountains, up steps and over marble terraces so shiny they looked slippery, between twin classical buildings that housed theatres and museums, the colour of smooth sand dried by a hot sun.

At the Trocadero, they went inside a café with cream drapes over mirrored walls for another drink – whisky and soda for her, gin and tonic for him; incredibly expensive but, what the hell, it was on exes. They smoked cigarettes, not talking much, Jacko thinking: What did she mean by 'There's more to love than hopping between the sheets'?

She tried and failed to catch the waiter's eye. 'You never drink whisky,' she said, for something to say.

He decided to find out what she meant. 'Sometimes. But it's like firewater to an Indian to me. Corrodes my barricades. Destroys my inhibitions.' He smiled casually. 'Makes me behave bizarrely in bed.'

She was wearing a look full of devilment when the waiter finally came and she placed the order in French. He was disappointed, felt rejected, when another gin was put before him.

He used a grey phone on a tiled wall next to unisex toilets to call Scott who said he had already been briefed and asked no questions. 'You're booked on the evening flight.'

'But, Scotty . . .'

'Be in my office first thing.' He slammed down the phone.

Out of chronology, which was always the way Jacko thought and, later, wrote, a silly little thing happened months after the case was over.

As he roughed his draft, no Tricia to help him, he struggled to find the right place for it in the narrative. Finally he came to regard it as a sort of postscript to Paris and Siobhan, so he decided to use it as a footnote there.

Late one night, very drunk in the Fairways, the HQ local, he spotted Silent Knight and his AT3 team strut in.

A red haze that often came with whisky descended over him; a professional death wish, almost; a career handicap, certainly.

He staggered up to him and slurred, 'Going to Scotty's duck do this weekend?'

'What's a duck do?' asked Silent, stiff, sober, unsuspecting.

'Quack, quack, quack,' quacked Jacko, marching up and down, fingering an imaginary oboe. 'Quack, quack, quack.'

Next morning he woke up, head pounding, harder still when the memory filtered through. Oh, Christ. Did I do that? Tell me, please, that I didn't do that.

11

'You dozy bastard.'

Eyes spun in the incident room. A score of pairs. Mournful ones of Happy, the collator. Greedy ones of Ginger Pig. Searching ones of the scrapyard alsatians from AT3. Tired ones from screens.

All rested on the lips of the Little Fat Man. They were in the reverse U, deeper than a Vatican dome. This was going to be the real thing, a major bollocking, a jewel of golden gossip for the King's Arms.

Before Scott stood Jacko and Tricia. His hazel eyes were alarmed, her brown ones calm.

Scott sensed the stares. 'In here', and he led the way out in a sort of pipe major's walk.

In the divisional super's office where even the empty space seemed to have been polished, he threw a green file on the desk. 'You've been conned.'

He sat down. From the folder Jacko withdrew a white sheet and held it so Tricia, standing next to him, could read it with him.

It was headed 'Union of Bottlemaking Allied Trades – Staff Expenses'. On top was Rich's name and insurance number. A series of vertical columns had their own sub-headings.

Date	Details	General	Car	Sundries
Mon 1	Abt Lincoln re May Day Rally – Ent visiting officials	5.60		
Tue 2	Grantham re PR – Lunch	4.00		
	Car-park			.60

Date	Details	General	Car	Sundries
Wed 3	Nottm – tribunal – Lunch			
	and tea	6.00		
	Car-park			1.30
	Petrol		18.50	
Thu 4	Newark and about re PR			
	Lunch	4.00		
	Car-park			.50
Fri 5	Abt Lincoln re dispute			
	Ent members	4.50		
	Phones out of office			1.00

The sub-totals had been added up to an overall total of £46. A block at the bottom declared that the expenses had been incurred in the performance of union duties. A scrawled signature: R. Richardson. A petrol receipt from Burton's garage was clipped to the back.

The item for 4 May, election day, his supposed day off, had been helpfully scored through in Happy's yellow highlight pen.

Scott ended their study. 'Well?'

'Where did you get it?' asked Jacko, rereading the sheet, playing for time.

'Anonymous. In yesterday afternoon's post. First class. Plain paper envelope addressed Police, Newark, Notts. It was postmarked Lincoln last post the previous day.' He paused. 'Well?'

Jacko gave a shrug, confused, and Tricia's eyes stayed on the sheet.

'So,' Scott said, slowly, 'while you have been sightseeing in Lincoln and Paris all week, your suspect has been committing murder and charging for it on his exes. He lied to you about working on the elections on Thursday and you let him get away with it, you dozy bastard.'

Jacko felt deeply embarrassed, inadequate somehow, but, sod it, he thought, I'm not taking all the blame. 'It was you who took us off this end and sent us to Paris.'

Tricia seemed to pull herself up taller than she really was, standing shoulder to shoulder with Jacko, a sort of symbol of their close comradeship. 'He told you we had a lot on.'

Scott, expecting no argument, certainly not from a WPC, gave her a stare of hostile disbelief.

A ringing phone saved her. Scott picked it up. 'Yes, sir.' Silent Knight, Jacko supposed, still sticking his nose in. Scott briefed him on the development, put down the phone.

'Have you two checked Richardson's alibi for Thursday?' he asked Jacko.

'Not fully.'

Scott leant back and swung in his chair, feet off the floor. 'He's on his way in under arrest. You and me will talk to him. She . . .' He nodded at Tricia. '. . . is going with the Ginger Pig, scavenging among his files.' He stood. 'And let's have no more cock-ups.'

He sat opposite them at a plain desk in a stuffy room with cream sound-proof panelling patterned with tiny holes. Between them were two small black microphones. Twin tapes spun slowly on a recorder on a wall shelf to the right of where Scott sat. 'It's my duty to caution you . . .' and he did.

Richardson nodded, unperturbed. He looked like a mature poly student in well-worn black leather jacket and yellow shirt, top button undone.

'Do you wish to have a solicitor present?'

'No thanks.' Rich appeared to give this very little thought.

Jacko guessed that as a law graduate and an advocate at scores of industrial tribunals he felt experienced enough to defend himself.

'Now, we'd like you to tell us the truth about your movements on Thursday.'

'I've already told him and his policewoman.' Rich gave Jacko a pale little smile.

Scott opened his green folder and slid the expenses sheet towards him, turning it. Rich met it with eyes that were watchful but untroubled. 'Then explain this.'

Mild puzzlement followed by enlightenment. 'It's a mistake.'

'Who by?'

His eyes had gone all the way down to his own signature. 'Me.' He turned the sheet round so Scott could read it. He pointed with a finger. 'I've transposed Tuesday and Thursday.'

79

Scott said nothing, making Rich obliged to go on. 'I dashed them off on Monday. I made a mistake. That's all.' A brief silence. 'Where did you get them?'

'I'm not at liberty to say at this stage.'

'If you're not talking, neither am I.' Rich crossed grey-flannelled right leg firmly over left and entwined his arms. After a few moments, he unfolded them, relenting. 'Look, I was in a hurry and got confused. I've been up to my eyes in elections, the strike at Lindum Crystal and a sick wife. He'll tell you. He knows.'

He looked at Jacko who asked, 'How can you transpose Tuesday with Thursday? You claimed you were off work on Thursday helping your father in the local elections. Were you?'

'Of course.'

'Then why charge your union for being on . . .' Jacko reined back his question as another came through on the rails. 'What's PR mean?'

'Not proportional rep . . .' He started to smile. Jacko set his face severely. The smile vanished. 'Public relations.'

'Why charge your union for a public relations visit to Newark when you were on a day off?'

'It was a mistake. I've told you.

'Newark is just down the road from Southview Cottage and a murder took place there that day. You realize . . .'

'I've had enough of this.' Rich resumed his defiant pose; only for a minute or two. Then, in an almost apologetic tone, 'The truth is I didn't go to Newark on Thursday. I put down a phoney trip. It was just to boost the total a bit. You know how it is.'

He looked hard at Jacko who felt a stab of guilt over the exes he'd been planning to submit from Paris.

'You're admitting fraud,' said Scott, very quietly.

'Come off it.' Unrepentant, unafraid. 'If you don't get them near fifty quid a week, head office moan that you're letting down field officers. Every other union meeting is in a boozer. I can't charge for buying our own members a round. It's an accepted and acknowledged way of getting a bit back.'

He held up the sheet between finger and thumb. 'This may be a minor fiddle. It doesn't make me a murderer. I was in Lincoln all day Thursday and I can prove it.'

They ran backwards and forwards through his movements

and expenditure for the whole week; spent a long time on them.

On Thursday he'd been off, he repeated, frankly admitting the total of £4.50 he charged for that day was a fraud. He'd been out of the ward committee room at his parents' home for an hour or so taking voters to the polling booths and for another hour around teatime on the picket line at Lindum Crystal, jollying up strikers. He listed the people, some top local politicians, he'd been with at the count.

They went back to the Tuesday when he claimed to have last seen Penny at Southview Cottage *en route* back from filming in Grantham. He began to speak in staccato sentences for effect. 'She was alive. When I left. Alive. And well. I knew her. I liked her. I did not kill her. OK?' He spread his hands, appealing.

'But', Scott insisted, 'you signed these exes the following Monday when the events of the previous week must have been fresh in your mind. Yet you expect us to believe this . . .' He pointed to the line in highlighted yellow. '. . . is an oversight, an admin error?'

Rich replied patiently, unruffled. 'Normally I do them at home on Sunday. That day I was in London for a union meeting. So I dashed them off on Monday. I keep telling you I had a domestic problem on Monday.'

Jacko moved slowly in for the kill. 'We have two witnesses who will testify that a car of similiar make and colour to yours was seen coming away from Southview Cottage at about nine forty-five on the night of the murder.'

A shocked look. 'Can't have been mine.'

Got you now, thought Jacko. 'The mileage you did last week doesn't add up.' He explained the figures. 'You were busy on the election on Thursday, you claim, when your car was in for service. You only did local mileage on Friday and Saturday. And yet . . .'

'Oh, look. I'm sorry.' Rich slapped his forehead. 'Saturday lunchtime I nipped away from the picket line at Lindum Crystal. I went to my sister-in-law's the other side of Newark. I should have told you. Sorry.'

'Why?'

Rich seemed surprised to have been asked. 'You know as well as I do that Ann's been ill. I wanted to see if her sister

81

would have her for a few days. Just to give her a break from the kids.'

'So her sister can verify that?'

'Afraid not.' Only passing concern. 'They were on holiday. I'd forgotten that, too. They didn't get back until Sunday.'

'Why didn't you phone her first?'

'I've told you. I was on picket. There are no phones on picket lines, in case you didn't know. I nipped out in my break.'

'Did anyone see you call – a neighbour perhaps?'

'No one was around. Everyone seemed to be at some sort of fete on the wharf next to the pub.'

'What time was this?'

'Two-ish.' Then, brightening: 'But I did leave a note asking her to ring me.'

Jacko felt as though an ace had been trumped. 'We'll need to check that.'

He stood and walked into the incident room to brief Happy, the collator.

'Seen that before?' Jacko placed a see-through packet on the table when the interview resumed.

Rich looked down and studied the silver Imp stick-pin. 'I gave something similar to Penny.' It was the first time he had used her shortened first name. 'Around Christmas time.'

'Why?'

'Why?' A frown forked lines up his forehead. 'She was a friend. Do you need a reason to give a gift to a friend?'

'You told me you knew her professionally. You mentioned nothing about friendship.'

Rich repeated the details of their meeting during the last election, their dinner at the seaside conference the following Easter and how they were co-operating on the TV project. 'OK,' he finally agreed, 'she had become a friend. It's only a keepsake from her old home town. It cost under a tenner from that shop near the Bow.'

Jacko sat back. In his mind, the interview had become like a duel on the cricket field, them as the bowlers, Rich as the batsman. They had tried fast balls and spin. Nothing disturbed him. They were being hit all over the ground.

Now Scott brought himself back into the attack. 'Do you, a married man, make a habit of buying unattached ladies such gifts?'

Rich went for the big hit. 'You listen to me. I don't like what you're implying. You're impugning the integrity of not only me.' His face twisted, enraged. 'Not just myself. But someone who can't defend herself.'

Jacko tried a softer ball. 'But you do see what we're aiming at?'

'All right. All right.' He breathed deeply to calm himself, to concentrate. 'Let me explain. She was important because of the work she was doing. Her programme was important to me. A wonderful platform for my union to get its point across in public. And it would have done me no harm, personally, in the Trent Valley seat.' He looked down, mumbling. 'Now, is that a motive for murder?'

Scott bowled his bouncer. 'Were you jealous because the woman you so admired had been seeing another man?'

'Nothing sexual happened.' He slashed out the words. 'Nothing. Nothing.' He glowered at Jacko, then back at Scott. 'Nothing happened between Penny and me. Never.'

Rich had let his head drop and he held his chin to his chest for a few seconds. Then his face came up and he looked at the expenses sheet. 'I know where you got that from.'

'Where?' said Scott, puzzled.

'Stands to reason, doesn't it?'

'What does?'

'The break-in.'

'What break-in?'

'Good Lord.' Rich laughed harshly. 'Don't you know about it? This force is worse than my union. One hand not knowing what the other's doing.'

'What are you talking about?'

'Yesterday morning. Got to work and found the office in a bigger shambles than usual. A window in the ground-floor toilet had been smashed.'

'Did you report this?'

'To the local CID. They've inspected the scene. Juveniles, they think.'

Jacko got up again and went out to phone the local CID, who

confirmed it all. They hadn't reported it to the incident room because they knew nothing about the murder squad's interest in Richardson.

Happy buttonholed him. 'How's it going in there?'

'He's winning hands down.'

What he had to say completed Rich's victory. Happy had contacted Mrs Richardson's sister. The family had been away at the weekend. They did not return from a holiday abroad until the early hours of Monday. Among the mail waiting for them on the doormat was a note. It was scribbled in biro across the top of a *Lincolnshire Echo*. It said: 'Shirl – Ring me please ASP – office. Rich.' It had been torn from the paper's front page. The date on the paper was Saturday 6 May, two days after the murder. Happy had checked with the local pub. 'A fete on the wharf started at two o'clock.'

'It explains the missing forty-eight miles,' said Jacko, mournfully. Game, set and match to Rich.

He went back into the interview room where Scott sat in silence. Rich looked up at him, smiling slyly.

Jacko sat down. 'So what stands to reason?'

'Eh?' Rich's concentration, lost during the interruption, soon returned. 'It's obvious, isn't it? Someone broke in and posted them to you.' He nodded at the expenses sheet on the desk.

'Why?'

'To implicate me.'

'Who'd do a thing like that?'

'A rival.' Pause. 'And who's my biggest opponent?'

'You're not seriously suggesting, are you, that a government minister broke into a union office to steal documents to implicate you in his sister's murder?'

'Oh, no,' said Rich, smiling. 'He won't commit crimes himself any more than he solves them. He has hired lackeys to do that, doesn't he?'

Jacko slumped in his chair next to Tricia. 'We've had to let the tricky little bastard go.' An exhausted sigh. He was bushed, as tired as a bowler who had taken no wickets but had been hit for plenty of runs. He just wanted to hide in the steam of a soothing shower.

'He's lying, you know.' She flicked through a file she'd brought back from the BATS office. 'These are copies of his exes going back months. At Christmas, he was charging bottles of wine and whisky, chocs and potted plants as seasonal gratuities to special contacts. If that silver Imp had been a PR thing, keeping a media contact sweet, he would have claimed for it. There's no mention on any sheet. He's claimed for everything else.'

'He's admitting she was more of a friend than a contact,' said Jacko after a yawn.

'I might just about buy that now, after they'd done all this working and filming together,' said Tricia, urgently, 'but he gave it to her at Christmas, more than four months ago.'

Jacko let it sink it, saying nothing. That's right. According to Rich, they had met only twice before last autumn when she got in touch with him about the TV project. They'd only got down to work on it together this year. At Christmas, she should have been no more than a one-drink, one-dinner, one-phone-call acquaintance.

'It was a Christmas gift for someone special,' Tricia went on, beginning to rekindle his enthusiasm. 'When did you buy something like that out of your own pocket? Your wife, your mum, your sister, your lover . . .' A playful smile. '. . . yes; but not a contact or a casual business acquaintance.'

This, Jacko realized, was one reason why he adored working with her. She saw things he missed. 'That silver Imp's hardly a crown jewel,' he said, testing her.

'It's not the cost.' Her eyes went a bit misty, he detected. 'It's the thought.'

'He certainly doesn't like being quizzed about Penny. Jumped down our throats every time we suggested they were close. He seems free with information until it infringes on his privacy. I suppose that's his party's official policy.' A brief laugh at his own joke, looking away. 'It was all too pat. His explanation for his exes and us getting them. The trip that explains the forty-eight missing miles.'

Tricia was shaking her head, disagreeing. 'He must have gone to his sister-in-law's. Happy's double-checked and the first edition of the *Echo* hit the street at noon on Saturday. By then Penny had been dead for more than thirty-six hours.'

They fell into a thoughtful silence which Jacko finally ended. 'Find anything else of interest?'

She pulled an uncertain face. 'He's got a diary date with a solicitor next week.'

Odd that he didn't call him out to witness the interrogation that had just ended. Union business, not personal; nothing in that, he decided. 'And?'

'In his main drive ...' She nodded towards their shared computer. '... he's got war games on hard disc. You know, air battles.'

Not much in that, either, Jacko thought. 'Every man is entitled to his fantasy.' A shared smile, and he guessed then that she knew exactly what he meant.

'What next?' asked Tricia, breaking off a long eye-contact.

'We've got to find an hour-long hole in his alibi for election day.'

12

Rat-a-tat-tat-tat. He felt as though he was under machine-gun fire.

The gun! Panic gripped him, forcing his fingers tight round the wheel, jolting him out of an angst-ridden reverie. I forgot all about the blasted gun, the murder weapon.

His right foot rode the brake until the tinny echoing of loose chippings beneath his car grew fainter. He was driving so badly these days, mind in terrible turmoil, that he'd missed a Slow Down sign and hit the newly surfaced stretch of road far too fast.

The gun. Where's the gun? Every other thought vacated his battered brain.

Should he ask? Pause. If he did, however gently, she'd have a relapse. God knows she's suffering enough.

But if the police ask? They wouldn't be so gentle. She'd break down again. Can't run that risk. He'd have to get her away, beyond their reach.

He couldn't go blundering about in search of it. But if that inspector and his woman colleague blundered in?

More than a vision this time. A kaleidoscope, chaotic, ghastly. In widening pools of blood Jackson and his WPC lay on the ground, legs twisted under them . . . A hand held a gun . . . The heavy footsteps of advancing marksmen in their flak-jackets.

He saw it all, wide-eyed, a spectator, looking in, wanting to scream 'Don't shoot,' but the words would not come.

Funerals now. Two coffins behind a slow-marching police band, streets lined, a huge send-off. One coffin being lowered into the ground and not a single mourner from outside his bereaved family to share their grief; all those back-slappers, all keeping their distance. He wasn't even there himself. He was a spectator again, watching it all through the bars of a cell.

So vivid were the pictures that for a second he screwed his eyes shut.

Stop this. You're hallucinating.

He opened his eyes.

Priorities. What did they teach you at all courses for candidates, those weekend schools, the party conferences? Priorities. Solve problem No.1 and problem No.2 will not arise.

Problem No.1 is to find a safe haven for her, until she is ready to face up to them. He had time. He'd outmanoeuvred them. They were fighting with their eyes to the sun.

Much calmer, fingers slackening, he was driving so slowly through the road works that the grey flint stones no longer sprayed up, just crunched on their wet bed of black tar. He no longer felt under fire.

He picked up speed when a sign said 'Sorry for the delay'.

A safe haven, he repeated to himself. How? Where?

13

Bored faces. Bewildered faces. Betrayed faces. No black faces, though.

The Brotherhood of Man had not yet embraced them, thought Jacko. Black sports and showbiz stars had always been granted a sort of honorary citizenship that never came the way of black labourers.

There was, he conjectured, only one organization more conservative than the Conservative Party and that was the trade union movement. He was in a bad mood, on duty for a second successive Saturday.

On a dicky megaphone Rich was demanding 'a return to the status quo, pending meaningful negotiations'.

They do love their status quos, do these union leaders, Jacko privately chuntered, standing out of the wind in a doorway, a black mac over his blue jacket. He could see and hear Rich but Rich couldn't see him.

The demo had been described in leaflets as a mass rally in support of the sacked workers at Lindum Crystal. Mass? He did a rough head count. Fewer than eighty were gathered round the loudspeaker van. Rich, in his black leather jacket, still claimed over his megaphone that the event was a huge success, 'showing the true depth of our support'.

Too true, thought Jacko. Unions had precious little support these days

He gazed round the sparse audience. Most of the out-of-towners turn up at Saturday demos in the way that sensible people, ordinary people went to football or cricket. They only came to sell their boring *Socialist Worker*s and *Militant*s.

A small knot, no more than a dozen, stood aside and apart from them, holding banners: 'Reinstate the 38'. The majority of the sacked workers, it seemed, had been too embarrassed or apathetic to turn up for their own demo.

A mixed bag of weather today, sunshine and showers. A dark, wind-whipped cloud started to spit rain on the small crowd on the downhill Cornhill. No shoppers stopped to listen. Those who had leaflets thrust in their hands dropped them, unread, in the nearest litter bin.

A complete waste of time, Jacko decided. He knew, because he'd heard it at his father's knee, that trade unionists love to hear the sound of men on the march for their rights. To Jacko, demos just snarled up the traffic and lost more hearts and minds than they won over. Difficult, he'd always found, to love your fellow man in a traffic jam.

Rich crackled on about 'the duty of every trade unionist to support them and not just with conscience money and a boycott of goods from their blacked workshops but with positive action'. There was desultory clapping, hardly worth the effort.

To an ear-splitting, echoing whine, he broadened his appeal, describing a recent and minor outbreak of strikes as 'the Spring of Discontent'.

Hype, Jacko groaned to himself. A decade ago, in that Winter of Discontent, outside Lindum's parent company, Browne and Green, they'd come in their hundreds, so many they needed mounted policemen to control them. Now just two policemen stood around. That's what Thatcher's Toryism had done to the trade union movement, their sympathy strikes and their riots. And a bloody good job, too. Bollocks to them.

'And', said Rich, loud and clear at last, 'the BATS are once again proud to be in the vanguard of the fight for trade union rights.'

This was greeted with warmer applause. Only, Jacko judged, because it was his pay-off line.

Rich put his megaphone in the back of the van and went into a huddle with the knot with the banners. Everyone else wandered aimlessly away into the covered flower-scented market or the old Corn Exchange with shopping arcades on raised walkways below a pillared balcony, their weekly orgasm of soul-searching and breast-beating having reached its usual disappointing climax.

Soon Rich departed and the knot unravelled itself, splitting into groups. At a distance Jacko followed the biggest group into and up the High Street, packed with slow-moving shoppers.

By the medieval Bow which spans the street, its big clock near to noon, they turned right in the direction of the head office and workshops of Lindum Crystal.

The building was big, of imported white stone and maintained with loving care. Some two hundred people worked there in the worldwide catalogue, outsales and seconds shop; forty-two more, all strikebreakers, in the basement glass-blowing shop.

Before they reached it, the group split up again. Two headed with placards towards the building, to resume their picket. The rest turned into a pub, the works' local.

He followed them into a busy back bar from which piped music was mercifully excluded, waited his turn to order an alcohol-free beer. He sipped, surveying them.

Most kept on their street coats, signalling an intention to stop for only as long as it took to drink a quick one. Two, older than the rest, took off their coats and settled at a corner table, slowly drinking halves of the cheapest draught bitter. He had found his targets but waited until they got near to the bottom of their glasses.

He sauntered up to their table. 'You boys with BATS?' They nodded, no suspicion on their strained faces. 'I'm looking for Rich Richardson. I was told I'd find him here.'

'Gone,' said a wiry man in a rough, thick tweed jacket, very well-worn.

'To see his missus,' said a tubby man in thick, round, wire-rimmed specs. 'In hospital.'

'I didn't know about that,' said Jacko, genuinely. 'I'll not trouble him then. Drink?'

He turned back to the bar, bought two pints of best and another alcohol-free half. He sat down as he put the glasses on the table and introduced himself. 'I was hoping to see him and chat to a few members he was with on Thursday.'

'Why?' said the tubby man, reasonably enough.

'You've read about Penny Browne?'

'It's been all over the *Echo* for days. I see you've let that Irishman go.'

'Mmmmm,' said Jacko, non-committal. 'Rich knew her professionally because of a TV programme she was making.'

They'd seen her, they confirmed, flitting about, directing filming at their May Day meeting.

'We need to eliminate everyone who knew her. Just routine.'

'We were here Thursday.'

'Was Rich?' Very casual.

They looked at each other in thought.

'It was local election day, if that helps,' said Jacko, helpfully.

'Yes,' said the man in the tweed jacket eventually. 'He was on a day off for the local elections. Still came up to see us, though. About six, would it be, Ted?'

Ted nodded. 'Stayed half an hour or so.'

That, Jacko worked out, still left half an hour unaccounted for, but not long enough to get to Southview Cottage and back.

Both men were about fifty. They had not worn their working overalls for the two months that the strike had lasted. On the second pint, they doubted whether they ever would again, blamed the union for their plight.

'We've been sold up the river,' said Tweed Jacket.

'Still,' said Ted, 'Rich works hard, done his best. He comes up every day. Even Saturdays.'

'Last Saturday?' Jacko asked, idly.

'All day.'

'Including lunchtime?'

'Had a drink with him, in here, didn't we?'

Tweed Jacket nodded.

They wandered on to sport and telly. Jacko let them, thinking: Rich has an alibi that stands up for Thursday but not Saturday. Was he lying? Does it matter? Penny Browne was stiff, white and cold by then.

Over a third pint, the talk got back to the murder and Jacko had become more-or-less a fly on the wall.

Neither knew Penny Browne to speak to but Ted knew Russell Browne. 'I know a hundred blokes who'd bump off that bastard. Rich's old man for a start.'

'Why?' asked Tweed Jacket.

'Dickie Richardson was shop steward at B and G in '79. After the strike they got rid of him and lots of others. I got fixed up here . . .' He yanked his head in the direction of Lindum Crystal. '. . . and what happens? B and G and bloody Browne take it over and here I am again.'

He told a story about Browne which, Jacko suspected, was apocryphal, but apposite.

After he'd smashed the strike and the closed shop, Browne ruled B and G with a rod of iron. He banned overtime. He banned union meetings on the firm's premises. He banned all booze from the factory even though the company made the bottles which contained it.

One day he came down the stairs in a floral shirt and kiss-me-quick hat. He announced to the receptionist, 'I'm going to Bangkok.'

91

'You may as well, sir,' replied the receptionist. 'You've banned everything else.'

Jacko laughed loudly, loving it, memorizing it for Tricia whose first stop next month was Thailand.

Still smiling, he said to Ted, 'You've got bottle coming out again.'

'I reckon I must be mad. It's just that ... well ... I'm a union man.'

'Better than being a scab,' said Tweed Jacket.

'Dunno.' Ted looked doubtful. 'All those who broke the strike at B and G in '79 did well out of it. Look at Alan Bond.'

A Lindum Crystal employee man and boy, Tweed Jacket didn't know Alan Bond. He'd been Dick Richardson's right-hand man in the union at the bottling factory in the seventies, said Ted. 'Great days. Old Man Green was the boss then, Dick and Alan Bond thick as thieves with him, wheeling and dealing, give and take in negotiations.'

In '79, Alan Bond wanted the dispute to be put to a shop floor ballot. Dick claimed it was an executive order which couldn't be voted on. Bond led the return-to-work which broke the strike.

He was expelled from the union, was made a middle manager, quit the Labour Party, joined the Democrats who'd broken from Labour when left-wingers sacked the city's pro-Common Market MP. He'd been elected to some council, made vice-chairman of the Parks, Markets and Cemeteries Committee, and, thought Jacko, amusing himself, only half listening, you can't get much higher than that.

Bond lost his council seat when the Democrats disintegrated, as all democrats are inclined to do, mused Jacko mischievously.

'Yeah, but ...' Ted still seemed unsure. 'He's never been happy since. Browne pensioned him off early. Saw him last week. His wife's just died. Cancer. No real mates. He even gave me a tenner for the hardship fund. Conscience money, I expect.'

A sad story to which Tweed Jacket couldn't add. Rather than stay silent he returned to an old subject. 'I reckon this Rich is a bit of a tosser, you know. All that solidarity stuff is shit. I mean, where were they today?'

Ted brooded, so Tweed Jacket went on, 'Sounds as though his old man was a wanker, too, the way he handled that B and G strike.'

Ted stirred himself. 'He was too occupied with the real thing. Well named, our Dickie. Always at it when he was an apprentice. He put a canteen lass up the stick. Married her. The one before her was real jailbait, they said.'

No wonder he looked so knackered when I saw him, thought Jacko.

Over a fourth pint, Ted and Derek decided, fuck it, they weren't going back to stand in the wind on a picket line. They declared a strike against the strike. Jacko bought them one for the road, excusing himself. He went into the lavatory and peed like a racehorse. Alcohol-free beer always did that to him.

Passing Lindum Crystal, he belched loudly. Alcohol-free beer always did that, too. In the shop window he saw a beautiful cut-glass fruit bowl, advertised as slightly imperfect, on bargain offer. He stopped and studied it.

Just what his wife Jackie had always wanted. He owed her something, to assuage the shame he felt over those unfaithful thoughts in Paris. He patted his pockets to find his credit-card wallet.

He saw the two pickets, cold and forlorn, holding their placards. He pictured himself looking away from their accusing gazes as he walked through their picket line into the Seconds Shop. He feared his long-dead dad would be spinning in his grave. He felt sinful – the sort of feeling that came with sex or snooker in the afternoon. You knew you didn't ought to be doing it.

These goods are blacked by the whole of organized labour, he told himself firmly. You can't scab on Ted and his mate. They deserve a bit of solidarity.

He walked on, whistling 'The Red Flag'. A man of principle, he agreed with himself, has to make sacrifices – or, at least, his wife does.

He felt good, clean, wholesome.

Tricia rose when he walked in. 'What will you have?' She was a modern girl, paid her corner. He asked for a Coke and sat with exaggerated weariness in a comfortable chair, helping himself to one of her Bensons from a gold packet on a polished table.

They'd made this early evening date to compare notes, run through their day. They picked this place, the Wig and Mitre, because it was round the corner from the castle and cathedral with which she had fallen in love.

Upstairs was all old beams with a bit of original wattle and daub, but downstairs was his favourite; a cosy mixture of pink blinds, brass rails, old timbers, a bit of brickwork, a bit of stone, plain plastered walls and a red-tiled floor. The sun was out again. The bar was cool from the shade of the narrow hill outside. The day's papers were scattered on an assortment of unmatched furniture. The customers, tourists mostly, seemed to have time to spare. For him the place had an Irish feel.

Tricia brought the glasses and sat down. He waited for her to take a long drink of cold bitter beer.

'Personally,' she began, fingering her lips dry, 'I got on well with Dickie Richardson. Can't understand why you took such a dislike to him.'

He'd invited her into the front room, the ward committee room, she went on, missing out nothing – the lists of voters pasted on bits of stiff paper on the flower stand; on a scrubbed table two sets of uncut registers; on the floor a box of undelivered election addresses; on the wall a map with the Riverside ward boundaries traced in red ink. A great eye for detail, thought Jacko, admiringly.

'Dickie confirms Rich arrived by bus about 9 a.m. on the day of the murder. He left twelve hours later when the polls closed. His mum, a homely lady, kept both supplied with cups of tea.

'Dickie's job, as the ward agent, was to answer the phone, to tell the loudspeaker van what roads and streets to annoy . . .' Jacko smiled. Just being with her bucked him up. '. . . and the volunteer workers where to do the pick-ups of voters wanting lifts to the polling stations.'

Dickie went up to his local club at the top of the street for an hour at lunchtime ('which he called dinner-time,' said Tricia, with a look of feigned disapproval). Rich manned the office and his mum had given him a snack.

'In the afternoon and evening, Rich borrowed that member's

car. His dad doesn't have one, just that ladies' bike in the passage.'

She nodded at her notebook. 'Dickie gave me Rich's pick-up lists. All of them by reference to household chores or TV programmes they were watching gave accurate times for the trips to the polling stations. Everything ties in.'

'You seem to have got on with the old bugger remarkably well,' said Jacko, grudgingly.

'It was first names when we parted. He's invited me for a drink at his working men's club. I explained the importance of it, from Rich's point of view. It was a case of family loyalty overcoming civil liberties, I suppose.'

Always did, even in left-wing families, Jacko acknowledged.

A shadow fell over Tricia's face. 'There was one odd thing. Rich's wife has been admitted to hospital . . .'

Jacko said he'd heard.

'. . . as a private patient?'

Her eyebrows were up. Jacko's followed. He had no strong feelings about private medicine or education. They just weren't for him, that's all. And he wasn't a Labour candidate who publicly rallied against health and education cuts. Rich Richardson was. Double standards, damaging if it ever leaked. Tory papers like the *Mail* and the *Express* would run it with great glee.

'How did that come out?' he asked.

'Well,' she said, 'Dickie was chattering about the delights of being a grandfather. He'd said more than once how fond he was of Ann Richardson. It's a devotion, by the way, his daughter-in-law didn't give me the impression of sharing when we talked earlier in the week.

'Dickie's wife was about to set off to visit Ann in hospital. She'd said to him, quite huffily, "If you care that much about her, why aren't you coming, too?"

'Very sheepishly, he said, "Better not, luv; not in a private ward."'

The old hypocrite, thought Jacko. He'd paid for his son's private elocution lessons but wouldn't visit his sick daughter-in-law because she was a private patient. 'Mmmmmm.' He let it stew. 'What else?'

She'd spoken to the party member who'd loaned his car to run voters to the polls. Less than twenty miles had been added to his mileage clock. 'There's no way he was missing for the hour we need, apart from when he went to Lindum Crystal. How did you get on?'

Jacko told her. 'And, after he left Dickie at nine, he went up straight up to the 'Sheaf. The landlord remembers him. He had two halves with a crowd and walked across the road to the Drill Hall. I've traced his ticket for the count. It was handed in about nine forty-five.'

'How can you be that sure?'

'Because the policeman on the door was the one who arrested him on the picket line at Browne and Green's ten years ago. They've been giving each other the evil eye since.' He shook his head gloomily. 'What's more, Rich has never made a song and dance about seeing that copper at the count. That's important. A suspect in any kind of murder would have made a point of it, laboured it, to prove an alibi. He's let us find out. 'They were locked in, Official Secrets and all that, until the results were declared. He went straight home after the vote of thanks to the returning officer. I've spoken to a councillor who dropped him outside his bungalow about eleven thirty.'

'So he's in the clear then?' said Tricia, frowning, infected by his gloom.

'Unless his wife or his parents are lying.'

Her brown eyes were deeply disappointed so he told her the Bangkok story and left her laughing to go for his sixth pee of the afternoon.

To make her stay for one more drink, just wanting to be with her, he returned to give her a longish account of the demo, his session with the two strikers which explained his frequent calls of nature, the gossip he'd picked up, repeating the sad story about Alan Bond.

Her eyes became alert. 'There was an A. Bond with a Lincoln number in Penny's contacts book. I called it when we were chasing up her nickname.'

'Let's drop in on him,' Jacko suggested, wondering where his tiredness had gone. 'Unless you've got a date.'

'I have now,' she said with enthusiasm that inspired him, made him want to work, to see it through, to crack it as a sort of farewell present to her.

14

The front garden of the semi-detached was without a single noticeable weed among the wide-open tulips and still-thriving wallflowers. A neat garden was always a sign to Jacko of someone with too much time on his hands, a good sign tonight.

Alan Bond opened the door to his knock. A tall body seemed shrunken within blue shirt and baggy, deeper blue trousers which hung off him. His facial skin was so tight that it looked like a whitewashed skull with a wig of wire wool on top. Cold hazel eyes had lost all trace of life; a man suffering in lonely despair.

Jacko stated their business, avoiding the word death. The Penny Browne tragedy, he called it. And he watched those eyes colour into a warmer brown and fleck themselves with greeny-grey. Bond opened the door to them, sat them down, offered them tea.

Jacko declined, to give his bladder a break.

Tricia accepted, stood up again and talked as he brewed it in the very tidy kitchen. 'You'll remember I phoned you midweek about Miss Browne's nickname.'

'Sorry I couldn't help.'

'That's all right. We sorted it out eventually.'

He led her back into the lounge, clean and neat but barren; no cut flowers from his colourful garden, not a place where a woman lived any more.

'How can I help now?' He lowered himself into a chair with wide arms and shiny gold fabric, putting his willow-patterned cup and saucer on the flowered carpet close to his feet.

Tricia sipped after she sat alongside Jacko in a matching couch. 'Your name and number are in her records. Perhaps you could tell us about your connections with her and with the firm and so on. That sort of thing.'

He said nothing.

'It's background we're after. Just chat for a while. If you've the time.'

As it turned out, time was about the only thing Alan Bond had.

He was almost sixty. He had joined Browne and Green as a clerk straight from school just after the war. Apart from his two years' National Service in the Pay Corps, he'd remained there until he was prematurely pensioned off.

For a quarter of a century he'd been uninterested to the point of apathy in union affairs, except for raising money for late members' widows and orphans.

His organizational flair having been spotted in a series of socials that profited the charity considerably, he was elected to the works committee in the mid-seventies.

'Changed my life,' he said.

Not for the better, Jacko suspected.

The chairman was Dickie Richardson, ten years younger than Bond, which made him around fifty. A surprise, this, to Jacko. To him Dickie looked mid-fifties at least, closer to sixty.

'A bloody bully,' Bond went on, vehemently. 'Rode roughshod over everybody. Even Old Man Green was frightened of him. Paid him sweeteners.'

Jacko visibly pulled his head back, his disbelieving look. 'The only extravagance we can find is payment for elocution lessons for his son Rich.'

'He doesn't even own a car,' Tricia added.

'Not for his own pocket.' Bond shook his head. 'For the union. His argument was that the company was paying donations to the Conservative Party. They ought to do the same for the Labour movement. You've no idea what muscle union barons had in those days. If the weather was hot, they'd demand a hot weather allowance. If it was cold, they'd demand a cold weather allowance. And they'd get them or there'd be a stoppage.'

All that changed when Old Man Green retired and Russell Browne became the boss. He'd been with the company since

98

electing to leave the RAF after failing flying training at Cranwell College just down the road.

Explains that Ballard book I saw in his study about the boy with a passion for planes, thought Jacko.

'Brought some military discipline with him,' Bond went on with a satisfied smirk. 'He'd have no truck with Spanish practices, wanted to introduce new tech and streamline.'

A strike was inevitable, but it was the way it was called that so disillusioned him. 'You see, Dickie always headed the district delegation to annual conferences where the policy was made. He moved a resolution calling for all-out resistance to new tech which was narrowly approved. But the vote was rigged.'

'How?' asked Jacko. He was completely lost on procedure, hadn't been to a meeting of the Police Federation in years.

'Dickie's card vote swung it at the conference. He was claiming to represent 3,000 members from our district, half of them at Browne and Green's. There were never more than 1,000 on the payroll. The other 500 were ghost members. He was paying their subs to the union out of the sweeteners he got from Old Man Green.'

'I don't follow,' said Jacko bleakly, lost.

'He wasn't pocketing the money. He was giving it to the union and, by affiliation, to the Labour Party. But he was claiming a district membership of 3,000 when it was under 2,500.'

'I still don't get it.'

'The more members you have, the bigger your block vote, the more power you have. His was the biggest card vote in the union. When he put up his hand, it could decide a motion's fate. It was his block vote that made resistance to new tech union policy. He was spoiling for a fight with Browne but wanted any strike to be official.'

'I see,' said Jacko, just about following.

Dickie called the strike. Bond objected. He wanted a shop-floor ballot. Dickie ruled him out-of-order, decreeing that it was a policy decision from the national conference, the union's supreme body.

'Totally undemocratic. I came out with the rest but all my department wanted to go back. I agonized for a week or so. I discussed it with Joan.'

Bond only just managed to hold back the tears as he recalled how Joan, his wife who had just died from cancer, told him, 'Do as your conscience dictates. You know I'll support you.'

He led his white collar members in the return to work and scores of dissident blue collar men joined them. Every morning, every evening they faced the pickets' taunts and their cries of 'scab'. 'We couldn't have got to and from work without your protection.' He gave Jacko a grateful little smile. 'Joan was spat on in a shop by a striker's wife. I opened one letter and a dog turd fell out of the envelope on to the breakfast table.'

The agony, the misery of lost lifelong friendships didn't end when the strike was over. Blacklegs like Bond were expelled from the union. Browne claimed this action reneged on an agreement, the usual bodge, which gave the union a modest face-saving rise for a new-tech deal in return for no victimization on either side. Within three months he'd torn up the closed shop agreement in retaliation. The union was too weak to resist.

Soon the redundancies began, Dickie among them, but not Bond. In a year he was assistant deputy in the finance department. His pieces of silver, Jacko guessed.

'It was during this time, going back through old payrolls, that my suspicions of Dickie's vote-rigging were substantiated,' he said.

All of this Jacko regarded as out-of-date background on the Richardson family, marginally interesting, if at times complex. Nothing that implicated his prime suspect, young Rich, who Bond knew of but didn't know personally. He moved him on. 'Tell us about your contacts with Penny.'

Three and a half months earlier, Bond resumed, she had walked unannounced into his office at the factory. He knew of her as a family shareholder but had never met her.

'She told me who she was, explained she was working on a TV programme and said she'd had lunch with brother Russell who'd OK'd her visit. A white lie, as it turned out.' Bond smiled a forgiving smile.

'She said the programme would be an examination of the company and union's fortunes over the past decade. Then and now, she called it. I recounted nasty experiences going through the picket line but I didn't want to say it in front of her camera. Joan was very ill. I didn't want it all brought back and Miss Browne understood that perfectly.

'She also said she wanted some financial information for graphics or something – profits before '79 and after to see how they compared. Since she was the boss's sister, I got it out for her.

'She dwelt a long time on the item "Political Donations", tracing them back though all the annual returns, making notes. She said she was going to find out how much BATS money went to the Labour Party and compare that with company donations to the Conservative Party.'

When she'd left, Bond, more curious than suspicious, looked back through the file himself. 'From the early sixties the company had sent an annual cheque to the Conservative Party. By the early seventies it became a legal requirement to record such donations in published accounts. The first record under the new law showed a donation of £2,000, doubled immediately after the strike. All were acknowledged in letters from the Conservative Central Office in Smith Square.

'In the early eighties Browne told me that the board had upped the donation to £6,000 but it should go in future to an account called CCO at a bank in the Strand, London.

'Every year since there were receipts, but no thank you letters, from an organization called the Conservative Census Office, care of the bank, all initialled R.B.'

Curiosity unsatiated, he wrote to the organization care of the bank, claiming the latest receipt had gone astray and the auditor needed it.

'Three days later, Mrs Browne called into the office.'

'Mrs Browne?' said Tricia, double-checking.

He nodded.

She asked him to describe her, triple-checking. The woman he described had been in the *Echo* photo they had seen and was not the horsy woman who served them coffee. She nodded him to continue.

'She had my letter to the bank in her hand. She insisted a receipt had been sent. Said she always handled the admin personally. It was true, of course. About the receipt, I mean. But I denied it, and she accused me of losing it.' He fell silent.

'That it?' asked Jacko, not sure what 'it' meant.

'Oh, no. That same evening Mr Browne came here. To my home. He'd never been before. He produced a duplicate receipt with the same heading and same initials. He told me I should approach him personally in future with any query.

'I told him the issue would not have cropped up but for Miss Browne's research. It was obviously the first he knew about her delving into the company files or of her programme.

'He seemed very shaken and took it out on me. He was exceptionally angry, said she was no longer even a shareholder and she should never have been allowed access.'

A month after that, out of the blue, Bond was offered early retirement on an enhanced pension; too good to turn down, with a wife in need of constant care.

Jacko wasn't really getting any of this and he said so. 'OK, he diverted the donations from national headquarters to a different fund. That doesn't mean he pocketed them for his own use any more than Dickie Richardson was doing in the seventies.'

Tricia came in. 'Russell Browne was on, what, fifty grand a year as managing director before he became a minister? Why should he be fiddling £120 a week?'

'Never suggested he was,' said Bond, evenly. 'I know no more than that.'

'So what did Miss Browne think about it?'

'I don't know.'

'Did you ever see or speak to her again?'

'Yes, but not about that.'

Tricia's head was back over her book, noting down that a week later Penny Browne phoned Bond and asked different questions.

'She couldn't understand why Browne and Green had not cashed in on their new tech. It was the most modern bottling plant in the country in the early eighties. Yet the shareholders were complaining about poor performance. She wanted to know if I knew anything about a Swiss company marketing new tech in which Mr Browne and his wife had major stakes.'

A Swiss company? Jacko recalled that Penny's Fleet Street fella had mentioned her interest in a Swiss company. 'And did you?'

'No.'

'Have you seen or spoken to Mr Browne since he got rid of you?'

'Only once.'

'Can we have it as near as possible to verbatim, please?' Tricia asked, pen poised.

Well, he began, the phone rang at his home last Sunday. 'Ah, Alan,' said a man's voice.

'I recognized the caller as Mr Browne immediately, though in all my years at the factory he never called me by my first name,' he went on.

'He said he'd tried two or three times to get me but kept missing me. Then he said, "I expect you've heard our sad news." I hadn't, as a matter of fact, because I'd been away from the kitchen radio in the garden. Mr Browne told me of Miss Penny's death. I expressed condolences and told him of my wife's death.'

'"So sorry," he said. "I just wasn't told."'

Bond looked a bit baffled. 'He kept calling me Alan. "We have a shared grief then, Alan," he said, "but as loyal old colleagues I know we can count on each other" or something like that.

'He said it wasn't the time, but in a week or so there'd be a project he wanted to talk over with me. It would mean a rather nice consultancy fee . . . I remember that phrase . . . but it wouldn't affect my pension. Then he promised to call again soon. "And, Alan, I am so, so sorry," he said, and we put down the phone. Strange, really.' He looked even more puzzled.

'What time was this on Sunday?' Jacko asked.

'Just before noon. I turned on the radio almost immediately and caught the midday news headlines.'

Jacko sat back and thought it through. After a morning when Russell Browne, Minister for Police, had spoken to the Prime Minister and was being chased by the whole of Fleet Street, within minutes of Tricia and me leaving him in his study, he'd found the time to phone an ex-middle manager who, in effect, he'd sacked.

Why?

To offer him what amounts to hush money.

Holy shit.

His bladder seemed set to burst again.

* * *

Scott closed his eyes and leant back in his desk chair on Sunday morning when Jacko and Tricia reported it all to him. 'Holy shit,' he said.

15

They had not seen each other for three days while Jacko had been away giving evidence in an almost forgotten case. Long days, to him.

In the King's Arms, Tricia updated him over drinks she'd bought. 'The Little Fat Man got a court order to view some accounts. Browne made a withdrawal of £30,000 from a high-interest account two days after Penny died. It travelled via Switzerland to wind up in the CCO account in the Strand.'

Jacko was always out of his depth on financial matters, had never served in Fraud, but even he recognized it as the classic conduct of someone about to be caught with his fingers in the till.

'Every year for nine years,' Tricia continued, 'there's been cash withdrawals of around £5,000. They were set against public opinion research. The recipients were listed as students at the three universities on the patch. The names don't tie up with the rolls of students.'

He whistled softly, said nothing.

'The donations from B and G date from the time Browne was first nominated as parliamentary candidate for Trent Valley. We've examined the financial returns from both his election campaigns since but there's no overspending breach of the Representation of the People's Act.'

Even so, Jacko acknowledged, curbing an inner excitement, if Penny had confronted him with all of this, threatening exposure, it's a powerful motive for arranging her murder. They'd never been close, professionally or personally. The more he'd heard about Penny, the better he'd liked her; the more about Browne, the less. A big job, a big house, a big car, a man of power, and still he wanted more. He was a product of the greedy society he'd help to create. 'What's he been using the money for, then?'

'An educated guess . . .' Tricia shrugged. '. . . a slush fund. Not to bribe voters but to oil the wheels with hospitality between campaigns.'

'Is it fraud?'

'The consensus is that it's well worth search warrants but the Little Fat Man is hanging fire.'

Why? Jacko asked himself. Scotty would not back away from anyone. In his time at Scotland Yard, he'd turned over two ministers bigger than Browne. So he asked why.

'He wants to know more about this Swiss account before he tackles him. That's proving trickier. You know how secretive they are over there. He's got a job in mind for you.'

'What?'

'Rich. A solo assignment. Don't know your brief though.'

Jacko groaned. He'd come to despise young Richardson, rated him as a self-regarding tub-thumper with a silver tongue which had talked his Lindum Crystal members into the dole queue while he kept his salary, his office car and his bumped-up exes; a throwback to the union-dominated seventies, every bit as bad as the money-grubbing eighties.

He went to the bar and returned with an orange and soda for her and a second pint of lager for himself. He was in a lunchtime drinking mood, feeling day-offish.

'Scotty had me in last night,' she said, handing him a cigarette. 'Wants me to withdraw my ticket and join the Major Crime Squad.'

Jacko's heart sang. 'And?'

'Don't know.' She pulled a face. Silence for a few seconds, then sadly: 'Sometimes I think I'm not cut out for this job.'

'Tricia!' He growled it, annoyed with her.

Her brown eyes went apologetic. 'Oh, I enjoy the chase. I'm loving all of this. I dread the kill. After an arrest I just can't sleep nights. I'm not like you.'

He was looking down at his lager, thinking fast but deeply. What he was about to say was important to him. 'I made a mistake when I took you on our grand tour of Lincoln. We missed the Magna Carta.' He shrugged. 'It's not much to look at, really. It's in a glass case and it's all Latin script. The first time I saw it I couldn't make head nor tail of it.'

An index finger ran round the rim of his wide glass. 'We had a teacher who took us on trips like that and she read out bits of the translation. There's an article in the charter. I can't remember the number now and I can't remember the exact words. Something like: "No free person shall be imprisoned except by the lawful judgement of his equals or by the law of the land."'

He had never said this, spoken like this, to anyone before and he wasn't quite finished yet.

'She explained how that became the inspiration for later concepts of trial by jury and due process of law, how men and women over the centuries had fought and died to bring it about. I knew there and then that, if I could grow a couple of inches, I wanted to be a part of that. I wanted to be a policeman. It took me five years to make it. Never regretted it. Not one single day.' He was finished now.

She touched the back of his hand with cool fingers. 'And you've made a good one, Jacko.'

He looked at her. 'Whoever we arrest won't be the kill. It won't be the end. Just the beginning, really. The judge and jury take over. All we do is present our case and let them decide. As long as we play it fairly and honestly, by the rules, don't threaten or fabricate, then the system can't fail really.'

Her hand rested on top of his now. 'Will you take me one day to see it?' A tiny pause. 'Before I go?'

He looked at her. He knew longing and sadness filled his face, giving him away, couldn't empty it. 'You're still going, then?'

'I have to. One day I'll wake up and overnight I'll be twice my age. As old as you.' Her eyes teased him but only for a second. Then, very seriously, 'With responsibilities, dedicated to a family and a job, and it will be too late.'

He nodded, glumly, heart heavy. 'Any day. I'll take you any day.'

Not a bad lot, this policeman's one, Jacko thought, walking into yet another bar. On this investigation, he was spending as much time in boozers as trade union leaders.

Rich Richardson was where his receptionist said he would be – in the lounge of the Nag's Head in Grantham; a pleasant pub, cool, with tinted bottle-bottom windows which, he assumed, was why local BATS members used it, as a form of solidarity.

Rich was surrounded at a wall table by four men wearing blue boiler suits and the end-of-the-world-is-nigh looks of harassed lay shop stewards with a piffling parity problem. They had dragged their district secretary away from his admin day at his office, his receptionist had said, to sort it out.

Without surprise or alarm, Rich looked away from his papers as Jacko walked in and up to a long bar.

Jacko had time for two Cokes, watching them occasionally, in earnest conversation, grumbling privately to himself that no one talks for longer, or repeats himself more often, than a union official. He thought on, for something to do, and added except, perhaps, parsons, headmasters, barristers and, with a couple of long-time press pals in mind, boring old journalists, and he smiled to himself.

Eventually the meeting broke up and the shop stewards departed, looking doomed, masks of their care-laden office. Who'd ever be a union official? Jacko asked himself. The job was on a par with social work – an ever-turning treadmill of other people's problems.

Rich, tieless and in his admin day black leather, walked up to him. 'Well, well.' Chipper and confident. He asked for a Coke and Jacko carried both glasses to the table his members had just vacated.

He sat down and, before Rich had time to resume his seat, he opened up, Scott's instructions, straight in. 'You've been holding back on me, haven't you?'

'What do you mean?' Rich remained standing, facing him, on guard.

'This TV project you were working on with Penny Browne – it was more than a political programme, wasn't it?'

Rich stood still, silent.

Jacko eyed him steadily. 'It was going to be an exposure, wasn't it?'

A smile filled Rich's face. 'It's taken you long enough, hasn't it?'

Jacko patted the cushion beside him. 'Stop pissing us about, sit down and tell me all about it.'

* * *

107

Penny Browne, Rich said, settled at last, had phoned him in February late one evening at home, very excited, and said she had documentary evidence that brother Russell had been syphoning off the firm's donations to the Tory Party.

February? thought Jacko. That's after her visit to see Alan Bond. 'Did she mention a B and G middle manager called Bond?'

'She was a professional. She never revealed sources.' A nettled reply.

Jacko pushed him, just as nettled. 'I never suggested he was a source. Did she ever mention him?'

'She asked for a bit of background on him, his union and political credentials and so on.'

'Were you able to help?'

'I didn't know much about him. I checked with my dad, a contemporary of his, and passed on a few details when we spoke next time.'

'Such as?'

'Bond's a scab and a Social Democrat.' Rich made both sound like some infectious illness, the same disease, like pox is VD. To a single-minded socialist, they probably were, Jacko supposed.

'That was all a long time ago,' Jacko said, shaking his head sadly.

Rich shrugged, awkwardly. 'Really, all she wanted to know was if he had an axe to grind that would make him an unreliable witness.'

'And does he?'

He looked down and said nothing. Jacko knew that he couldn't bring himself to answer with a truthful 'no'.

He asked a speculative question, but made it sound positive and knowledgeable; to hide his ignorance. 'What about the Swiss account?'

Rich answered immediately. 'I don't know what led her to that.' Penny, he said, had discovered that brother Russell and his wife were major stock holders in a company registered in Zurich which marketed computerized machinery to the bottling industry.

'All of it was devised and developed at B and G. Instead of setting up a subsidiary, which would have benefited the shareholders and, I might add, employees through a bonus scheme, he was cashing in personally.'

'How do you know that?'

'Penny went to Zurich and came back with balance sheets to prove it.'

'Did you see those documents?'

A nod. 'On the Tuesday when I went to Southview Cottage after we'd been on a recce round here.' His eyes went to the open door and the main street, still sultry after a mid-morning cloudburst of monsoon intensity.

'Did Browne know she had got hold of them?'

'Yes. The day before, May Day Monday, Penny filmed the Lindum Crystal demo and interviewed Browne at the factory. Afterwards both went to Southview Cottage where she confronted him with her evidence. She told me next day that he'd threatened her with an injunction.'

'Apart from Browne, did Penny tell any other member of her family what she'd discovered – her mother and her sister, for instance?'

Rich seemed to wince slightly. 'She can't have done. Both died in a car crash just before Christmas. She knew nothing about it then.'

A thought hit Jacko, as sudden and as frightening as that morning's storm. Browne's mother and two sisters were all shareholders at some time. All died within six months. Holy Christ. You don't think, do you, that our Minister for Police is a triple killer? Would have to be checked. Might as well start here and now. 'Did she ever express any nagging doubts to you about that accident?'

'It was the other driver's fault, wasn't it?' Jacko experienced relief that Rich had missed the significance of the question.

He needed time to think things through and bought it by asking Rich to go back so he could look at the story from his favourite chronological viewpoint.

Rich went back over it all – his first meeting with Penny at the last election, strictly business; the next meeting at the seaside conference, partly social; the contact in the autumn about the TV programme, business again; the double road fatality just before Christmas; Penny's visit to Alan Bond that unearthed the CCO account and the phone calls to Rich's home about it;

her Zurich trip; her May Day confrontation with Browne and Rich's visit to Southview Cottage the following day when he saw Penny for the last time.

Jacko had a firm, clear picture now and felt in control. 'Why the hell didn't you tell us about this CCO and Swiss business when we first saw you?'

'How could I?' A protesting voice.

'This could be a motive for murder. You were holding back on us. Why?' Jacko used his stroppy tone.

Rich showed no signs of agitation. 'Everyone knows there are dirty tricks in politics. But I couldn't expose Browne to the police. He's your minister. I wasn't sure if you'd believe me. How would it look? His rival unmasking him as a swindler to force a by-election? It would have looked like naked ambition.'

'But you, aided and abetted by his own sister, were going to do just that in your TV programme.'

'It wasn't going to work that way.'

'What way was it going to work?'

Rich finished his drink and began to get up. 'Come on. I'll show you.'

'Been in the job long?' asked Rich, just making conversation, not really interested.

'Twenty-five years or so.'

Nearer twenty-eight, really, but just lately Jacko had become coy about his length of service. Not because it signposted his age, but because he couldn't accept how short was the span he had left. He'd got into the habit of lying, like an ageing Hollywood film star, in the unattainable hope that time would stand still.

'What will you do when you leave?'

Jacko hated that question. Every week someone asked it. What he wanted to do was write. What he feared was that he didn't have the talent. The alternative was a security consultant or some other desk-bound job, a prospect he dreaded. 'Dunno.'

They were in the town centre of Grantham walking past a square with two statues. One was Isaac Newton, a local boy who, sitting under an apple tree, discovered what, Jacko had a hunch, Russell Browne was about to find out the hard way: What goes up must come down.

'Was your old man in the force?' asked Rich.

'No.' Stiffly. 'Unlike you, I didn't follow my father's footsteps. He worked at a factory.'

'Hope he was in the union.' A sideways look with a snide smile.

'AEU and a lifelong member of your party, too.' Jacko wondered why he was telling Rich this. But he liked talking about his long-dead father so he added, 'And an atheist.' He chuckled at a memory he decided to share. 'Yet he played snooker for the Con Club and the Catholic Club. His excuse was that they had the best tables in town.'

You and your party could do with a bit of his pragmatism, he added privately.

'Interested in politics?' Rich posed the question like a time-serving recruiting sergeant at a schools careers convention, not really bothered about the reply.

Jacko wasn't going to bother with an answer. 'Where the hell are we going?'

'There soon,' said Rich, speeding up from a stroll into a brisk walk on wet pavements that steamed with heat from an unclouded orange sun.

Most of the programme, Rich was saying, would have been based in and around Browne and Green's factory. A bit of old footage of the '79 strike. A where-are-they-now with strikers and scabs (as he insisted on calling the strikebreakers) reflecting on how the dispute had altered their lives.

Jacko was having trouble keeping up. People in the main street took their time. Rich rushed on.

'Talking heads explaining how the industrial scene had changed in the decade. Statistics about falling union membership, days lost by strikes, how both parties were funded. The walkabout scene in Grantham had been pencilled in for about four minutes.'

'Why Grantham?'

'To point up the irony of two families on opposite sides in an industrial dispute fighting each other for a marginal seat just up the road from Mrs Thatcher's home town.'

111

Contrived that, thought Jacko, but then you know these arty-farty producers on BBC2 and Channel Four.

Rich came to a stop at last. 'Here was the starting point.'

Both looked at an old corner shop which had PREMIER written in unpatriotic red where Roberts, the Grocer, was once painted; Mrs Thatcher's birthplace, a restaurant now. Through the door credit card signs were on display on a counter with old-fashioned tins of fruit and coffee. A poster menu in the window listed a collection of fine wines. Jacko's eyes automatically homed in on the cheapest – Capalleti: £5.30. Never heard of it.

'Then a shot of her old grammar school.'

Impossible to pass up this, thought Jacko, smiling impishly. 'Is that where she lost her local accent in elocution lessons?'

No reaction, no guilty look, and Jacko knew then that he was dealing with a consummate actor, the complete politician.

The slower walk back suited him. Rich's non-stop commentary didn't. 'Firms that haven't taken on apprentices throughout the eighties . . . The plight of inner-city kids in high-rises . . . Schools that sold off their sports field so kids weren't taught games.'

'Or elocution,' added Jacko, smiling straight ahead. But he was wasting his time. He'd worked him out now. Rich was a man who talked a lot, but never listened, a know-all.

They passed an old, grey-stoned coaching house offering sanctuary from the humidity. Jacko would have loved to have gone in, to talk about the form of the Aussies; better still, have an Aussie lager. Rich walked and talked on. 'A few shots of factories closed down, here in her own home town. And replaced with what?'

A year or so back, Jacko recalled reading, Grantham had been voted the most boring town in Britain. Penny Browne's programme would have confirmed that unenviable reputation for all time.

'A bit of film of a big RAF camp on the outskirts where the police were billeted when the miners took her on. Hundreds of them.'

Isaac Newton's reappearance put Jacko in a better mood so he made a quick quip. 'I'll bet there were a lot of babies born here

112

nine months later with outsized feet whose first three words were "Hallo, hallo, hallo."'

Quick that, and clever, he congratulated himself, but wasted on him. Rich was totally without humour.

On a green, in front of the gabled Victorian town hall, Rich spread his hands. 'Then we planned to wrap it all up here. What do you think?'

Seems a long four minutes to me, thought Jacko, sweating in his thickish blue jacket. 'How were you going to dish the dirt on Russell Browne?'

'We hadn't scripted it. That's what we discussed at her cottage on the Tuesday before . . .' His words dribbled away.

Jacko looked at his anguished face, knew for certain then that Tricia had been right all along. Rich had loved Penny Browne.

He gathered himself, the politician in him surfacing. 'She wanted to consult libel lawyers first. We weren't going to accuse him outright. I was going to say . . .' He looked up into the clear blue sky in thought. '. . . something like . . .' Still thinking, finally getting it, he lowered his head. 'I was going to point out that we are open and frank about our contributions to the Labour Party, yet official Conservative records show nothing received by them from the company. I was going to add something about new-tech advances that cost so many of our members their jobs having brought no advantage to the company or the country because the expertise had been shipped abroad. Something like that. The shareholders would have done the rest with demands for an inquiry.'

Jacko wore a troubled frown. 'The balloon would have gone up for Browne, wouldn't it? A real scandal. At worst, a fraud charge. At best, it would have cost him his job.'

Rich nodded with a detectable hint of eagerness.

Jacko was still perplexed. 'And Penny was going to do that to her own brother?'

'They weren't close.'

'Even so . . .'

Rich bit his lip, said nothing.

'I mean . . .' Jacko was still struggling with it. 'You said what a professional she was. Wouldn't she have had to declare an interest or something?'

'She was going to make any personal . . .' Rich corrected himself, trying to disguise it. '. . . any family involvement plain in a personal voice-over in the opening few lines.'

'Saying what?'

'She hadn't worked it out.' Rich's face set hard, then melted. 'She wasn't from the same mould as her brother, you know.'

'So I gather.'

'She was, well, closer to my brand of politics. She thought truth was important . . .' An exceptionally sad face, in great pain. 'Totally committed to the project, she was. A piece of social and economic history, she said it was.'

'Her university speciality.'

Rich smiled at last, impressed. 'So what do you think?'

Jacko gave this some thought. 'I don't know much about civil law but it all sounds a bit dicy without documentary proof.'

He was smiling broadly now. 'She had it.'

'We didn't find it at her office or Southview Cottage.'

That snide look again. 'Well, you wouldn't, would you?'

'Why not?'

'I've got it.'

Jacko gave him an angry stare.

'She gave it to me. For safekeeping.'

'Why?'

'She was worried that Browne might take out his injunction, claim breach of confidentiality or even that the papers were stolen. She thought his police might be knocking on the door of Southview Cottage. If you raided the BBC over the Zircon affair, you're not going to be too worried about a small company like hers, are you?'

'We never saw them when we searched your office after someone sent us your exes. Where are they?'

'Come on. I'll show you.'

There were a dozen sets of different dabs on the documents, the fingerprint bureau reported next morning. Some, they suspected, would be those of clerks who'd handled the papers in Zurich. From the exhibits already collected in the incident room, they had identified four sets – Penny Browne, Rich

114

Richardson, Jacko's own when he collected the evidence from Rich's bungalow, and Russell Browne, Minister for Police.

'OK,' said Scott, looking up from the report at Jacko. 'Fetch him in.'

16

Kind faces. Confident faces. Complacent faces. No coloured faces, though.

The ruling classes were taking their time sharing a bit of their power with people whose skins weren't white, Jacko reflected, as he surveyed the scene from a hot terrace.

'A good three hundred,' said Tricia next to him. 'There's some money here.'

They had arrived in his specially cleaned Montego with an hour to spare. 'A short speech at three thirty,' his agent had told them, 'and he'll make himself available after that.'

The place was on the southern edge of the Trent Valley constituency, a short drive from Grantham, not a town that tempts a visitor to linger long. That summer a local entrepreneur launched Thatcher trail tours by luxury coach to see the shop where she had been born, the two schools she attended, the chapel where she worshipped with her lay preacher father. No one, not a single person, booked.

Its attraction as a tourist centre lies in the stately homes in the rolling huntin', fishin', shootin' countryside around. They ooze elegance, power and privilege, except for the sad shell of one whose destruction years before, Jacko recalled for Tricia, was reported under the headline: EARL'S SEAT ABLAZE – ANCIENT PILE DESTROYED.

'You gotta laugh, ain't you?' Jacko added. She threw back her head and laughed, easing a terrible tension he felt within.

This place was not on the guided tours. The owner was only a Sir, among the other ranks around here. He had been born into a family that had managed its finances well and he was able to maintain his Regency manor with its mere twenty rooms and twenty acres without sightseers trampling all over it, thanks all the same. Except for a day like today, of course, which was in aid of the Cause.

A banner, blue letters on a long thin strip of cream canvas, was strung along a clipped privet hedge from one gated entrance to another: TRENT VALLEY CONSERVATIVE FETE.

Jacko had parked in a field which smelt of sweet fresh-mown grass surrounded by acre upon acre of yellow rape, the cash crop these days. Never mind if its fumes give you a sickly, heavy headache, he grumbled to himself, it's bankable and, therefore, acceptable in rural areas. In the tidy rows were two Rolls Royces and a handful of Mercedes, several horseboxes but only one other Montego.

Ahead of them, as they walked up to the house, two men wearing brand-name short-sleeve shirts, arms reddened by the sun, dawdled and discussed cars. 'We have a scale,' said Lemon Shirt. 'Three thou for the board, 2.4 for us and 1.3 for the reps. Sally runs around in mine all the time. I still take the train into town.'

Tricia looked at Jacko, shook her head and smiled bleakly. They followed stragglers up a pine-scented driveway. The red-brick house, draped with two strands of small triangular Union Jacks, was surrounded by large lawns. No one was calling the host Sir. He was off duty today, Harold to those who knew him. He was dressed off duty, too, in brown open-toed sandals, fawn slacks and a maroon long-sleeve shirt. He had a silvery, well-trimmed moustache which ran up the nostrils of his nose and silvery strands of hair over a mottled bald patch.

'It's a lot easier now we have a YTS boy,' he was saying to a buxom woman in a flowery dress.

'Yes,' she agreed. 'Good gardeners are so hard to find.' Cheap gardeners, she means, Jacko privately fumed.

He felt overdressed in his slate grey court appearance suit for his third successive Saturday on duty. He was on edge, nerves tingling – scared, frankly – but he told himself that it was not every day a policeman lifts the Minister for Police for questioning and makes a bit of force history.

As he stood on the slabbed terrace in the bright sun, sheltered from a fresh breeze by the house, he felt the heat burning the top of his forehead through his thinning hair and had to fight off an urge to yank down his striped Service Corps tie and undo his top collar button.

Tricia looked cooler in a shirt-style blouse, white and blue patterned with an open neck, under a grey check jacket and straight navy skirt; simple, stylish. Her brown hair was held in a pony tail by a navy velvet band and made her look businesslike. Only her brown eyes betrayed her anxiety.

On the long walled terrace stood chatting, laughing groups, informally but expensively dressed, the women in knitted and braided Chanel and Jaeger, the colours classic – cherry red, bottle green and lots of black, odd on a hot day.

There were floating skirts of jade green cheesecloth. 'Very in this year,' Tricia whispered. A few cotton flying suits. 'Very out.' Some of the younger women looked debby in long white pleats. One had her raven hair spiked to establish her credentials, an art student home from college, he guessed.

Showing the same sartorial independence, a handful of young men had come in T-shirts and jeans to mark themselves out as sons of the soil among the City blazers, thick-stripe shirts and brand-name casuals.

Browne had caught the carefully casual mood of the Tory Party at play. His lightweight suit was that of a Western diplomat in a hot country, thread-thin stripes of deep blue and cream. On his tie, a flock of silver cranes had taken flight across an air-force blue sky.

'His Old Cranwellian tie,' Tricia said. Jacko frowned. 'Used to date a pilot,' she explained. 'Ditched him.'

Poor sod, he thought. 'Did your brokenhearted Biggles become a kamikaze pilot?' She laughed again. He thought: I would.

Browne was moving slowly between rows of stalls whose covering cloths fluttered in the breeze in exposed parts of the grounds. In his entourage his horsy PA looked jolly hockey sticks in her multi-coloured blazer and sensible shoes. 'No Mrs Browne again,' Tricia noted.

Browne smiled, but not too brightly. He spent, but not too lavishly. A jar of preserves here, a box of home-made shortbread there, an unsuccessful go at the tombola stand where torn straws littered the grass.

'Fancy a flutter?' said Tricia, brightly.

117

'Not bloody likely', growled Jacko. 'My dad's ghost would haunt me if I contributed a penny to this lot.'

This was Browne's first public appearance since the murder of his sister. The story was still news, though relegated to inside pages these days.

Three photographers whose idea of informal dress was track suits and dirty trainers backed away from him, crouching, clicking. Trailing behind was one of Silent Knight's men, a secretive sergeant called Harris who everyone called Hush-Hush and hated. Jacko knew there would be reporters there, too, probably in the drinks tent which stood to the left of the stalls. If this goes wrong, he fretted, I'll be front-page news all round the world tomorrow.

Beyond the stalls where the grass grew longer and greener a pony-jumping competition was in progress. A loudspeaker, not crackling today like Rich's, announced each competitor to a ripple of applause from spectators lining the ropes.

From that direction one girl, no more than twelve, in heavy jodhpurs and carrying a hard hat, returned to the terrace. She was hot and bothered with a temper to match. 'She's too small and too old for me now,' she told a pale, thin, bespectacled Enid Blytonish sort of woman. 'I need another, Mummy.'

'See what your birthday brings,' said Mummy, rather shrilly so others could hear.

Jacko raised a disapproving eyebrow at Tricia. They sauntered down the terrace steps, bypassing the stalls, and caught another sight of Browne, sitting on a borrowed shooting stick, watching the pony riders. No cigar today, but then the government was in the middle of one of its health fads, berating northerners for smoking and eating chips and clogging up their arteries and hospitals, so, Jacko supposed, examples had to be set.

Browne was about to set another, it occurred to him: Never get caught. All these people surrounding him now would soon be ditching him, like Tricia dropped that poor pilot.

'Thank you. Thank you.' Sir Harold wore a dark blue blazer with silver buttons for the formalities, addressing a semicircular crowd at the foot of the terrace steps as a subaltern would

118

his platoon. 'And thank you for digging so deep into your impoverished pockets.'

There was a self-conscious titter which grew into laughter when he added, 'I hope our member will take that back with him to Westminster as a reminder from the grass roots of our pledges for further tax cuts.'

Browne smiled uneasily.

'Seriously though, our main purpose is to welcome back Russell. We said when we picked him that he was ministerial material. We're happy to have been proved right by his recent promotion.'

The young farmers hear-heared.

'Sadly we all know of the tragedy that has befallen his family. Like the statesman that he is, he insisted on being with you today.' An appreciative murmur now. 'So let's give him a typical Trent Valley welcome.'

Browne took a lightweight hand microphone from the chairman to long applause mixed with the sort of hoots jazz musicians give each other at the end of a solo.

'Thank you, my friends. I haven't prepared a long speech.'

Some of the crowd did their duty and groaned.

'In the same way that doctors make poor patients, politicians can make poor speeches. That's because we listen to so many of them from the Opposition benches.' Ribald laughter and above it he said, 'Such bunkum and balderdash.'

A five-minute eulogy on the government's first ten years followed – the expansion of the property-owning, shareholding democracy, the drawing of the unions' teeth, the taming of spendthrift local government.

Another five minutes were spent on the ten years ahead – the freeing of more industries from state control, better value for money from the public services, safeguarding sovereignty within Europe.

He ended by inviting questions. On a TV talent show, Jacko gauged, the clap-o-meter would have registered eight out of ten. Some, their duty done, edged towards the drinks tent as half a dozen reporters strolled out.

In Jacko's early days as a uniformed constable, standing guard on the door at public election meetings, an invitation to an audience to ask questions was met with mixed response. At Liberal rallies, a bit of well-meaning waffle, statements rather than questions. At Labour events, finger-pointing debates, good, aggressive fun. At Tory rallies, the invitation was frequently met with embarrassed silence as if questioning the great and good was somehow impolite. Not today though.

A hand shot up immediately. A laid-back student-type was on the end of if. His question, so topical that Jacko just knew a pressman or Browne's own agent had planted it, was, 'Will the Minister tell us how he stands on capital punishment?'

Browne raised his mike to his mouth and repeated it. This technique is sometimes seen as a courtesy to the crowd at the back who may not have heard it. Jacko knew better. It allows the speaker thinking time. President Kennedy was a past master at it.

'My record shows I have always voted for hanging along with our leader.' A low and slow beginning. 'Long before . . .' He hesitated and looked pensive. '. . . recent tragic events, I was in favour of it. Sadly the majority of MPs from all parties are out of touch with grass-root feeling on this subject. They are wrong.'

The hear-hears swelled up and so did his chest and his voice.

'In my new position I am all too well aware of the dangers faced by our dedicated police officers. Nothing I have ever heard in this on-going debate dissuades me from my view that murder in the furtherance of crime or the killing of a police officer on duty should be treated as a hanging offence. If, because of my misguided colleagues, I cannot offer them that protection – though I never give up hope – the least I can do is push on with legislation to make their job easier by withdrawing the right of silence to wrongdoers under questioning.'

The crowd gave Browne ten out of ten. The cameras clicked. The reporters headed for their cars and their car phones.

A demand for some form of community service for those school-leavers who did not take up training schemes got seven. A long rambling question from a City type was succinctly summed up by Browne as 'Whither the unions now?' His view that they were no longer needed in a well-run country any more than they were of use in a well-run company got nine.

'Have you a message for Ted Heath?' shouted a Hooray Henry.

'Get lost,' shouted a young farmer, even louder.

Christ, thought Jacko, just over a decade ago Heath, a decent old stick, was their Prime Minister. Now they mock him. A tough business, politics; harder than the police service.

The jibe got eleven out of ten. Browne wisely did not try to top it. 'Need I say more?' he asked amid roars of laughter.

Sir Harold reclaimed the mike and said thank you to Russell and thank you everybody for raising more than ever before.

Tricia and Jacko stepped on their cigarettes, walked slowly round the side of the house where Sergeant Harris stood by the big blue Volvo.

'OK,' said Jacko, huskily, 'Mr Scott wants us to take over from here.'

'Where're you taking him?'

'That, Sergeant, is hush-hush.'

Browne approached in short, slow strides. 'I gather you want me again. How can I help you?' He seemed to be speaking from a great height.

'We'd like you to come with us to the station to assist in our inquiries,' said Jacko, accurately and judicially.

'Developments?' He lowered an eyebrow.

Jacko nodded.

Browne turned to his agent, the golf partner who had chauffeured him to the mortuary on the first night Jacko had seen him. 'Go ahead in the car. This won't take long.' He turned back to Jacko. 'Am I all right for a lift?'

'Oh, yes, sir.' With his anal muscles twitching, Jacko had no difficulty in keeping a straight face.

Scott looked up, grim-faced, when Jacko showed the Minister for Police into his office at the headquarters of the East Midlands Combined Constabulary, an old manor house ten minutes' drive away from the prying eyes of the incident room. He nodded him to a chair across his big, file-filled desk.

Jacko sat on a long fawn bench, a side-on view, beneath a collection of framed cartoons, most of them anti-police. Russell Browne didn't give them a glance.

He sat down slowly, reluctantly almost, as if offended because he hadn't been greeted at attention.

Scott, in a brilliant white shirt and dark sober tie, leant forward, clasping his hands together over a red file. 'First, let me explain.' He spoke coolly and clearly. 'You are here as a witness to help our inquiries into the murder of Miss Penny . . .'

'Penelope,' Browne corrected him with a pedantic little smile.

'. . . Browne.' Scott ignored it. 'You are free to leave at any time. You may have a solicitor present, if you wish.'

'That won't be necessary.' A hurried little gesture with a hand, let's get on with it; then, obviously thinking: 'Is this normal when dealing with next-of-kin?'

Scott looked witheringly across the desk at him. 'It's a legal requirement when dealing with someone who, we have reason to believe, has not been frank with us.'

Browne tried to conceal his shock with a short laugh that came out as a snort. 'What on earth is this all about?'

'Why didn't you tell us you quarrelled with your sister when you saw her on the Monday, three days before her death?'

'Why?' Browne repeated the word, his face questioning, but came up with no answer. 'I don't know what you mean.'

Scott opened the red file. 'We have a witness who called at Southview Cottage on bank holiday Monday. He saw your car parked outside. He heard what he describes as a fierce row.'

'A fierce row?' Browne echoed it, buying time. 'On Monday?' Then, smiling, relieved: 'Good Lord. That. The Irishman you arrested.'

Browne inched his bottom more comfortably in his chair, relaxing. 'Yes,' he agreed, unconcerned, 'the Irishman who called may have heard a few sharp words exchanged.'

'About what?'

'Good Lord.' Irritated this time. 'Isn't that obvious?' He sighed and put on the bemused look of a parent who can't understand a child. 'She was buying contraband spirits, evading duty. She told me so. How would that have looked if it ever came out? Police Minister's sister buys bootleg booze? The *Mirror* would have made a great play with that.' His face became cross, scolding. 'It may have been a giggle to her and her media friends but it could have had serious consequences for me, which I pointed out.'

Scott bit his bottom lip. 'How did you know the Irishman was selling bootleg booze?'

Penelope had admitted it to him and Assistant Chief Constable Knight had confirmed it, he said. He and Silent had been in touch on an almost daily basis. 'Mr Knight explained why you had to release Riordan.'

Jacko screwed his face, angrily. That fucking creep Knight has been buttering up to him and shown him our hand.

Scott's poker face dropped, just slightly. 'We have another witness who says that the following day your sister told him that you two had an argument that had nothing to do with bootleg booze.'

'The following day?' Browne repeated, looking down, then up, enlightened. 'Richardson!' A scornful look. 'Surely, you can't believe him?'

'Why not?'

Browne sat up, back erect. 'He's as crooked as his father. And he's a political opponent. He'd say anything to discredit me. If he claims that, he's wrong and you're wrong to believe him. I'm surprised. That's all I can say.' A conciliatory shrug. 'Still . . . I appreciate you're doing your job . . . doing it most thoroughly . . . without bias.'

'Do you know Mr Richardson?'

'I can't say I've had that pleasure.' Very sarcastic. 'His avaricious father, unfortunately, yes. The son, fortunately, no.'

'Then how do you know we've interviewed him?' asked Scott.

That blabbermouth Knight again, Jacko thought, seething.

He was surprised at Browne's reply. 'Penelope. She told me she was dealing with Richardson Junior over her TV programme and had an appointment to see him in Grantham on the Tuesday. I assume you're talking to everyone as a matter of routine.'

As he talked, he searched in a pocket of his diplomat's suit and produced an unopened packet of Hamlets. Noisily he removed the wrapping and took out a small cigar which he lit with a gold lighter. The smell of Christmas filled the office. Jacko, dying for a cigarette, decided against.

Scott had waited for Browne. 'Richardson states that you threatened your sister with an injunction over that programme.'

'Nonsense.' It came out with a quiver of his head.

'You'll be aware that we have questioned him at length.'

'Why should I be?' A truculent look.

'Well,' said Scott, cleverly reintroducing an old subject, 'Mr Knight clearly discussed the Irish aspect with you. Did he mention Richardson?'

'No.'

'Were you aware that there was a break-in at his union office?'

Browne's gaunt face set austerely. 'No.'

'And the following day we received this.' Scott slid a photocopy of Richardson's expenses across the desk. 'Seen them before?'

He studied them with his cigar held between two fingers and his teeth. 'No.'

'Mr Richardson suspects you may have been behind the break-in and our receiving that.' Scott nodded at the exhibit.

Browne pulled the cigar away from his mouth and released a thin jet of smoke. 'You're going to have to do better than this, Mr Scott.' There was great menace in his voice. He sat back and thought better of it. 'You are dealing with a troublemaker.'

Jacko came in then, pre-arranged. 'Do you know a Mr Alan Bond?'

Browne looked sideways, surprised. 'Of course.'

Jacko slouched forward, elbows on knees. 'He states you pensioned him off within a month of him allowing your sister access to certain documents. Is he a troublemaker, too?'

'Good God.' His head swung back towards Scott. 'I allowed him early retirement because of his dying wife and now . . .' He checked himself. 'He's unwell.'

'If . . .' Jacko stopped until he'd got his attention again. 'If he's unwell, why were you offering him a job as a consultant?'

Browne stopped, too, but only for a second; then, acidly: 'It was supposed to be an act of kindness.'

'Because of your ministerial position, Mr Browne, you told us you'd severed your administrative links with your firm. You had no authority to offer him anything.'

Browne shifted in his seat, silent, stumped.

124

'This offer was made within minutes of my leaving you at your home on Sunday.'

Browne recovered, sighing. 'Remorse, I suppose. There was I, inundated with messages of condolence, and I hadn't made contact with Alan since the death of his wife. I just felt I ought to . . . needed to . . .' His mind was wandering.

'According to Mr Bond, you weren't aware of his wife's death when you made that phone call. Now.' Pause. 'What job did you have in mind for him?'

'This . . .' His whole tall frame stiffened. '. . . is disgraceful. What are you trying to prove? Your independence from the government? Is this a sick game you're playing?'

As if to atone for his outburst, he turned back to Scott, half appealing, half cautioning. 'You're making a mistake going down this road.'

'We'll see,' said Scott, almost under his breath. 'Is it true that you and your sister were in a legal dispute over the estate of your late mother and sister?'

'I don't quite see . . .' Browne addressed him as though he was a distant speck on an ocean. '. . . that as any concern of yours.'

'The difference between half a million and a third of a million is a matter of concern . . .'

Browne held his cigar up in his fingers at temple height. 'But not to you. It's a civil matter which will be sorted out civilly.'

'This also concerns us.' Scott pulled a bundle of photocopied documents from the file, spreading them, like a winning poker hand, turning them so Browne could read them. He patted them. 'Mr Richardson says your dispute with your sister was over those.'

Browne looked down at the Swiss and CCO accounts, fanned out before him. He breathed out a bluish-grey cloud of cigar smoke and Jacko couldn't read his face.

'Seen them before?' Scott nodded at them.

'I see countless documents every day,' he replied rather too quickly.

'Seen them before, Mr Browne?'

'I can't say that I have.'

'Then perhaps you will explain what your fingerprints are doing on them.' Scott leaned back, a DA resting his case.

125

Browne stared down at them. His brushed-back fair hair had darkened and glistened as though held in place by gel. His chin dropped. Twice he opened his mouth to speak but failed, a goldfish in a bowl. Finally he made it. 'I'd like to exercise my right to see my solicitor, please.'

One of those rushed-off-their feet solicitors, silver-haired, sixtyish and sweating beneath his grey three-piece suit, bustled, breathless, into the panelled foyer of HQ, where Jacko waited.

He asked for a private half-hour with his client and it stretched into more than an hour.

In their absence, Scott swung his feet up on to his desk and gave Jacko his saucer smile. 'A bit of fun, eh, old man?'

Fun? thought Jacko. If this collapses, we'll both be pensioned off faster than old Alan Bond. Yet the Little Fat Man was enjoying it.

They'd been together now for five years. Scott had changed his life. Under his tough tutelage, he had flowered late in his career from a run-of-the-mill detective into a good one. No mystery about that, he realized. You get from average to good by working hard – and Scott made sure that he did. Good, but not great. He regarded Scott as great. Great moral courage and a high intellect hid behind his boyish humour. His work rate was phenomenal. His honesty was beyond question. A genius, and Jacko loved the man. 'I suppose so.'

Scott clasped his hands behind the back of his head. 'Ah, come on. We've got him.'

'For fraud, maybe. Not murder.'

'He's got a terrific motive, his reputation.' Pause. 'He can't have done it himself. His alibi checks. I've spoken to Downing Street. He was dining there all right.'

'What do they think about it?'

Scott didn't answer. Instead, a confident, who-cares shrug. 'If he's hired anyone, we'll find him.'

The phone rang. Tricia for Jacko. 'At Beck Manor,' she said. 'No Mrs Browne. The gardener last saw her two weeks today.'

126

Two weeks today? Jacko thought. The day they found her sister-in-law's body.

The solicitor led Browne back into the room. The interview resumed.

Scott went through all the questions again. To everything the solicitor said, 'We note your question.' Browne, who just a few hours earlier had been calling publicly for an end to the right of silence, sat motionless and speechless.

Scott repeated the questions in a variety of forms, and second time round the solicitor shortened his reply to, 'Noted.'

Only once did he deviate from a legal tactic designed to force the police to show their hand and plan counter-measures. When the question of the wills was raised, he said, 'That action was instituted on QC's advice and with great reluctance. It's a valid exercise to test an important point of civil law.'

The questioning moved on to the CCO and Swiss accounts which Scott suggested were the real cause of the quarrel between Browne and Penny, and the lawyer fell back on 'Noted' again.

'When am I going to get some answers?' Scott snapped.

'You will have a full, signed statement in a matter of days,' said the solicitor.

'We shall also want to see Mrs Browne.' Browne looked long and hard at Scott. 'She's not at home. We'd like to know her whereabouts.'

At last Browne broke his silence. 'She's ill.'

'We'll still want to see her. She's a major shareholder in the Swiss company. Where is she?'

The solicitor shot Browne a silencing look. 'That information will also be forthcoming,'

'Soon, I hope.' Scott's mouth was in a reverse U.

The interview ended. Browne stood. Like Alan Bond he seemed to have shrunk inside his striped suit. Grieving, not for his sister, Jacko suspected, but for the end of a political career.

17

Near exhaustion now, wondering how much longer he could keep this thing off the ground.

Two weeks now. Two weeks and, in almost every car trip, he saw himself flying through a high-sided valley in a fog that refused to lift.

The diversion had bought precious thinking time. No peace of mind, though.

That hard-nosed chief, his inspector and policewoman were closing in, getting closer.

She's no better. I have to get her completely away, he told himself. To somewhere, anywhere where they can't trouble her, tackle her.

One firm question-and-answer session and she'll tell them everything. Even he still didn't know everything.

She'd gabbled out what details she hadn't blanked out. Incoherent, much of it. Garbled.

Where was the gun? In one private, tender moment, holding her head to his chest, he'd tried to find out. In the panic and the trauma, she didn't know for certain, wasn't sure. Or so she claimed, weeping. He couldn't ask again, daren't. Hadn't he told her, 'Put it out of your mind. I'll take care of everything'?

If they found the gun, it was all over for everybody. Where was it? It was a question he asked himself constantly.

Would it be used again? The thought haunted him. Could be. Possibly. When they, that superintendent, inspector and WPC, work it out.

Possibly became probably, then a certainty and he saw chilling visions of funerals again.

No thought of abandoning his family to their fate, of baling out, even in this, his darkest hour. It was all a misunderstanding, his fault, his stupidity.

Guilt filled him to overflowing, forcing tears out of the corners of his eyes, running down each side of his nose, strapped-in body shaking. My fault. All my fault. I'll not desert you.

For a tearful mile or so, he wondered if he should tell the police, to save more life, wrestling at the controls of his conscience.

A calming question. What was that great Washington saying? If the clock's working, why alter it? And it is working, you know. Two weeks now and, really, you know, they are no nearer the truth.

If they can't get to her, talk to her, he decided, there need be no more lost life, no more funerals.

Besides, that gun was probably at the bottom of some river, out of harm's way.

His tears dried. He was strong again, strong enough to take all the flak they could throw up at him.

18

His hotel bedroom commanded a view of the Thames where it bends, broad and beautiful, from Waterloo Bridge and beyond up to Westminster.

A small team of them (no Tricia, though) were based in what Scotland Yard modestly called an out-station: an elegant four-storey building, with mellow purple brickwork, home to the diplomatic protection corps, good cover on what was a top-secret assignment.

His short walk to work was studded with breathtaking buildings, brilliant white in the morning sun. On slack days – and there were plenty of those – he could wander through Trafalgar Square and amble round the bookshops in Charing Cross Road.

Scott loved almost every minute of the fortnight that followed in London. One of the great capitals of the world, he called it. The theatres, the restaurants, the dive bars, his haunts in his days as a detective superintendent in the Met before he became a provincial CID chief to gain the experience needed so he could return here, as Jacko was certain he would, as a commander, then on and up to commissioner, the top job, and police this great capital his way – straight and fair.

Jacko was unhappy. It wasn't just that he didn't know of the cases and characters they talked about in the bars. Or that he was a small city boy. It wasn't just that he missed the green fields as he travelled underground in the tube or was stuck in traffic, not travelling at all. Or that in his many sleepless, mind-wandering hours he missed his wife, his son, his dog and Tricia; to his shame, not always in that order.

He was waking up tired. By noon his shirt collar was grubby. His socks stuck to him in the airless heat. Most nights he had far too much to drink.

It was not the sort of job he liked. The Yard intelligence branch obligingly listed all suspected 'contractors' – men, they said, who would do anything if the price was right. *Agents provocateurs*, wired for sound, were dispatched. Plainclothes policewomen offered sizeable shares of the insurance pay-outs if only their brutal husbands met with an accident. Policemen posing as businessmen sought the permanent removal of partners and rivals. Phones were tapped, suspects lifted and held until their movements had been checked for the night Penny Browne was shot. Most were more Mitty than Mafia.

One was an ex-cop who'd been invalided out after a mental breakdown. He talked very tough at the start of his interrogation, ended up weeping over a wife who had walked out on him with their three children because she could no longer stand his drunken rages. He was packed off to hospital again, a stop on the way to Skid Row and cider and a cardboard box under Waterloo Bridge. Once, said Scott sadly, he'd been a fine detective sergeant.

London, Jacko decided, is a great place to discover how lucky you are to live and work where you do.

One by one the suspects were being crossed off the list. Never got close to a link with Russell Browne; not a whiff.

'Just a day trip,' said Tricia, gliding into his borrowed office.

130

'The Little Fat Man wanted this hand delivered.' She dropped a file on his borrowed desk.

Jacko barely gave it a glance. He hadn't seen her for almost two weeks, though he'd spoken to her most days (aimless chit-chat mainly so he could listen to her seductively quiet cadences, her wisecracks, her laughter) as she'd helped to plough through paperwork back at the incident room.

Now he just wanted to gaze upon her, all over her. Being in London, he decided, is a great way to discover who you really miss in your life. In ten days he'd have to start getting used to missing her for ever.

The thought of having to say goodbye to her soon made his heart begin to sink, nag. He could physically feel the pain. In a flood of conflicting emotions, yearning and fear predominating, he made up his mind in that instant. Tonight would be sleepless but without tiredness, without pain.

That evening Scott held court over an hotel dinner for three.

He hadn't taken Jacko with him for the second interview with Russell Browne. 'You know fuck all about fraud, apart from filling in your own exes,' he'd explained. Instead he took Tricia.

'His solicitor handed over a typed statement in which Browne concedes he reprimanded Penny at Southview Cottage for buying poteen,' Scott began, breaking off from the lamb fillet coated with an asparagus truffle cream.

'He admits he threatened her with legal action claiming breach of commercial confidentiality when she confronted him with the Swiss and CCO documents,' Scott went on.

'He agrees he flipped through them. Had to, to explain his fingerprints on them.

'He denies fraud's involved in either account. He says he sent £30,000 to Zurich but the bank there mistakenly transferred it to the CCO account.'

An irritated sigh. 'In any case, his agent provided a statement claiming sole responsibility for administering the CCO account. If the names the pollsters he hired proved to be fictitious, for tax reasons, sorry, he says, but what can he do about it? It was his idea, he claims, to engage someone with clerical and financial

131

experience part-time to sort out the CCO account from its tangle. Browne backs that up by claiming he had Alan Bond in mind for a short-term contract.

'He insists he hadn't seen or heard from his sister in the three days between his visit to Southview Cottage and her murder.'

Jacko shook his head, despondently. 'Browne and his agent are doing what bent cops do under investigation – covering up. We're not going to get him for anything.'

Scott wiped his mouth flamboyantly with a pink napkin. 'Oh, I don't know.' He nodded at Tricia. 'She's been through all the exes he claimed against CCO. He charged a train fare to London when he was travelling first-class on a free MP's voucher and he hasn't got an explanation for it. That's fraud.'

'Are you going to do him?'

'I'll report him to the DPP, who will doubtless inform the Attorney General, and he'll see the PM.' He flicked his head backwards, in the direction of Downing Street.

Christ, thought Jacko. The career of a politician who'd been tipped in one quality Sunday as the next Prime Minister but one over because of a forty-quid fiddle. He resolved that his own expenses for these two weeks in London would be copper-bottom.

'If Browne isn't charged,' Scott continued, 'we can hardly do Rich over his phoney trip on election day to Newark, can we?'

Especially, thought Jacko, if Rich uses the privilege of court to publicly query why he was in the dock and not a government minister. 'What about Mrs Browne?'

'Under treatment, they say. A breakdown. In a clinic in Geneva.'

'Are you going to see her?' Jacko asked.

'When her doctor OKs it.' Scott looked at Tricia. 'Coming with me?'

'I could be gone by then,' said Tricia, very quietly, speaking for the first time in a long time.

Oh, God, thought Jacko. Gone. Goodbye. He was no good at goodbyes.

Scott tossed his napkin in a rolled ball on the table. 'If it isn't Browne, it has to be Richardson.' He looked at Jacko. 'I don't care how watertight that little leftie's alibi is. Take another look at him and that dad of his.'

On any other night Jacko would have skipped cheese, made a dash for the first train from St Pancras, before Scott had time to change his mind, and sat entirely on his own, drinking beer from a can, gazing at the green fields all the way home.

Not tonight. 'First,' he said, 'there's someone I want to see down here.' He explained who and why.

Scott listened attentively, addressing Tricia when Jacko had finished. 'So, what is it then?' Lips in their undecided straight line, he flicked his head towards Jacko. 'His love triangle or the country house cosy with me?'

She made up her mind immediately, smiling towards Jacko. 'I'd like to stick with him.'

Oh, lord, he thought, if I must die, and die I must, then take me now because never again will I know such happiness.

'Stay over then,' said Scott, more or less to both of them, rising from the table, leaving them alone together.

Jacko skipped cheese anyway, too tense to eat now.

'I ought to be making tracks,' said Tricia on their second black coffee and third cigarettes.

'Why?'

'You won't want me around tomorrow.'

'Why?' Christ, he chastised himself, stop parroting.

'It sounds like man's work to me.'

'Stay anyway.'

She looked away, said nothing, not even 'Why'?

'We could travel back together.'

Nothing still, as her disturbed brown eyes searched his.

Tell her, for christsake. Tell her all you know is that you want to hold her and hug her and kiss her . . . Would it end there? I don't know . . . To kiss her shoulders, stroke her lovely legs . . . Then you know it wouldn't end there. It would alter things. Things would change between us. Do you want that? His nerve went completely, vanished without a trace.

'Better not.' Tricia shook her head ever so slightly. She started to rise. 'You can see me off at the station, if you like.'

Too much like *Brief Encounter* for me, he thought dejectedly. She smiled warmly. 'With a chum's kiss for your cold nose.'

Now she's making me feel like Fred, her old, dead dog.

133

In the lobby a porter called a taxi. They parted without a kiss. Not even a chum's kiss.

The wine bar was dark and should have felt cool but was greenhouse-hot, clammier than the harshly bright, noisy, fume-filled street outside, from the body heat its customers were generating.

The tables and stools had been cut from wine barrels and sawdust was sprinkled on the wooden floor. Jacko guessed the clientele couldn't enjoy their shellfish and iced champers unless they pretended to be slumming in a sweat-shop. They didn't look like artisans in their expensive City suits.

Before his eyes had adjusted to the dimness, a warm northern voice came over his shoulder. 'Mr Jackson?'

Anthony Hollins, Penny Browne's Fleet Street fella, had identified him by the description he'd given him over the phone when he fixed the appointment. His off-the-peg blue jacket, much too thick today, and his ice blue slacks must have been conspicuous among the pin-stripes.

Hollins had a smile to match his voice. He was surprisingly small. His face was shiny smooth, handsome with even white teeth, bright blue eyes and fair curly hair. His suit was a charcoal grey.

The bar was his local – half-way between the City and Fleet Street where he worked on a daily's financial staff. They ordered rare beef rolls (no cobs down here) and a carafe of house red.

Hollins listened, amusement in his eyes, while Jacko groaned about London living and traffic to explain why he was ten minutes late. He'd never worked out that London miles were not the same as provincial miles, always misjudged travelling time in the capital. In the provinces he prided himself on punctuality, he waffled apologetically. Hollins understood.

Soon they found space alongside a wall with a shelf for their plates, glasses and elbows.

'How can I help?' Hollins asked at last.

Jacko was hot, not just from the furnace heat of the packed bar and the thick jacket. He was about to pry into deeply personal matters. There was only one way of tackling it, he'd decided, and that was honestly. He began slowly, saying he'd read the statement Hollins had given to the Yard, thanks very much, but since then he'd interviewed a close friend of Penny's, a musician.

'Siobhan!' Hollins gave a delighted exclamation. She, Penny and he had lunched together in London, he said. He'd obviously found her every bit as engaging as Jacko had. 'How is she?'

He listened, interested, to the details of their lunch in Paris and her tour. 'I don't want you to think she put us on to you. We'd already got your name from a family source. We saw you a long time before we traced her.' A smart sentence that, he complimented himself. It cleared Siobhan of gossiping, protected Browne as his informant.

Hollins nodded, message received.

'We've had to look closely at Penny's background,' Jacko went on,' and you've been helpful. Can I ask you a couple more personal questions and the answers will go no further?'

Another nod, tentative this time.

'Our information is that Penny viewed motherhood as a woman's God-given right. Marriage she could do without, but not a child.'

Hollins chewed on this with a mouthful of beef. 'I think that sums it up.'

'The Yard man told you that she'd been pregnant in the last twelve months or so?'

Hollins shook his head, very sadly. 'It wasn't me.'

'I know that from your statement,' said Jacko so quietly that Hollins seemed to ignore it.

'We made love regularly without taking precautions. I didn't make her pregnant.' He looked down. 'My own marriage is childless. The reason, I've been told at a fertility clinic, is that I fire blanks.' He gave a tiny laugh, to ease any embarrassment.

All Jacko could think of saying was, 'You're being very frank. Thanks.'

Hollins recapped and expanded on his statement to the Yard man. He was thirty-five. They'd met at a press briefing six years earlier.

Yes, he said, she was an intellectual left-winger, highly regarded in her profession. No, she didn't like brother Russell and tended to avoid contact with him. 'Completely opposite outlooks. He's as reactionary as she was radical.'

135

'Where did she get it from?'

A shrug, unsure. 'Met her mother and sister only the once. A lovely home, well-to-do. Old-fashioned Tory, I'd say. Macmillan's era. Know what I mean?'

Jacko knew. *Noblesse oblige.* Memorial village halls and endowed hospital wings; patronizing and paternalistic, certainly, but better than the new breed of asset-strippers.

'University, maybe,' Hollins continued uncertainly, 'or just being in this job.'

For five years he and Penny saw each other for supper, then back to her place, when professional and domestic duties permitted.

'Setting up together was never discussed. Not with my commitments. Penny accepted that.' He stared into his glass, his mood suddenly darker than the claret. 'Do you think it's possible to love two women at the same time?'

Let me know when you come up with an answer, Jacko brooded.

Both fell into a pained silence. Jacko looked around him. On one table a greying man was holding hands tightly with a pretty girl half his age. Agony was etched deeply on both their faces. Lovers, he speculated for no real reason, about to say goodbye. Your turn soon. Oh God.

He forced himself to concentrate again. 'If, throughout your relationship, you were committed to your wife and Penny knew that, is it possible she had another man in her life?'

'It's obvious, isn't it?' Hollins stated the obvious without any sharpness.

'Any idea who?'

He pursed his lips and swished wine round his glass. He couldn't really answer that, he said. Hadn't seen much of Penny since she left the BBC and went into the provinces to start her own company. Wasn't just that she'd given up her Notting Hill flat, their love nest. 'It was more a mutual realization that we had to phase it out.'

They'd kept in fairly close contact, phone calls when she wanted something like how to locate financial records in Zurich or needed a long-distance shoulder to cry on when her mother and sister were killed, the occasional gossipy letter, an even rarer dinner.

They had, Jacko recognized with admiration, made the difficult transition from lovers to friends.

'She talked about dinner dates with professional colleagues and contacts and so on. I didn't get the impression there was a steady man in her life.'

The swirling wine seemed to dredge a memory to the surface. 'In the last year or so she only ever talked with detectable enthusiasm about one.'

'Who was that?'

'Some chap she met about a year ago.' He closed an eye in thought. 'A bit earlier. Over Easter. On a job for the BBC. Covering some union conference at Scarborough.'

'What did she say about him?'

'Only that he was a rising star.' A nostalgic smile. 'She fancied herself as a political talent-spotter. He was a bit left, she said, for the way the Labour Party was going, but full of long-term promise. Youngish. A bit younger than her. I remember her saying that. She was impressed by him, but whether that was a professional, political or personal appreciation I don't know.' He looked straight into Jacko's eyes. 'And I don't know his name.'

I do, thought Jacko.

He got his can of beer, found his window-seat and gazed out on the green fields without seeing them.

What, he kept asking himself, was Penny Browne doing terminating Rich's child? OK, the offspring might have been a bolshie, humourless little bastard, but to a woman desperate for a child it was better than drinking poteen and dreaming of motherhood. There was nothing wrong with Rich's genes. He had two healthy kids at home. There was nothing wrong with an accent that elocution lessons couldn't cure.

The train didn't go into a tunnel but he imagined that it had. A light beckoned. Just a glimmer and a long way away, but beckoning.

19

At the side door, half-way down the tiled passage that echoed to their footsteps, Tricia turned her anxious eyes away from Jacko. He watched them switch on to full beam as an unshaven Dickie Richardson answered her knock. 'We've just dropped round to tell you that your Rich is in the clear.'

'Come into the living room,' he said over his shoulder, turning. 'Mary,' he called loudly, 'didn't I say there was nothing to worry about? Wasn't I right? Aren't you pleased?'

Mary emerged from the back kitchen to greet them in a small lounge which families who live in terraced streets like this, Jacko's streets, call the living room. It is always in the centre of the ground floor sandwiched between the front (or best) room and the kitchen (or scullery) which always looks out on to a backyard.

As a small boy, in the years just after the war, Jacko mistakenly assumed that it was called the living room to distinguish it from the front room which he thought of as the dying room. In those days, before chapels of rest, corpses would be laid out in opened coffins on stands like carpenters' benches behind the closed curtains of the street bay windows. All the neighbours would troop in, view the body, say something suitable and have a cup of tea.

By his mid-teens he'd had many such cups of tea and seen many such humble lyings-in-state, most with exceptionally peaceful faces. Death held no great fear for him, though not for a while yet, he half-heartedly hoped.

The furniture was old and smelt of wax polish. Photos stood on a grey marble mantelpiece. *Daily Mirrors* and TV and women's magazines were stacked in a pile on a thick, warmly coloured carpet beside a brown easy chair with a lace runner as a head-rest.

Mrs Mary Richardson looked unworried, as though doubt had never crossed her mind. 'Tea?' she inquired, wiping her hands on a flowered apron.

'No thanks,' said Jacko, who'd brought up the rear. The taste of the lunchtime lager over which they'd shared their thoughts and worked out their tactics lingered.

Tricia would do most of the talking, flashing those eyes, bedazzling him, softening him up. They had twin aims – more background on Rich, looking for a chink in that alibi, and to discover if his father could drive – and had decided on a roundabout route to achieve them.

She started straight away. 'We thought we'd ask Dickie for a drink to say thank you for all his help, if that's OK.'

Dickie didn't wait for his wife's consenting nod. 'Just a quick wash and change.' He disappeared through a door that led to the foot of the stairs which ran up between the living and dying rooms.

'I'll finish these pots.' Mary went back into the kitchen from where she called. 'Sit down.'

'Been sitting all morning,' said Jacko.

Tricia walked on into the kitchen to engage her in small talk.

For a moment or two, Jacko stood, watching Mary at work at the sink. He was not a tall man – five feet ten throughout his police career. Rich was about the same. He'd wondered where his height came from. Now he knew. Mary was Jacko's height, three inches taller than her husband and much, much slimmer. Facially she looked no younger, her auburn hair streaked with grey.

He stepped on to a plain fawn hearthrug, square, with little tassels running round the edges, in front of a modern gas fire. On the old mantelpiece were three framed photographs. One was coloured, of Rich in cricketing whites holding a trophy. 'Good cricketer, your lad, then?'

'In his day.' A reply from the sink.

Another photo, black and white; Dickie as a youth, lean-faced with a full head of dark wavy hair. Beside him, Mary, a teenager, tall and pretty then, in a pale-coloured jacket. Both wore dark buttonholes. Red, Jacko guessed. The photo was cropped at chest height. A register office wedding. Around thirty years ago. Not common then. That old Lindum Crystal striker he'd got drunk after the rally had been right. Mary was in the club when they wed. Otherwise, it would have been a white church wedding with full-length photos.

The third photo was sepia, of a small man in army uniform with a row of campaign ribbons: Dickie's dad by the look of him.

Dickie reappeared, clumsily shaven with a nail-size bit of bloodied blue toilet paper over a razor nick. He had washed and polished his bald head. He was in a blue sleeveless pullover over a lighter blue shirt and darker blue trousers, only slightly smarter than the pair he'd changed out of.

He sat on a low stool in the kitchen, pulling on and lacing up black shoes. 'Won't be long,' he said to his wife.

They walked up the shaded side of the street at an easy pace. Dickie peeled the paper from his cut chin, looked at it briefly and dropped it in the gutter. This minor first aid stirred a memory. 'We had a health service here in Green Street before Beveridge and Bevan, you know.'

Tricia said she didn't know.

'Me grandad used to run it. The Sick and Dividing Club, he called it. Everyone put in tuppence a week. Got their doctors' bills paid. With what was left they'd have a right beano at the club.' He nodded towards the top of the street. 'A concert party, free booze and loads of mushy peas.'

Strewth, thought Jacko, lagging slightly behind, smiling to himself, I bet Green Street was a place to be avoided next morning.

His grandad, Dickie explained, had been one of the original members of the work-force which opened Browne and Green's. His own father had started there as an apprentice, was called up during the war and stayed on as a regular.

Riverside Club (they'd dropped Working Men's in the middle) had been modernized since it hosted the Green Street Sick and Dividing Club annual blow-out.

It resembled a Swiss chalet with a huge triangular wooden fascia. It needed a backdrop of snow-covered mountains and looked out of place among the terraced streets.

Dickie ignored the lounge sign and they entered the bar. Jacko seemed to have stepped back into the NAAFI of his army days. The room was big, bright, almost bare. In the centre stood a small pool table with plenty of space around it. Along three walls were tables and chairs, easily breakable and affordably replaceable.

Nods came from groups of men beyond their middle years sitting and standing around. They seemed surprised when Dickie didn't join them.

He stood at the bar where Jacko ordered half-pints for Tricia and himself and a pint for Dickie, who signed them in in a ledger which was pushed across the bar.

He lit a cigarette after his first swallow. Jacko took his Zippo lighter from him, turning it in his hands, feeling it with pleasure. 'I used to have one of these. Terrific, they are.'

'Especially when you're sitting on a river bank, fishing, and there's a big wind on.'

Jacko explained that his had been a farewell present from his army buddies in Paris, subsequently lost on a drunken night out. Dickie said he'd just missed National Service and Jacko hurriedly added that so had he, but he did three years anyway, just to get away, to experience a bit of the world.

'You'd never catch me volunteering.' Dickie injected a note of disdain into his flat, local accent.

Jacko handed the Zippo back. Dickie studied it himself. 'Belonged to my dad.' He'd been called up at twenty, he said, served in Europe, signed on, finished up in Korea where he was captured and badly mistreated by the Chinese. He came home a broken man, died aged thirty-five, when Dickie was in his last year at school.

Jacko guessed his father's experience at the hands of the Communists had kept Dickie to the right of the Labour Party.

Dickie slipped the lighter back into his trouser pocket and, with it, the memories. 'What do you want to know?'

'Well,' said Tricia, 'as we said, we've cleared Rich, thanks to you, among others. There was just no opportunity for him to get to Southview Cottage that day.'

A belligerent glare so she added quickly, 'Even if he wanted to.' Slower: 'But someone landed him in it by breaking into the BATS office and sending us those exes. Someone wanted us to think he killed Penny. Who'd do that to him?'

'You make enemies when you're a union activist.'

'Like who?'

'Browne for one. He's frightened he'll lose the next election to Rich. And he will.'

'He wouldn't break in.'

'He could have a mole.'

'Not in the union, surely?'

'Lord, yes. In the B and G dispute Browne was always getting tip-offs about our committee's decisions. Never did catch the grass. And your lot . . .' A glance at Jacko. '. . . were tapping our phone. You knew about every demo we staged.'

Jacko said nothing, sticking to the game plan, leaving Tricia in charge. 'Has anyone in the union got it in for him?' she asked.

'When there's trouble, the strikers blame the union official for calling them out. The scabs blame him for losing their cards.'

Hardly sounds like that great movement of brotherly love, thought Jacko.

'Could this sort of aggro be happening now with the current Lindum Crystal dispute?' Tricia asked.

'Could be.'

She asked for names. Dickie gave her question long consideration but no names. She didn't push. Today was to be just a gentle probe, they'd agreed.

'It would have to be someone who goes to the BATS office and knows which papers are kept where,' Jacko ventured.

'A union office is like Piccadilly Circus when there's a dispute on. People in and out all day.'

Tricia bought the next round and rounded this subject off, head closer to his. 'So what we're saying is this: It might have been someone in Browne's pay?'

Dickie nodded.

'On the other hand, it might be an enemy within the union?'

Another nod.

'Or the break-in at the BATS office could have been coincidental, the work of juveniles, as the local CID suspect?'

A shrug this time, not speculating.

Dickie reminisced for a while about his time at B and G, fumed at Browne's union-bashing and bemoaned his current ill-paid job on shift work at a small plant on an industrial estate, his third in a decade, long lay-offs in between because managements had him blacklisted as a troublemaker.

He returned to his management conspiracy theory. 'They belittle union leaders these days, spread lies, anything to discredit them. In the old days a good official was promoted out of harm's way into middle management.'

'Like Alan Bond, you mean?' said Jacko, casually.

The colour drained from Dickie's face.

'It's just that we've seen him during our inquiries. He was quite helpful to us.' Jacko wondered what chord he'd struck. 'And to Penny Browne and her programme.'

Dickie audibly sucked up phlegm from the back of his throat and flicked his chin down as if to spit on the floor, swallowed it, bringing his head up again. 'He's a scab. We don't mention him here. This is a working men's club.'

Jacko smiled feebly. 'What was Old Man Green like in the old days before Russell Browne became MD?'

Dickie screwed the first two fingers together on his right hand and smirked, colour restored. 'We were like that. Great days. Never any real trouble.'

'Have you seen Browne since he got rid of you?'

'Only spouting off on the telly.'

'How about his sister Penny?'

'Whatderyermean?' Another fierce look.

'Well, Rich had dealings with her over the TV programme. Did you ever meet her?'

A headshake. 'She filmed the May Day rally, I'm told, but I don't recall seeing her.'

Tricia leaned closer, pushing now. 'Did Rich's wife ever meet her?'

Dickie pulled his head away, alarmed. 'No. And don't you go bothering her. She's poorly.'

'We were sorry to hear that. Having to rear two youngsters when Rich is so busy with the strike and campaigning must be a great strain. How is she?'

'Not good.'

'Been to see her in hospital?'

'Rich goes most days and takes my missus sometimes.'

Dickie blew out as if to exude some sadness. 'It came on all of a sudden.' He fumbled to find his cigarettes. Jacko found his first. All three were lit by Dickie. His hand shook slightly as he used his Zippo.

He changed the subject abruptly to the Euro elections and the canvassing he was doing, predicting big gains for his party.

'What with shift work and politics you won't have much time for your fishing.' Tricia put on a sympathetic face. 'I used to go with my father after trout.'

'Oh,' said Dickie, modestly, 'it's just coarse water round here.'

'Pike?' asked Tricia, expertly.

'Sometimes.' And he listed the types of fish he'd caught, the biggest he'd ever netted, the match-angling money he'd won. She listened, apparently enthralled. Jacko could tell that he was hooked.

The season on the Witham which flowed under Green Street bridge was only a week, he said, but he planned to go to the Trent. 'Tricky there but great pike on the weir where the tide down from the Humber stops.'

Jacko finally went fishing himself. 'It's a hell of a long way to cycle.'

'I train it to Newark with the bike in the guard's van, then pedal up the old Great North Road. It's not far. Less than an hour door-to-door. Well worth it.'

'Have you never driven?' asked Tricia, catching on quickly.

Another headshake. Browne and Green's had been two minutes' walk away, he explained, over the bridge from home. When he lost his job there, he'd never bothered to learn, never got round to it.

Shit, thought Jacko. No wheels. Can't have been him, acting for and on behalf of his son, or taking a dreadful vengeance on the Browne family on his own behalf for the havoc they had brought to his working and political life. He couldn't have made the forty-eight-mile trip by bike. His wife had said he was in the house by ten thirty at the latest on the night of the murder. Shit.

Can't just take his word for it, he decided. Maybe he learned years ago but never got round to taking a test or owning a car. How can I check that? Who can I ask?

Dickie was talking fishing successes again, Tricia giving him her full attention. 'Does Rich fish, too?' she asked.

144

'No time. Not even for cricket these days.'

'How about his wife?' asked Tricia, pushing to the limit.

'Whatderyermean?' A growl, startling her.

'I go with my dad. Lots of women go. Don't you ever take her?'

'No.'

'You must.' Tricia spoke with real enthusiasm, like a games mistress. 'It's wonderfully relaxing. You must take her with a picnic when she comes home from hospital.'

'If she comes home,' he said, more mysterious than sad, his mind far away.

No reply to the front door at Alan Bond's semi in a tree-lined cul-de-sac, the domain of white collar workers, over the bridge and beyond Browne and Green's factory.

They opened a lattice gate, newly coated with sharp-smelling preservative, at the side of the house. He was where Jacko guessed he'd be – in a back garden, immaculately laid out with young bedding plants, well-established, making good progress in the warmth of early June.

A welcoming smile flowed through his weary face. He laid aside his hoe, told them to sit down, went indoors and reappeared with three glasses of lemonade in which ice cubes tinkled.

He sat beside Tricia on a wooden garden seat in the dappled shade of a lilac tree heavy with white, delicately scented blossom.

Jacko was inspecting the veg patch, thinking through the question-line. Again, they had dual targets: Did Bond tell Penny Browne about Dickie's union vote-rigging? Had Dickie ever been able to drive?

He returned from his tour, complimented him on his onions, noted Tricia's dark skirt was riding provocatively high.

He sat down on the springy, weedless lawn where he could get a good look at her smooth, shapely calf muscles. She crossed her legs at the knees, very pertly, wrapping left instep round her right ankle to deny him the view, one step ahead of him again.

Jacko smiled, gracious in defeat.

He craned his neck up towards Bond, summarized the Browne inquiries, flannelling, not telling him much, apart from reassuring him that his assistance wouldn't jeopardize his pension.

'The promised consultancy job's a goner, though, I'm afraid,' he added.

'Never believed it anyway.' Bond smiled thinly.

Jacko nodded towards Tricia. 'We've just had a drink with your old workmate Dickie Richardson.' Bond didn't ask why. 'Seems unhappy in his new job,' Jacko added.

'A lot of people were unhappy following the Browne and Green strike,' said Bond. 'Since he was largely responsible . . .' He shrugged. More or less serves him right, he was going to say.

Jacko plucked a blade of grass and began to chew. 'When Penny Browne called at your office, did you tell her how Dickie used to inflate his union membership roll to increase his block vote?'

'Why?' A look of genuine surprise. 'She was only interested in company donations to the Tory Party.'

'So the subject of donations via the union to the Labour Party never came up? You're sure of that?' Jacko was vandalizing the grass blade now, frustrated.

'Certain.'

'The donations to the Conservative Party were recorded officially in B and G's accounts. Was there any record kept of Old Man Green's sweeteners to Dickie?'

'They'd been lost under various headings – hospitality, cash payments. Easy to do. Nothing was computerized in those days.'

Shit, thought Jacko again.

Tricia filled the conversational void, talking about Dickie's passion for fishing, which Bond didn't share. Then she said, 'His wife seems a homely enough sort. Remember her?'

'No'.

'A canteen girl at B and G's. A shotgun wedding by the sound of things.'

'Just like him,' said Bond in a lighter tone, no malice.

Jacko began speaking and smiling very knowingly. 'Not much to look at now – then listen to who's talking – but a bit of a lad in his time was Dickie, they say.'

'So they say.'

Casually now. 'Did he have a passion wagon?'

Too casual, Jacko realized, as Bond gave him an uncomprehending look. 'You know. Wheels. A car. For trips to the woods?'

'Do you know . . .' Bond gave it some thought '. . . I don't think I've seen him driving. Ever. I used to take him to union meetings sometimes. No.' Positive.

Shit, shit, shit, thought Jacko. No transport, no motive. He lapsed into silence, sulking really.

Tricia prattled on, Jacko hardly listening. 'You liked Penny, didn't you?' No response. 'Despite the problem her visit caused you?'

'She was a bonny little lass, certainly; very engaging manner.'

'More so than her brother Russell?' Tricia put on a shrewd smile. Bond smiled carefully. 'Their mother, the colonel's wife, was a fine lady, too, they say,' Tricia went on.

'Oh, yes,' Bond agreed without hesitation.

In the seventies, before the trouble, he said, she always showed up for Christmas and retirement parties, mixing with the men and their womenfolk, but never daughters Caroline or Penny. In fact, he'd never seen Penny till she turned up unannounced in the office ('and surprisingly diminutive she turned out to be'). He'd never seen Caroline at all. Not once in more than forty years' service.

A nostalgic sigh. 'They were good days before . . .' He turned to Jacko, silent for some time. '. . . Richardson ruined them.' The mention of his name prompted a resumption of the topic of conversation Jacko had dropped. 'Having no car didn't stop him.'

'Stop what?' asked Jacko moodily.

'You know.' A shy look at Tricia.

'No,' she said, sweetly, 'but tell me, please.'

Bond's bit of gossip went back to the mid-fifties. He'd just been demobbed from National Service. Dickie was a teenager, an apprentice, not long out of school.

'There was a whisper in the works canteen that Dickie had

147

been up to something naughty with a bigwig's daughter,' said Bond. 'Under-age sex of some sort, but no one was sure how far it went.'

'If it was the daughter of some bigwig, a major shareholder or a company executive, say, why wasn't Dickie fired?' asked Tricia

'His dad, I suppose. He died after being a POW in Korea. Both the Brownes and the Greens were military families. Russell, too.'

'You told us,' Tricia reminded him. 'A short spell in the RAF.'

'Dickie became his family's breadwinner after his father died,' Bond continued. 'And his grandfather had been a good servant, retired with his gold watch.'

Jacko had sat up on the grass, absorbed, alert.

Flash. Like a camera bulb popping. Two photos were instantly developed in his mind – of a family group of four in colour in a leafy garden and of a black and white photo of a register office wedding.

In his mind's eye, they became negatives and he held one on top of the other. It came to him in that blinding flash, not slowly, as on the train trip home. Good God, he thought, stunned, what a fertile family.

He asked his next question with his heart in his mouth, eyelids blinking in the after-flash. 'Whose bigwig's daughter was it?'

'All I remember was a rumour about Sandy Banks. I never did understand it. Never asked. Never was a boss connected with B and G with that name.'

Jacko seemed to swallow his heart into his stomach. His face dropped with it.

Bond saw his disappointment. 'I told you it was just gossip,' he said apologetically.

Shit, shit, shit, thought Jacko. He'd been sure he was on the brink. One name – that's all he was short of, and Bond had come up with the wrong one. Sandy Banks, for christsake. Sounds like a sodding stand-up comic who's not fucking funny. Who, in God's name, is or was Sandy Banks?

Tricia broke into his black depression. 'Seek and ye shall find.'

148

She unwound her legs. He waited for a close-up flash of thigh as well as calf. She nipped her knees and ankles together, pushing herself, hand on the garden seat.

Nothing.

Everyone, everybody was conspiring against him today.

20

'Sperm Bank?' Jacko wasn't quite sure why he'd said it and regretted it immediately he saw Tricia's eyes frost over.

Any matter remotely connected with sex was never mentioned between them. Everything else they'd discussed, openly and honestly. But not that. It was as if it might give him Paris or London ideas, but he never really related sperm to sex.

In his school-days sperm was spunk. Every time a cowboy in the Saturday morning serial at the Ritz referred to one of his womenfolk as being 'spunky' or 'full of spunk' the cinema would erupt with gales of delighted, dirty laughter, so a new word was substituted. Someone found sperm which he'd always associated with whales.

Funny, he reflected, the way the permissive society of the sixties stole your words – like gay, grass and spunk.

The truth, he decided with a yawn, was that he was bored and, when he was bored, he was inclined to say and do silly things.

They had gone back through half a century of B and G records but Alan Bond had been right; they could find no Bank, singular or plural, who had been an executive or even a shareholder of the company.

They had culled the names of more than a hundred Banks from two phone books. Only a dozen or so answered to the nickname of Sandy. One was a carpenter who smoothed wood for a living. One was an incompetent golfer who kept visiting bunkers. One was an ageing prostitute, a goodtime girl from the days of GIs. Jacko checked her out personally. She had black roots in her ginger hair. He guessed she wasn't sandy all over, didn't check her out that far. None had any connection with Browne and Green's.

They switched their attention from people to places. They had trotted out the obvious jokes. Bottle Bank from Tricia; Dogger Bank from Jacko just before he'd come out with Sperm Bank and bombed.

He looked across the desk at her, longing for a conciliatory smile. Her eyes were down, peevish, at his breach of their unwritten rules. His head dropped and his eyes rested on the doodles on his pad where 'Bank' had an 's' added, circled, then crossed out, and he'd drawn distorted fish, their mouths hanging open.

He looked out on a dull day through the window of a tiny, airless office they were sharing in Lincoln's modern police station at the foot of a hill leading up to the cathedral; not the hill or the rabbit warren of a station where he'd served his early years in the police force. They were, he realized, going back into events that took place while he was still at school, long before Tricia was born. A hopeless task.

His clanger nagged him still. If he'd called her spunky, he could have understood Tricia's displeasure. But sperm? Why did I say that? Dogger Bank was linked in his mind with fish and the sea, which meant whales, which meant sperm whales.

Or, working it back the other way, sperm meant whales, meant sea, meant Dogger Bank, meant fishing grounds, meant Dickie Richardson.

He looked back at his doodles, studied them, suddenly staring at them, and there was the beginnings of an answer.

Not Dogger Bank. A fishing ground on a river, not one stuck half-way out into the North Sea.

He looked up Water in the phone book and called the river authority. Their clerk had heard of Sincil Bank, a drain after which the home of the city's football club took its name, but not Sandy Bank or Banks. 'Try the bailiffs,' he suggested.

'Upper or Lower Witham,' said a female voice when he finally got through. She gave two numbers.

He gave Tricia Lower whose bailiff had heard of Bardney Bank and Five Mile Bank but not Sandy Bank.

Upper told Jacko with a juvenile giggle that he'd heard of the Co-op Bank and the Blood Bank. Jacko only liked silly jokes when he was cracking them. 'How long have you been on the bloody job, mate?' he asked testily.

'Don't make my debut on patrol until the new season opens,'

150

said bailiff, suitably subdued. He gave the name and address of the man he'd replaced. He lived in a terrace street near Green Street, with a blocked-off end because it backed up to the river.

'Sandy Banks?' he repeated over the phone. 'Christ, you're going back a bit, son.'

Jacko started scribbling, a stupid smile spreading over his face as he wondered whether Tricia would call him a spunky old sod when he broke the news that he had sought and he had found.

They lowered themselves on to a foot-high concrete wall separating a tarmac towpath from the bank which sloped steeply down to the river.

Tricia sat side-saddle, knees together, the hem of her black skirt tugged down. No reward, Jacko realized, for solving the riddle of Sandy Bank.

Each side of them the bank was waist-high with tall weeds and lanky white-flowered cow parsley. In front the grass had been trodden short all the way down to a patch of caked, cracked clay at which the water lapped.

Where the grass grew longer a pair of upright cylinders, gunmetal grey, rose out of the bank like ugly air vents. On the other side of the river, fifteen to eighteen yards across, another pair of cylinders stood. Behind them the bank rose steeply.

'So what's so sandy about this place?' Jacko looked across the brown water, smoking a cigarette which failed to mask the muddy smells of summer by the river.

The old bailiff, a tiny man, standing behind them, laughed. He put his hand on Jacko's shoulder, stepped over the wall and sat lightly beside him. Like a bird on a branch, he was missing nothing that moved within his vision, every ring that appeared in the water being observed and noted. His face was creased, nose hooked, dark eyes alert. His body had the hardy agility of a young, fit man.

Cloudy and cold today, with an easterly wind which blew down the river. Jacko was pleased he was wearing his thick blue jacket. Just looking at the old bailiff in his khaki cotton trousers and red shirt buttoned at the wrists, no sweater, made him feel the chill, a wimp.

'See those supports?' The old bailiff gestured across the river.

They were so obscenely obvious that Jacko didn't answer. 'A railway bridge rested on them and ran all the way back.'

All three turned. More pairs of cylinders were dotted at intervals as they approached another high man-made embankment.

'In the war,' the bailiff went on, 'they built a bloody big barricade directly under the bridge with a gap for the river. Over there . . .' All three faced the front again as he pointed across the river. '. . . where the bridge and bank joined, they built a pill box for the sentries.'

'What were they guarding?' asked Tricia.

The old bailiff jerked his head towards a sprawling factory, clad with grey corrugated iron, standing on the bank further to the north. 'Made munitions there in the war. The barricade was a good six feet high and four feet thick. They didn't demolish it for ages. More important things to do, I expect. Like building houses. When they did get round to it the inside was full of sand. They carted the bricks away as hard core and dumped the sand on the banks. Kids played here for years afterwards. More sand than Skeggy beach until the floods gradually took it away.'

'When did they take it down?' asked Jacko.

The old bailiff screwed an eye in thought. 'Ten years after the war; a bit longer, perhaps.'

Around 1955. Jacko did some mental arithmetic, not his strong point. Dickie was born in 1940, left school at fifteen to become a B and G apprentice. So the pill box could still have been standing then.

He could see it in his mind's eye, jerry-built with a sand-covered floor. Not a very romantic place to lose your virginity but more going for it than the open banks with clumps of nettles beyond Green Street bridge where Jacko had tried and failed with Olive Oyl around the same time.

Tricia, who always seemed to sense when he needed private thinking time, was chatting knowledgeably about angling. The bailiff told her he planned to spend his summer fishing the stretch he'd patrolled all these years.

He stood, nimbly. 'If that's it then . . .'

Jacko nodded. 'Thanks.' He smiled. 'Don't forget to take out your licence.' They parted with friendly waves.

* * *

152

They sat on the wall for a long time. He shared all his thoughts with her. Except his Olive Oyl memory, of course.

'You mean . . .' She pulled a disgusted face. '. . . they actually had sex in places like that?'

'It was before duvets, central heating, flats, hotel rooms on exes, even the back seats of cars,' Jacko explained, feeling very old.

She pulled his thoughts and theories about, examining them in great detail. 'It will alter the whole course of the inquiry.'

'I could be wrong.' Doubt descended, engulfing him. If so, it was a massive intrusion, a terrible slur, a blatant breach of civil rights. If it leaked, the combined weight of the Conservative Party and the whole Labour movement would crash down on his head, crushing him.

'Let's find out if you're right,' she said, positively.

'How?'

'Get a body fluid sample.'

Jacko groaned. He pictured Dickie talking about the Sick and Dividing Club and walking up Green Street with the bit of loo paper on his shaving cut which he dropped into the gutter.

All Jacko had had to do was leave him chatting up Tricia in the club, double back and pick it up. He hadn't. It would have been swept up days ago and buried deep in the council's refuse tip.

'I can hardly punch him on the nose and give him my hankie to bleed in, can I?' he said.

'There must be a way without him catching on.' Tricia fell silent. Slowly a gleam rose in those brown eyes.

21

'I can see clearly now the rain has gone. I can see all obstacles in my way.'

The song over the car radio seemed to reach him via his imagined headphones.

Music. The first he had listened to, actually heard, in nearly five weeks.

He felt he was soaring over clouds, his course charted. It

would mean the end of his political dreams. For a while anyway. Better than ruin and prison. He'd plead personal commitments. His chance would come again. When she was better.

This time next week she'd be out of the law's reach. Just for a month. Time enough to settle her down, rehearse her story for when they came after her again.

They wouldn't be able to touch her there. He'd checked it out carefully. They couldn't extradite a reluctant witness; an accused, yes; not a witness. By the time they came back he'd have coached and coaxed her.

If they came back, he corrected himself. He had doubts, glorious, soothing doubts, about that now.

The crisis was over. He was certain of that. The acid test had been and gone. He was sure now that the gun must be on some riverbed. No gun, no drama, no more loss of life. No visions now of that inspector and WPC lying shot dead.

And there I'd been in a sweat, fearing all sorts of appalling consequences. He laughed at himself. A short laugh. A mirthless laugh. But a laugh. The first in almost five weeks.

'*Gone are the dark clouds that had me blind,*' Johnny Nash sang. '*It's gonna be a bright, bright, sunshiny day.*'

22

A bright, sunny day. Only gloom for Jacko. In less than a week, she'd be gone.

He'd dropped into the Swiss NAAFI, unannounced. Her idea. 'Men-only work,' she'd said. 'You'll manage without me. Besides, I've got to arrange my farewell party.'

Dickie had been pleased to see him and signed him in. Jacko, following Tricia's script, told him he'd been closing down the local operation. 'All loose ends tied up here.' So far, so good.

But then Dickie's curious friends joined them. Jokes about blacks and homosexuals and sex. Dickie laughed at them all. Chat about a gang who had murdered a homeless boy. 'Hanging's too good for them,' Dickie declared. Almost every sentence contained a fuck or a fucking. Had Tricia been present, not a swear word would have been uttered. No one's more chauvinistic (or polite in mixed company, depending on which way you view it) than middle-aged, white, working-class men.

Dickie had an elbow on the bar, eyes on a TV with a big screen in the far corner. He started shouting pointless advice to a well-beaten jockey on a course miles away.

A wasted trip, thought Jacko. Saturday lunchtime at the Swiss NAAFI was not the time or place. He ordered a sizeable round, glanced at his watch, working out an excuse to leave.

He'd made a conscious effort to dress off-duty. The younger he dressed, the older he felt. Over a yellow crew-neck he was wearing a fawn cotton jacket washed so often that it was almost see-through.

His blue slacks no longer fitted at the waist. He had lost six pounds. Major inquiries always did that to him. Couldn't eat, couldn't sleep. Like being in . . . For christsake, forget it. She'll be gone within a week.

'I ought to be making tracks.' God, I'm even using her phrases now.

He was surprised when Dickie broke off a conversation with a fellow punter. 'I'll come with you.'

Outside Dickie immediately removed the *Mirror* from a pocket of a grey-green jacket a size too small. 'Seen this?'

He held the paper taut as it tried to escape on a warm breeze that blew up the High Street. TRAGIC TORY QUITS, said the banner headline. The Browne case was back on the front page. Jacko had read it over breakfast but he read it again:

A top minister whose sister was murdered last month quit his government post last night.

Rising politician Russell Browne's departure came after talks with the Home Secretary who consulted Downing Street before making the shock announcement.

No official reason was given for his resignation and the customary exchange of letters between the Prime Minister and an outgoing minister has not yet been made public.

This fuelled speculation in Westminster last night that

there had been 'a conflict of interest' between him and police investigating the shooting of his sister Penny, 33.

Friends said he felt unable to carry on in the post of Minister for Police after his sister's murder, which came just months after the tragic deaths in a road crash of his mother and elder sister. 'He's grief-stricken,' said one.

His agent said in his Trent Valley constituency: 'He has gone away for a long rest. A decision on his position as our MP will not be made until he returns.'

Labour have already picked their candidate to fight the seat, which has a Tory majority of just over 5,000. He is Rich Richardson, 31, full-time official of the Union of Bottlemaking Allied Trades.

His union and the MP's family firm have been locked in past and present industrial disputes.

The story continued on page two but Dickie did not turn over. He refolded the paper and put it back in his pocket.

They crossed the High Street. As they reached the quieter Green Street, Dickie said, 'Did he arrange it?'

'Official Secrets.' Jacko looked sideways and pulled a face with clenched teeth. Both laughed. Then he added, 'Ask Rich if you want the full SP.'

Dickie shook his head. 'He's tighter with info than you.'

At the house he said, 'Come in,' and led the way down the passage without waiting for an answer.

Here, thought Jacko, in front of Mary, is most certainly not the time and place. He was sitting on a couch and, in answer to a question he guessed Mary asked every visitor, he requested tea without.

'You look dead beat,' said Dickie in an easy chair opposite a thankfully blank TV set. 'You coppers should get yourself a decent union.'

Adrenalin begin to stir. Take your time, Jacko ordered himself. He put on a weary smile. 'Matter of fact, my missus was on to me last night to find a hobby. I get no exercise or fresh air.'

'Take up fishing.' A prompt, enthusiastic reply.

Low-key, slow-burn, nice and easy does it, Jacko told himself.

'I'm not sure the big match-angling and the pike you were talking about to Tricia are for me.'

'Go pleasure fishing.'

'The Trent's near enough to my home but you say it's a tricky river.'

'Start on a smaller one. Like ours here.' He flicked his head westwards, towards the bridge. 'I often fish there. It's good fun.'

'Show him, Dickie,' Mary encouraged.

'When he's finished his tea.'

He restrained himself from gulping it down. When the drink was finished, he stood. Dickie went ahead to the passage door.

Jacko turned to Mary, said thanks for the tea, then, 'Where's he taking me?'

'Just round the corner.' An innocent smile. 'To Sandy Bank.'

Will he? Jacko was asking himself. Won't he?

He did. He stopped within feet of the spot where Jacko and Tricia had sat on the wall with the old bailiff the day before. 'Look for a place like this. No high weeds on the bank to interfere with your casting. No rubbish in the river to snag your line.' Three rings appeared on the water's rippling surface, spreading outwards. 'And a fair few fish about.'

'As good as the Trent?' Jacko asked.

'No pike.' Dickie rubbed his hands, beaming. 'I shall be after them next week. At Cromwell Lock. Know it?' Jacko nodded. 'Too tricky for you yet.'

Tricky? thought Jacko. Treacherous is a better word. Some years back a boatload of TA soldiers had gone over the weir instead of through the locks. Only one survived.

He asked beginner's questions about baits and hook sizes and began to dry up. Sit him down and change the subject to something you know about, he told himself.

'Phew.' He put his hands on his knees and lowered his right buttock on to the wall. Dickie stepped over the wall and sat. He lit a cigarette with his Zippo.

Jacko swung his legs over. 'Ever get a midweek day off?'

'Can do. Sure. I'll take you.'

He'd misunderstood. 'I didn't mean that. It's nice of you, though. I was thinking of a day at the Test at Trent Bridge.'

They talked for some time of Botham and Border and the stars of the past. 'Agreed then,' said Dickie, as though summing up a resolution in his days as a shop steward. 'A day's fishing on me. A day's cricket on you.'

The bond was sealed. The time was right. The topic, as so often in men-only talk, was about to change from sport to sex.

Jacko arched his back and threw an elbow into a shot-putter's position. 'A-r-r-r-r-gghh.'

'You are buggered.' A trace of alarm in Dickie's face. 'You need a holiday.'

'Had one just before I started on this case.' Jacko slumped forward, resting his elbows on his knees, his chin in his hands. 'No. It's Friday night, ain't it?'

Dickie looked puzzled.

'Friday night,' Jacko repeated. 'You know. Pay night, bath night and leg-over-night.'

Rocking laughter. 'Give her a good seeing-to then?'

'Beats cricket, doesn't it?'

'Not half.' He was smiling mischievously. 'Still at it regularly, are you?'

'Mmmmm.' Casual, almost modest. He let his brow furrow. 'Not as much as when I was a youth.'

'How old were you when you first cracked it?'

Jacko knew that a little white lie wouldn't work. He went for a fisherman's whopper, a sperm whale of a lie. He put the palm of his hand over his mouth, speaking out of the corner. 'Fifteen. I had this convent girl.' He looked to his right beyond the bridge. 'Down there. Near the baths. I've still not seen a better pair of knockers.' He shook his head in amazement. 'You?'

'I was married by eighteen.' A serious face brightened into a sly grin. 'Didn't do too badly before that, though.' He nodded across the river. 'See over there?'

'What?' Jacko removed his hand from his mouth. 'In full view of the towpath? It's a wonder you weren't nicked.'

'There used to be a Home Guard post there. Just the job. Warm and cosy.'

'Go on.' Interested, not dismissive.

'Sixteen I was when I lost my cherry over there. One better

158

than you. A boarding school lass. Met her at the roller-skating rink behind the Ritz.' He inclined his head sideways, northwards, in the direction of the only cinema left in the city.

'Very classy.' Jacko spoke with admiration.

No response.

Keep it going, son, he urged himself. 'I used to take my convent girl there on a Saturday morning.'

Dickie appeared to be lost in his thoughts.

'Funny thing.' Jacko kept going. 'Know what? I saw her for a couple of years on and off until she went to university. Never saw her again until two weeks ago. On this job. In a pub up near the cathedral. A bit embarrassing really. I was with my policewoman.'

'She's a bit tasty.' Dickie was back with him. 'Have you given her one?'

'Too close to home.' Then, hurriedly: 'Anyway, we recognized each other straight off and had a drink. She's still got a lovely pair. She's married, of course. Twice, in fact. But I reckon it's still on.' He paused, then quieter: 'Ever see your boarding school girl again?'

'No.' A slight sigh. 'No, never. She wrote once. From school. That's all. It was never on, really, not long-term. Her family was, you know . . .' A slight shrug. '. . . well, pretty posh.'

Jacko knew he couldn't ask outright: Who was the lucky lady then? So he said, very sincerely, 'Maybe she thinks of you still. Now and then.'

Dickie shook his head, very sadly. 'She was killed in a crash. I read it in the *Echo*. A shock it was. Even after all these years.'

He sat, shoulders rounded, staring across the river.

One more thing, Jacko knew, would prove it beyond doubt. He put a hand on Dickie's shoulder. 'Come on.' He stood.

'Where to?'

'I want to see your tackle, as the missus said last night.' More rocking laughter, like schoolboys sharing a rude joke.

At the bottom of the backyard Dickie went into a washhouse chaotically filled with fishing and gardening gear. Jacko stood at the door, idly watching him.

He removed a brown square wickerwork basket, placing it

carefully to one side, to reach a similiar-sized wooden box with a cushion nailed to the lid. He carried it outside, the first of several trips.

Jacko got out of his way, surveying the tiny vegetable plot. The seeds had turned into neat rows of seedlings protected against birds by black thread.

He turned back. Dickie was crouched now. A long, black and white plastic bag rested on one knee. From it he drew a black rod in three separate pieces. He fitted them together, lining up a series of wire eye-holes. It reached half-way back to the kitchen door. 'Carbon fibre. Nice and light. Here. Feel.'

Jacko took the cork handle. He barely cocked his wrist and the tip of the rod thirteen feet away sprang into quivering life.

No good, thought Jacko. He laid it carefully on the concrete path.

Dickie opened the lid of the cushioned box, the size of a footstool. He rummaged through green waterproofs, dirty rags, and withdrew a bag which he unzipped to reveal a reel. 'You'll need one of these.' The line was knotted and tangled into the reel handle.

Dickie pulled out a black plastic tray containing something like dry-cleaners' coat-hangers which, he explained, screwed together to make a keep net.

No good, Jacko decided.

At the bottom of the tray was a can opener. 'No pincers?' asked Jacko, disappointed.

'Don't need them with non-toxic lead. It's so soft you just nip it on with your fingers.'

Last out of the basket was a tin box with plastic disgorgers, floats and hooks in packets which Dickie made no attempt to open.

This isn't going to work, Jacko fretted. Then he saw the penknife. Dickie saw it, too. 'Always carry one of those.'

'Why?'

'For birds' nests.'

Jacko cocked his head, quizzically.

'Tangles. Like that.' Dickie nodded to the reel. He picked up the reel and tried to take off the spool but the knotted line wouldn't release it fully.

'Here.' Jacko opened the knife.

160

The entwined line was tight between Dickie's thumbs and forefingers.

'About here . . . *shit.*' A sharp gasp of pain.

'Sorry.'

'Jesus.'

'I'm sorry.'

Dickie sucked his right index finger and reached for a dirty rag.

Jacko snatched a white handkerchief from his pocket. 'Here. It's clean.'

Dickie took the finger out of his mouth and offered it towards him. Skin had been sliced just below a grubby fingernail and was bleeding badly. 'I'm sorry.' He closed the handkerchief round it. The blood slowly crept over the white cotton.

'It's just a nick,' said Dickie.

'Keep it there another tick.' Jacko held on for a few more seconds before releasing the finger. He fumbled in another pocket and took out a fabric plaster, tore away the wrapping with his teeth. He stuck the plaster over the cut which still oozed blood.

'You're a bloody Boy Scout,' said Dickie, admiringly. 'Always prepared.'

The wet bloodstained handkerchief was stuffed in a pocket lined with clingfilm. 'You never know when you're going to draw blood in this bloody business.' Jacko smiled a smile of mock grimness.

Dickie laughed. There was genuine mateyness in it.

In the few days that it took Forensics to break down, band and compare the blood on the handkerchief with a post-mortem sample from Penny Browne that the pathologist had kept, Jacko and Tricia skived.

One afternoon, he parked near Lindum Crystal, where two pickets with placards still stood on dispirited sentinel.

They walked in the sunshine towards the Drill Hall, where Rich had been locked in on election night, at the time of the shooting, throughout the count.

Before they reached it, they went into the museum, a cool, fusty, quaint stone building that looked no more than an ancient outhouse to the impressive domed library next door.

161

He led the way through echoing gangways flanked with glass cases containing bits of flint and pots until they reached an enclosed illuminated stand on which the Magna Carta stood, bathed in light.

Tricia lowered her head to study it, then lifted it to read the translations framed on the walls above, repeating the movement several times, saying nothing.

Jacko stood behind her, saying nothing either, a trifle embarrassed, afraid she might find it boring or disappointing and wonder what the fuss was about. 'It's not much to look at, is it?'

She turned to face him. Her brown eyes seemed to shine on him, lighting him up, like the Magna Carta itself. 'It's wonderful.'

They strolled up the cobbled hill to give her one last close-up look at the cathedral and castle, not saying much, then dropped into the Wig and Mitre for one last drink.

'You'll come to my party,' she said, quite suddenly.

Jacko sipped, said nothing.

'Just pop in.' She wasn't making it sound very inviting.

He sipped on.

'Please.'

He put down his glass. 'I'm not very good at goodbyes.'

She was silent for a while. Then: 'Is anything the matter?'

'No.'

'Sure?'

'Yes.'

Silence.

She tried again. 'Are you offended about, you know . . .' A worried little smile. '. . . about London?'

'No.'

'What is it then?'

He took a long swallow, thoughtful. 'It was the way you made me feel like your old dog.'

She closed her eyes, sighing. 'Oh dear.' She opened her eyes. He had never seen them so full of affection. 'Then you should be flattered.'

A short grunt.

'Yes, you should.' She looked away. 'You see.' Back at him. 'I think of him still, miss him. Always will.'

162

Jacko felt himself blush, could find no words.

'I hope all of this is telling you something, Jacko.'

He wanted to find his cigarettes, for something to do, to collect himself. He started to lift a hand from the round table. She stopped him, hand lightly resting on his.

'Pity you never picked up French. They have a beautiful word for it. *Tendresse*. Everyone should experience it. Only a lucky few do.'

He swallowed again, hard. An affair of the heart, she means. Soulmates. A love that would last. No sex, no sin, but no guilt or remorse. Better to have met her, to have worked with her, to have drawn from her than never to have known her at all. Wonderful. No, her word – beautiful – was the right one to describe his feelings right now.

Ever so gently she squeezed his hand. 'So you'll come? To the party?'

He nodded, smiling, just.

'And, don't worry, we don't have to say goodbye.'

23

Dickie Richardson *was* Penny Browne's father.

For the umpteenth time, Jacko read the laboratory report on the DNA testing which not only matches scene-of-crime samples to the body fluids of suspects, but also proves parentage. Finally he accepted its verdict, confirmation of what had begun to dawn on him on the train home from London, affirmation of that blinding flash of insight (rare for him) in Bond's back garden.

'Do you think Dickie knows?' Tricia's brown eyes were deeply troubled.

'No.' Jacko shook his head without looking across the desk at her, sitting opposite. 'He hasn't the first clue, the tiniest inkling, that he put Caroline in the club all those years ago. It was just a teenage fling. He never saw her again after Sandy Bank.'

'Do you think Rich knows?'

163

This, Jacko realized, was harder to answer. They knew the sequence of events, could fill in the gaps with conjecture, educated guesses. 'Let's work it out.'

He began after long thought. 'Penny and Rich fizzed for each other over dinner at the BATS Easter conference in Scarborough.'

'Easy to see why.' Tricia took over. 'Rich married young. Maybe it was love or maybe just good sex or maybe he was lonely living away from home for the first time at college. His wife never kept pace with his intellectual development. He'd grown bored with her.

'Sitting across the table at that cliff-top hotel was this attractive, articulate, liberated woman, fancying him.'

'What was in it for her?'

'Young, virile and bright, with ambitions she could motivate and mould.' Tricia continued, always the more fluent. 'Coming from families on opposite sides of an industrial dispute a decade earlier would only make him more intriguing. Being stuffed shirt Russell's political rival, irresistible.'

'Maybe it was the booze. Maybe it was lust. Maybe it was love.' Jacko was flowing now. 'What we're sure of is that one or other's hotel bed wasn't slept in that night.'

He looked, a touch guiltily, at Tricia who smiled slyly.

'A couple of months later, pregnancy's confirmed. She's delighted. It's what she'd wanted for years.

'She goes home. Over cucumber sandwiches at the Big House tells her tolerant, indulgent mother she's going to be a grandmother. "Who's the father?" she'd be asked.

'"Rich Richardson, would you believe? Big brother Russell's rival for the MP's job in Trent Valley. Old Dickie Richardson's son. We get on like a house on fire. Next week he's coming round to my place and I'm cooking him a meal. Small world, eh?" Something like that.'

She nodded.

'What alternative did her mother have but to sit her down and tell her the truth? Or maybe Caroline did it. "I'm not your sister. I'm your mother. Your mother is your grandmother. And your lover is your half-brother." Imagine it. Holy Moses.' He shook his head and noisily blew out cigarette smoke.

It would all have had to come out then, they agreed – Caroline home from boarding school three decades ago, meeting up with Dickie at the roller-skating rink. Sandy Bank. Too young and inexperienced to know any better. The missed periods when she's back at school, too frightened to tell anyone. No abortion in those days, except in the back streets. No woman's right to choose.

'She probably kept it secret until it was too late anyway,' Tricia ventured.

'And all this was happening about the time Caroline's soldier father was being killed on active service in Cyprus,' Jacko added.

So what would the colonel's widow do? they asked each other.

'She'd leave son Russell in his boarding school and take Caroline off to Switzerland for the birth,' Tricia suggested. 'When they came back, Mrs Browne passed off the baby as her own, the result of a last night of passion on late husband's embarkation leave, and Russell had a baby sister.'

'Wouldn't happen today,' said Jacko, thankfully. 'No one bothers these days. But they did in the mid-fifties.'

'Imagine the shock, the pain, Penny must have gone through hearing all of that.' Tricia eyes were downcast. 'Think of Mrs Browne or Caroline having to tell her.'

Jacko lapsed into private thoughts. He was certain they'd all be very stoic about it. The middle and upper classes are like that. Comes from public schools and reading Evelyn Waugh. They came to terms with adversity and so would Penny.

So what would Penny do? Get rid. That's what; explains the abortion.

Policemen, especially those who have worked in isolated places like the Lincolnshire Fens, sometimes make jokes about incest. And when he thought about the subject, which wasn't often, he always recalled a film set in the swamps of the Deep South, and a strange pale little fellow with even stranger eyes sitting in a tree playing 'Duelling Banjos'. For some perverse reason, he'd always smile. He wasn't smiling now.

He was imagining the conversation when Rich called round with flowers in one hand, a bottle of wine in the other and a packet of five in his top pocket because last time, by the seaside, he'd been pissed and he didn't want to run any more risks.

165

'Sorry,' Penny would say. 'You can't be my lover because you're my brother.' Enough to dampen anyone's ardour, isn't it?

(He kept these musings strictly to himself. Tricia sometimes affected a who-gives-a-shit attitude to life, but only, he'd realized, to hide a deeply compassionate nature. She did give a shit, did care. She would have rebuked him for expressing himself in such poor taste. But the only way he could prevent a heavy truth weighing him down was to make light of it. Many detectives are like that. They have to be.)

To give both Penny and Rich credit, they'd accepted it. After all, he'd found a sister. That would mean something to him, the only child of his parents' union.

They agreed to maintain their secret for the sake of Dickie and, above all, his wife, Rich's dear, unsuspecting, innocent mum.

They'd keep in loose touch, as brothers and sisters do. She'd phoned him with her TV idea. Of course, he'd dig out for her. She'd phoned him with the tragic news that Mrs Browne and Caroline had been killed in the car crash. He'd have been tremendously supportive. She regarded him as family, was closer to him than Russell.

Tricia interrupted, tired of waiting for him. 'I'm certain Rich knew. That silver Imp he gave Penny for Christmas. He never regarded it as a gratuity to a union contact, chargeable on exes. It was for family or lover. She'd been both. It was to let her know that he cared. A nice gesture, really.' A wistful look.

'You're right,' Jacko nodded, very positive. 'Look at the way he reacted when we asked him if he'd become closer to Penny than just a friend. He couldn't bear the question. Innocently, accidentally, he'd committed incest. He had to blank it.'

He paused, concentrating, looking for and finally finding the clincher to their theory. 'And look at her and her old Fleet Street flame. He'd changed in her eyes from lover to friend. Rich went from lover to brother. She had a kind of phlegmatic ability to accept relationships for what they'd become and still cherish them. In affairs of the heart she was a pragmatist.'

Yes, they agreed, Rich knew.

With Penny, Caroline and Mrs Browne all dead, he was the only person in the world who did know. Apart from them. Jacko

166

felt the tremendous burden of that knowledge, a peeping Tom who didn't like what he was seeing.

Tricia sighed heavily. 'One thing's for certain. Rich can't be guilty. Apart from his cast-iron alibi, you don't kill your sister, do you?'

Jacko didn't know about that. When he'd been five or six, his own sister had taken him to the swimming baths down the towpath. He was paddling quite happily when she and her friends ducked him. His eyes smarted, his ears deadened. His lungs seemed set to burst. He thought he was going to die. When they let him up for air, he'd been sick on the water and the attendant ordered him out and home. He never went back, never learned to swim. He could have cheerfully murdered his own sister that day. But it was all a long time ago. 'I suppose not.'

'So it has to be Rich's wife.' Tricia looked away from him, out of the window, her thoughts ahead of his.

His began to catch up. Ann Richardson could have been sorting through drawers or checking that her husband's suit pockets were empty before she went in the car on her regular run to the dry-cleaner's. She finds the box from the jeweller's. Oh, lovely, she thinks, a little surprise present for my Christmas stocking.

Christmas arrives. She doesn't get it. She starts to wonder about a card that's addressed only to him from someone called Penny, to worry about the phone calls he's getting at home in which she overhears the odd term of endearment.

She starts to suspect he is playing around while she is heavily pregnant. When the baby's born she becomes more and more withdrawn – classic symptoms of post-natal depression. Tearing around like a blue-arsed fly, Rich doesn't cotton on. You know what union leaders are like; solving everyone's problems while ignoring their own.

By last month she's a very sick woman. Her husband is always out. There's this mystery lady in his life. Then he tells her about the TV programme and Penny Browne. He's very excited about it. He might even have told her that he had visited Southview Cottage and that she and the kids would love it. Some simple remark, well-intentioned, preparing the ground for telling her about his new-found sister, when the timing was right.

She thinks it's all an elaborate smokescreen for a bit on the side. Instead of having it out with him, she broods. Come election day, she has a fatal impulse to confront her supposed rival for Rich's love. She knows he is locked in at the count. The car is back from its service at the garage, standing in the drive with the keys in the ignition, but . . .

'No opportunity.' Jacko's train of thought hit the buffers. 'She may have a motive but she had no opportunity. The mileage since the service is fully accounted for.'

Tricia was still ahead of him. 'It's possible that she's confessed to Rich and, between them, they somehow fiddled the mileometer to clear her and to con us.'

Jacko pulled on his chin, getting his mind back on the rails.

The big bony head of the black and tan devil's dog emerged with dramatic suddenness from behind pink honeysuckle which had invaded the hawthorn hedge in front of two almost identical detached houses.

Tricia gasped, surprised. She took a pace sideways behind Jacko who made a staccato chucking noise with the tip of his tongue on the back of his teeth. 'Hallo, beautiful.'

A woman appeared behind the dog, being tugged on a strong leather lead. The Rottweiler slavered over Jacko's proffered fingers.

The woman stopped as the dog stood still, gazing up at Jacko with a worried face, a mirror reflection of his own. 'It's nice to meet someone who's not terrified of them,' she said.

'My little dog plays with one every night,' said Jacko, avoiding contact with the dog's dark, gleaming eyes.

'You're the first person I've met in weeks who doesn't think he's about to be gobbled.'

Not by him, I hope, madam, thought Jacko, holding back a smile.

Tricia stepped from behind Jacko. 'Mrs Shirley Trigg?'

Ann Richardson's sister, mid-thirties and wearing a pink track suit, said she was. Tricia made the introductions.

'I'm afraid Ann's in hospital,' said Mrs Trigg.

Jacko vigorously scratched the black bony head just above its tanned eyebrows. All four started to walk. 'A severe bout of depression, I'm afraid,' Mrs Trigg went on.

'Mind if we stretch our legs with you?' Jacko still tickled the dog's head as they walked side by side.

'Please.' A delighted smile.

Jacko knew he had captured her heart. Some women who are childless or whose children have flown the nest adopt dogs as substitutes. They lavish more affection on them than would be good for any child. They buy them sweets, toys and treats. They talk baby talk to them. They give them silly names.

'What's he called?' He released a smile now and made it ingratiating.

'Little Rexie.'

All three looked down on an animal that was nine stone, had jaws as strong as a shark's and the shoulders of an all-in wrestler. Ever since a spate of attacks by the breed on harmless old ladies and small children – one of them fatal – Little Rexie would have been treated like a leper on his walks. Now Jacko was treating him like a human being. He was in with Mrs Trigg, had her eating out of his hand, like his own mongrel took Good Boy chocs.

As they walked, Mrs Trigg said, 'I thought you were more or less finished with Rich. His mother said you were.'

'We wanted Ann to sign a statement.' Tricia patted a black bag which hung from one shoulder of her loose cotton trouser suit which had broad black and white stripes.

It was a cool, grey day for June, just right for Jacko's thickish blue jacket.

'Hope that's all,' said Mrs Trigg. 'Rich is taking her away tomorrow.'

'That's a . . . Fine . . . Good idea.' Tricia gushed it, shocked, stammering. 'She needs a rest. Where to?'

'A secret, he says. A second honeymoon.'

'I gather you've been away. Good time?' Tricia had recovered rapidly.

'The Italian lakes.' Pause. 'A bit windy.'

Rexie led them into a car-park. On the right was a boat builders' works, an old building whose deep red bricks wept white salt. Outside on blocks stood a squat glass fibre boat and a long wooden boat, badly holed in its black bottom.

On the left was a cream-painted pub which overlooked the River Trent. More boats bobbed at their moorings at the foot of a deep wall. The car-park was filled with cars, though the pub was not yet open.

'I was on holiday first week in May, too – in Ireland,' said Jacko, very slowly. 'It meant we could take Lucy, our dog. She hates kennels. Where does Rexie go?'

'Oh, we never put Rexie in kennels either. He'd pine. Besides, he's a wonderful guard dog.' A confident smile. 'You may think you're a pal of his now but try knocking on the door when we're not in. He'd let the whole village know.'

'Who looks after him then?'

'Nancy, next door. The milkman, the dustman, the postman. All get the same reception. She's the only person I'd trust with him.'

Rexie led the way on to a towpath and Jacko could see why the pub car-park was full. Anglers sat on their baskets at thirty-yard intervals, grumbling to each other about a long barge which was churning the water white, sending waves lapping on the stones at the foot of the bank opposite, making their floats jump frantically up and down.

They chatted about dogs and holidays for another 300 yards. They parted at a white gate which had a 'Private Fishing' sign. Tricia said goodbye to Mrs Trigg.

Jacko said to Rexie, 'See you, sexy.'

They linked arms for the stroll back, as they had done in Paris. They did not notice the sun which peeped from the one gap in clouds of three-tone grey. They did not feel the spots of rain. They did not see the swallows and martins sweeping along the river, wings almost touching the fast-flowing water.

They did not congratulate themselves on a job well done on Mrs Trigg. They were talking of jobs still to do, discussing tactics.

Next-door Nancy's pleasant plumpness was due, Jacko guessed, to the four young children whose photos were on a window ledge in the lounge.

They talked about Ann first. 'She's getting no better. I visited

170

her last week. She looked really awful. Her husband must be worried sick.'

'Do you know Ann's husband well?' asked Tricia.

'Only since he's been calling every day at Shirl's to see his wife.'

'Did you see him on that Saturday when there was a big fete on the wharf?'

Nancy shook her head.

'Did you go to the fete yourself?'

A second shake but this time she added, 'I couldn't have gone even if I'd wanted to. It was the first day of the cricket season and I was rostered for the teas. My hubby Bob plays.'

A bit of a chore, she went on. She had to collect the cold meat from the butcher in the morning, wash the salad and butter two loaves of bread.

'Were you in that lunchtime?'

'All the time. You don't have to be at the pavilion until about four.'

'Did anyone call at Shirley's, say, between one and three?' – which more than spanned the time Rich had been missing from the Lindum Crystal picket line.

She remembered straight away. 'A raffle ticket seller from the fete.'

'Did Rexie bark?'

'I should say so. Always does.'

'Did anyone else call that lunchtime?'

'No.'

'Sure?'

'Positive. Rexie would have let me know.'

A dead end. Jacko felt the excitement flow out of his veins to be replaced with anxiety and depression. A dead end.

Apart from the opening pleasantries, he hadn't spoken. Now he took up the questioning, urgently, their last shot.

'When Rexie barked were you always able to get out of your house round to Shirley's in time to see who the caller was?'

'If you're bathing one of the children or something like that, you don't drop everything. You just let him bark.'

'Did that happen any time during that weekend?'

'Oh, yes.' An instant reply. 'Just before midnight on the

Sunday. We'd gone to bed early because Bob was as stiff as a board.'

Flushing slightly, she hurried into an explanation. 'From his first game of cricket. He could hardly move a muscle. Rexie barked and I thought Shirl and her hubby were home a bit early because their plane wasn't due in until the early hours. I had to get out of bed and look out of the window because Bob refused.'

'Did you see anything or anybody?'

'Only a car pulling away.'

'What sort?'

'I don't know the different names.'

She stopped in thought.

Jacko waited.

'One like Shirl's brother-in-law's. Same colour, too.'

The excitement rushed back in a huge wave.

24

Outsmarted, thought Jacko, bitter, angry. The scheming socialist shit.

Oh, Rich Richardson would have gone to the top in politics all right. Not any more. He was finished now. Like his rival Russell Browne.

Over the car phone they had briefed Happy, the collator, who'd promised back-up. 'Want 'em armed?' Happy asked routinely.

'Nar,' replied Jacko, dismissively. 'It's just a domestic, the old equation – three into one bed won't go.' He clipped back the phone.

They headed west away from the river, working it out for themselves, only the hum of the engine and monotonous squeaking of the wiper blades on the rain-spattered windscreen breaking the silence in the car.

As usual Tricia finished first. 'Rich would come home on election night. Ann would be waiting up. Even if she looked or acted odd, he suspected nothing. She'd been odd for weeks.

Not a word, I'll bet, did she say about her trip to Southview Cottage while he'd been locked in the count.'

Jacko's turn to theorize. 'Rich didn't drive to his sister-in-law's on Saturday. That was bullshit. He was drinking with his sacked strikers from Lindum Crystal, still unaware, like the rest of the world, that Penny was dead. That picket I got pissed. Remember?'

'Of course.'

'He was one hundred per cent right about everything. Should have listened to him. Should have started to see through it then.'

'Seen what?'

Rich, Jacko speculated, arrived home on Sunday evening from his union executive meeting in London. Another heavy day. Head aching from all those motions, deploring this and condemning that. Stiff from travelling a 250-mile round trip as a passenger in his branch chairman's old banger.

'Without a car radio, he still wouldn't know about Penny.'

Jacko drew a word picture for Tricia of Rich walking into the bungalow, looking in on his sleeping kids, eating his warmed-up meat and two veg on a tray in front of the TV.

'Then his world would cave in. First, the newscaster reports the murder of Penny over stills of her and her minister brother and film of police guarding Southview Cottage. Then his wife would say, accusingly, perhaps, "You were in love with her, weren't you?"'

'And the whole truth would come out,' Tricia concurred.

His poignant, hers terrible, thought Jacko.

'She'd tell Rich we'd already been round and looked inside his Cavalier,' she continued. 'He probably got it firmly fixed in his head, quite wrongly, that we suspected her from the outset and that we'd . . .'

'A choice,' Jacko broke in. 'He had a choice. He could turn her in. Or he could cover for her. All his adult life he's been a committee man. In the party. In his union. Every decision he's ever made was debated round a table and voted on. This time he's on his own. He has to make up his own mind. And he makes the wrong decision.'

'Don't hold that too much against him,' said Tricia.

Jacko hadn't really heard, so fast were his thoughts. 'He'd be

173

ridden with guilt for not sharing the secret of his new-found sister with his wife, for not recognizing how ill Ann had become. One woman has died because it. He was determined his wife wasn't going to suffer, too. He may have neglected her before but, by Christ, he came to her aid now.'

'Rich knows he's got to account for those forty-eight miles.' Tricia was thinking positive again. 'He has got to get them on the clock. He drove to his sister-in-law's *after* you'd seen the mileometer. That Sunday night, late on, he made the trip. Not Saturday lunchtime.'

'Clever that.' Jacko nodded agreement. 'Not only did it explain those missing miles, he arranged to get Ann out of our way, too. Sister Shirl's was just a temporary safe house until he'd found and fixed up a private hospital.'

'Now' – Tricia's eyes were alight with enlightenment – 'we know what his old man Dickie meant when he said, "If she comes home."'

He nodded grimly. 'A sham. Her illness could be a sham. Rich is planning to discharge her and whisk her away.'

Automatically his right foot raised his speed, unusual for him, on winding country lanes.

Tricia asked a question that the Little Fat Man was bound to raise. 'Should we have seen through this before?'

'How could we?' asked Jacko, defensively, eyes on the road. 'We were concentrating on his movements on Thursday, the day Penny died.'

'How could he know about the fete on the wharf on Saturday if he wasn't there?'

'He probably heard about it when he came to the village on the Monday to drop Ann off at her sister's. He threw it in to support his story. It backed up the note torn from Saturday evening's *Echo*.'

That note was clever, too, Jacko privately conceded. Now he was blaming himself.

In his mind's eye, he was back, glancing idly around inside Rich's car, as he saw it on that Sunday evening. There were stacks of scrap paper in the back seat, including headed union notepaper. He didn't have to write a note on top of that night's *Echo* and tear it off. He did that for effect, to underline the phoney story that he'd made the trip on Saturday, as he claimed.

Should have seen through that, he chaffed.

Out of the corner of his mind's eye he saw a transparent file folder on the back seat. Could it have been . . . ?

Surely not.

Come on, face it. Could it have been the folder with the Swiss and the CCO documents taken from Southview Cottage?

It would explain why Rich kept them at home, not at the BATS office.

But why should a wife in a supposed love triangle steal business documents from the scene of a murder?

He didn't know. It was one of the questions they were on their way to ask.

They were on a main road now, bound for Nottingham.

Tricia swivelled in the passenger seat. 'Who sent us Rich's exes through the post?'

'Rich himself.' Pause. 'Put yourself in his position. Rich knew who'd killed Penny. And it was no Irish terrorist. He reads we're holding someone under the Prevention of Terrorism Act. He's a big campaigner for the Guildford Four and the Birmingham Six. He'll believe everything he's ever read, true or false, about those cases – the allegations of confessions being beaten out of them or fabricated, the brutality they were subjected to in prison.

'How could he, a rising star of the left, let that happen to Riordan? Protecting a sick wife is one thing. Letting an innocent man do thirty years for her is another. So he staged the break-in at the BATS office and sent us his own concocted exes to divert attention from Riordan to him.'

'Dangerous,' said Tricia, not buying it.

'Not really. He didn't kill Penny and had a solid alibi to prove it. In his view, we could have beaten him up, fitted him up. Anything. Nothing would have altered that. Besides, he can handle pressure.'

They travelled some distance in silence.

'Anyway . . .' A new thought was dawning. They passed a field full of bedraggled cows before it was fully formed. '. . . if we had charged Riordan, the inquiry would have been finished. We would never have gone on to unearth those Swiss and CCO documents. With Penny dead so was the TV programme. He wanted them found to embarrass Browne. If Riordan had been charged, Browne would still be the Minister for Police.'

'Why keep them at home?' Tricia was not completely sold on it yet. 'Why not keep them at his office? He must have known we'd search it after he reported the break-in and we'd got hold of his exes.'

'We're dealing with a law graduate used to preparing defences for arrested pickets and union activists. He'd know that any search warrant wouldn't be open-ended and would only cover his exes file. He wanted things to come out gradually, drip-feeding us, to keep us busy looking at Browne and away from his wife.'

Machiavellian bastard, thought Jacko. He'd have made a far better Minister for Police than Browne.

Tricia was seeing it differently, a woman's way. 'It was a remarkable, if belated, act of love on Rich's part. Not many husbands would have done that.'

'Oh.' Uncertain. 'I don't know.'

And he didn't know; didn't know what he would have done, could have brought himself to do, for his own wife in such circumstances.

What he did know was that married men shouldn't become bedazzled by other women. He felt a terrible shaft of guilt, a complete hypocrite. He didn't like the feeling but he knew he had to find a moral somewhere. He decided that travelling men shouldn't flam up their exes. He made a mental note to knock a fiver off when he got round to them. He felt a lot better.

They were in the built-up suburbs now, talking tactics. 'It's woman's work,' he ordered, pulling rank for the first time in their partnership.

Tricia went very quiet, her brown eyes dull. She'd enjoyed the chase, loved it. He knew that. She'd told him so. Now, in her final two days as a police officer, he was asking her to blood herself with the kill; the arrest of a sadly mixed-up mother driven to murder.

The medical superintendent greeted them in his chaotic office. 'She's very sick.'

'I thought she was due for discharge,' said Jacko, not really believing him.

'Her husband calls it convalescence.' A disapproving face. 'We can't detain her. She's here voluntarily.'

'Does he visit often?'

'Every afternoon. Do you want to wait for him?'

'We'll see her now, if that's all right.'

'I'll ask a nurse and social worker to sit in, if you've no objections.'

'Fine.' Jacko spread his hands: the more, the merrier.

Just before they entered the room, he briefed the two-man back-up team.

Tricia unzipped her shoulder bag and reached inside for her notebook and pen. He turned, laid a hand on hers. 'You ask the questions, I'll take the notes. Don't go too fast, that's all.'

Ann Richardson sat huddled in a big armchair in the day room, which was spotlessly clean and smelt of pine. She had a blue cardigan over the thin shoulders of her pink dress. Jacko was shocked by the sight of her. No sham this.

She seemed to have faded away since he last saw her, as if melting in a room that was hotter than an old folks' home. Her short dark hair was lifeless, her pale face lined, her cheeks sunken. She looked fifty, not thirty. She was knitting baby clothes with blue wool, for the baby daughter she'd never see grow up.

'Hallo, Ann.' Tricia slid a stiff-backed chair closer. A buxom middle-aged nurse, watch and name tag pinned to the bosom of her dark blue uniform, sat upright in a similar chair.

Another woman, tweedy, white-haired, older than Jacko, sat on a deep couch. Jacko settled next to her. He took a small hard-backed notebook from an inside pocket and a biro from his top pocket. He crossed right leg over left and rested the notebook on his knee.

'How are you?' Tricia sat down.

'A lot better.' A pitifully brave smile.

'You know I'm WPC Floyd-Moore and you've met Detective Inspector Jackson, too, haven't you?'

A weak smile and nod.

'You know that we are inquiring into the tragic death of Miss Penny Browne?'

She tucked her knitting behind her at the back of the roomy chair. 'Yes.'

'I want to ask you a few more questions but before I do I have a duty to tell you . . .' Tricia used the words of the formal caution. '. . . and I also have to tell you that you have a right to a solicitor.'

Mrs Richardson seemed to perk up. 'Rich doesn't like them. Says they're expensive for what they do. He doesn't like policemen much either.'

'I know.' Smiling. 'Do you think that he originally got that dislike from his father?'

Mrs Richardson shuddered slightly. Tricia went on quickly, 'Though, I must say, Dickie has been very help . . .'

Mrs Richardson started to weep, noiselessly, tears running down those hollow cheeks. She held out her hands and took Tricia's fingers in them. Tricia waited, close to tears herself. 'You don't have to talk, if you don't want to.'

'Will it help Rich?'

'I can't promise that.' A very truthful answer. 'All I know is that it would help me understand things.'

Her hands gripped Tricia's tightly. 'All I wanted to do was talk to her, plead with her. You must believe that.'

Tricia nodded. 'Tell me what happened, Ann.'

Many more tears were shed in the next two hours, bringing many interruptions to the questions that Tricia so softly asked, as they talked woman-to-woman.

Jacko had no difficulty in getting all her rambling replies down in his scribbled longhand.

They'd been right about nearly all the details; wrong about the major one.

Jacko closed the door quietly before he spoke to the squad sergeant waiting in the corridor outside. 'When Richardson comes, nick him.'

The sergeant nodded.

'And bring him in.'

Another nod.

'Let him have a few minutes with his wife first.' Tricia's eyes begged him. 'Please.'

He looked back at the sergeant, nodding consent.

25

A glance in his wing mirror as he was inching, barely moving, nose-first, into a tight parking space in the hospital grounds. The sight froze him.

He had to force his neck further right for a longer look. His worst fears were confirmed, his nightmare had come true. That inspector and his policewoman were rounding a bed of variegated heathers on their way out in his car.

Rich Richardson faced front. Too late to stop his Cavalier from hitting a low dividing fence.

Just a fender bump. That's all.

A juddering explosion to him. The plane, his world, seemed to disintegrate around him. Behind him, the agonized screams of passengers, his family. He clapped his hands to his ears.

Flames of fear engulfed him, choking him.

He didn't try to unfasten his safety belt.

No point.

There'd be no survivors, no escape from this disaster.

26

'Ah, well.' Jacko belted up. 'In the great scorebook of crime, he'll go down as stumped by the tea lady, bowled by Sexy Rexie. But he had a good innings.'

'For God's sake.' Tricia slammed the passenger door and spoke sharply. 'How can you be so flip after listening to a harrowing story like that?'

Easy, thought Jacko, starting up and driving round the heather bed. In this job you either make a joke of it or finish up in a place like this. He wasn't going to apologize. What was that line from that Hollywood weepie, *Love Story*? 'Love is never having to say sorry.' Load of old cock, of course. 'Sorry,' he said.

Both missed the sound of splitting timber from the car-park to their left.

Tricia threw her head back in its rest. 'No wonder she's ill.'

Jacko nodded. 'Post-natal nothing. A trauma like that would have unhinged anybody.'

'He conned her, didn't he?' Her eyes were angry. 'She was being torn apart, and he conned her.'

She stopped suddenly, a question occurring. 'Think it was the car your beloved Siobhan saw driving away from Southview Cottage?'

'Certain. Two adults up front, a toddler in the back. The baby was on the back seat out of view.'

'Fancy taking her kids.'

'She had no one to babysit. It's not unique.' Jacko told her of a double-killer, the first murderer to be trapped in DNA testing, who had taken his sleeping child out in the car on a stalking trip while his wife was at evening classes. 'Ann didn't know she was going out on a murder mission.'

'Where did the gun come from?' Tricia said more or less to herself.

Where is the gun? Jacko asked himself. Dumped, he guessed. The frogmen had searched the wrong river. He may have tossed it from the bridge at the very spot where I stood, knees against the metal plaque, day-dreaming. I've been within spitting distance of a solution for five weeks without realizing it.

They didn't have to use much imagination on this journey. They had the basic facts down in black biro on white paper in Jacko's notebook.

180

Everyone, he brooded, everyone, left, right and centre, is blessed or cursed by their genes.

Jacko shook his head, to shake away these thoughts, to concentrate.

They branched left at a Y-bend on the approach to Newark, avoiding the town centre, driving through a busy broad street. At a roundabout by the ruined castle, they took another left over the level crossings up the old Great North Road to join the A1 for a couple of junctions.

A sign pointed them to Cromwell.

He drove beneath a line of ash trees at the end of a long rutted track. He could hear the roar of the water in the weir above the sound of his engine.

He parked the car close to a slab of granite hewn into a triangle on which had been fixed a memorial plaque to the ten soldiers who died in the night exercise disaster fourteen years earlier.

They walked down a wide concrete path towards the lock-keeper's cabin, like a railway signal box, standing in front of a white house with purple-tiled eaves.

It was a long lock, about 150 yards, high-sided, with three big black gates.

At right angles to it, even longer, was the weir, 200 yards wide at least. The water was a smooth, shiny grey upriver; a brilliant boiling white downriver after its fast, curved six-feet fall, like a monstrous washing machine, noisily churning steaming suds.

He skipped up the metal steps, his shoes making a tinny sound, to the door of the cabin. A bearded man in a flat cap and royal blue boiler suit answered his knock.

'Seen a fisherman? Short, bald, tubby. On a ladies' black bike.'

The keeper nodded upriver. 'First peg.'

'Thanks.' Jacko skipped down again and joined Tricia at the bottom. 'Wait here. I'll fetch him.'

'Sure?' Her brown eyes were worried.

'Man's work.' He smiled, confident.

* * *

A quarter of a mile, a pleasant stroll. No rush, he decided. He'd do it by the book. He subconsciously felt for his notebook in the inside pocket of his blue jacket. All they really needed to locate was the murder weapon.

Easy.

He walked on a sloping grass bank, recently cut, beyond two blue dredgers, hardly moving at their moorings in the shelter of the lock wall. At regular intervals to his left were the white handrails of steps down the sheer sides. Red stands with lifebelts were dotted to his right.

A watery sun had broken through the clouds, but there was no warmth in it. A stiff breeze blew in his face and hurried the river past lines of red navigation buoys and a safety barrage, like a series of huge beer canisters, thirty or more, strung together from bank to bank.

The noise of the weir became no more than a low rumble and the wall was replaced by wide steps leading down to the water.

On the bottom step sat Dickie Richardson. On a brown wicker basket. Not the cushioned box he'd opened up in his backyard.

He was wearing a dark green weatherproof, hood up against the wind, concentrating on his float.

He didn't notice Jacko until he stood next to him. Then he cocked his head over his left shoulder, looked up, startled.

'Hallo, Dickie.' Jacko tried to force a sympathetic smile, failed. He knew his look was giving him away.

'What's up?' Hopelessness in his eyes that Jacko had seen many times when making arrests; the defeated look of the hunted fox when the hounds have finally caught up for the kill.

'I'm here to arrest you.'

'Ann.' He sighed her name.

'. . . and I have to caution . . .'

'You've seen Ann, haven't you?' His face twisted, enraged.

Jacko gabbled on through the caution.

'Sick, she is,' said Dickie over the formal words. 'And you've been pestering her. I warned you not to.'

Jacko, talking fast, failed to detect the warning note in his tone. He completed the caution before answering him. 'Yes.' He patted his pocket. 'We have her statement.'

'You promised . . .'

Jacko cut in. 'She's ill because of what she saw, what she knows. Get yourself a solicitor and save it for the station, Dickie.'

He sat still, as if frozen solid by shock, on his basket. Only his lips moved. 'She's ill because of that woman.' He turned his face away, talking to the river. 'What she was doing to Rich.'

'Stop playing politics,' said Jacko, bitterly. 'You did it to save your own reputation. Ann turned to you in desperation, and you used her. We've got her words down in writing.' He patted his pocket again. 'Remember them, Dickie? "I'm sure Rich is having an affair. He keeps getting calls from a woman. They talk very affectionately. He even bought her a Christmas present." Remember, Dickie?'

'Conniving bitch.'

'Who?' Jacko used his sharp tone.

'That Browne bitch.'

Holy cow, thought Jacko, alarmed. He still doesn't know she was his daughter. 'Why?' Softer.

'She was doing a big exposé on Browne and Green. My lad told me.'

'About what?'

'On the union, of course. She'd asked him about that scab Bond, too.'

'Yes.' Jacko's sarcastic voice. 'The one person alive, now that Old Man Green's dead, who knew about the way you perverted your union power for years. But Bond never told Penny about that and she never asked.'

Eyes still front, Dickie didn't appear to be listening. 'It was all a right-wing media plot – to discredit Rich and the union by exposing me. To save her brother's seat. The bitch was even prepared to sleep with Rich, a married man, to get what she wanted.'

Jacko reverted to his softer tone. 'Rich has since told Ann, and Ann has just told us, that they were never lovers.'

'He would say that.' Mumbling. 'Wouldn't you?'

True, Jacko conceded. If things had gone differently with

Tricia in London – if she hadn't saved me from my own stupid self – I'd have never owned up to my wife. Every detective knows that hot denials get you into far less trouble than frank confessions.

'Do you want to tell me what happened?' Jacko tried to sound indifferent, it's up to you.

'Don't mind.' His waterproofs tightened at the shoulders as he shrugged. He pulled down his hood but still faced front. 'I told Ann we ought to go and have it out with her. About the affair with Rich, I mean. She wanted that, for the kids' sake.

'She picked me up from the bridge just after nine when the polls closed and Rich was out of the way and could prove where he was. I wanted it that way, see. I knew you bastards would suspect him, them being lovers and all.

'We got there in half an hour. I told Ann to sit outside in Rich's car. I wanted to talk to her first, to try to make her see reason, to realize the damage she was doing.'

'You normally negotiate with a pistol at someone's head, do you?' Jacko smiled caustically down on his bald patch.

'I thought her brother might be there. He's twice my size.'

'What happened?'

'She screamed. She thought I was a robber. She went for me. It was an accident.'

'It was robbery. You took a plastic folder.'

'There was nothing in it. Nothing that I could see. Nothing about the union, anyway.'

Even then the dumb bastard couldn't see it, thought Jacko, angrily. He'd never dreamt that Penny Browne's TV exposé was going to be about her own MP brother, the Minister for Police. Capitalist families, Dickie would reason, rat on each other as often as leopards change their spots; unthinkable to a closed, ·class warrior's mind, like his.

Jacko was still looking down. 'I know. We've got it and your prints will be on it.'

'Expect so.' He turned, just slightly, sort of cocking an ear. 'We were there and back within the hour. She dropped me at the bridge. I told her to say nothing to nobody – but she has, hasn't she?' He shook his head sorrowfully.

'Not for three days. She wasn't sure what happened in the cottage . . .'

Dickie broke in. 'No reason why she should. She didn't go in. Got that, have you?' He looked up, very sharply, a point to make. 'She never set foot inside and I told her nothing. She was too shocked.'

A curt nod. 'She certainly kept it secret from Rich until he got home from his London meeting that Sunday and it came out on TV.'

'He knows?' He jerked his head fully round and up, face a mystified mask.

Jacko nodded again, convinced now that Rich had told his father nothing, absolutely nothing. He decided to tell him, a bit of it anyway.

'Know what Rich did? He gave her a sleeping pill and held her and told her, "Put it out your mind. Leave everything to me." And while she was sleeping, he sneaked out and hand delivered a note to her sister's and then he posted us phoney exes to point us away from you.'

'Never told me.' He sounded gutted.

'There's a lot you don't know, Dickie. Like you told me once, your Rich is tighter with info than I am.'

So tight, Jacko now knew, that he never admitted to his adultery (or incest, call it what you like) to his wife; never told Dickie he'd killed his own daughter, a daughter he never knew he had; never told anyone about Penny's pregnancy, who got her that way and the abortion.

It was clear to him now, much, much clearer than the river water. Rich had borne the cross single-handed, the poor lonely sod. He'd not only followed his father's footsteps into union politics. He'd become an accomplice by trying to hush up his father's crime, the whole, sorry scandal.

'Is he in trouble?' A worried tone.

'He'll have some questions to answer. I've one more for you. The gun . . .'

'Is he in trouble, I said?' He spaced out the words, his tone menacing.

'. . . was it a war souvenir belonging to your dad, like his Zippo lighter? Russian, according to Ballistics. The Russians equipped the North Koreans, didn't they? Where is it, Dickie?'

'Is he in fucking trouble?' Almost a shout.

'A fair amount. Not as much as you.'

He stood suddenly, turning. He transferred his rod from right to left hand, still holding it over the water. Stooping, he flicked open the basket lid. His right hand went inside.

'I fucking warned you. Bastard.' It came out like a drum roll from the back of his throat. 'All coppers are . . .'

His rod dropped into the water. The current snatched it and carried it away, taking Jacko's eyes with it for just a second.

Dickie's freed left hand started towards his right, holding something. Jacko's eyes returned. They only caught a glimpse. All they needed. A rusting black revolver.

No time to think, let alone talk. Jacko lunged, hands outstretched. Palms slapped against the backs of Dickie's hands, twisting the gun skywards.

A blast ran from his fingers to his toes. His shoe soles went beneath him, as though he had slipped on ice. He and Dickie were in mid-air, falling. He knew exactly what was happening; knew he was in dire danger, was unable to do a thing about it.

He didn't really hear the splash, only felt shocking cold stings on his face and the dead weight of his wet clothes. He closed his eyes. His ears, mouth and lungs filled with rushing water. Blindness, deafness, dumbness, breathlessness. He had never felt more wide awake, more alive, more paralysingly handicapped.

An age. A lifetime. Finally his soles touched the bottom and sank into clinging mud, sucking him downwards. Trapped. I'm trapped. Do something.

He curled his toes, making his feet small, but couldn't free them.

He tightened his lips, ballooned his cheeks.

He squatted on his haunches.

He rammed his feet into the mud.

Mightily, he pushed. Up. I'm going up. Sweet mercy.

Water washed off his spectacles. Daylight. Thank Christ. Daylight. His ears took in rushing sounds.

He filled his aching lungs with one great gulp.

More sounds. Close by. Dickie beside him, arms flaying.

'Bastard.' A scream as he rose out of the water and pressed down on Jacko's head with both hands.

Brown, airless silence again. He kept his knees flexed and kicked his legs sideways. He was being swept away, a parachutist on hurricane winds.

Didn't matter. As long as he was out of Dickie's reach. He was astonished at his clarity of thought. No panic. Just practical considerations.

To the surface again, surprising himself. On his back this time. More greedy gulps of air.

Get your coat off. It's dragging you down. He tried to pull it apart and off his shoulders, splashing, struggling. Everything was stuck to him, immovable, an extra skin.

Get some bearings. Where's the bank? He tilted his head forward. The rounded end of an island between the lock and the weir was bearing down on him, the bows of a liner.

The current was pulling him away from the still calm waters of the lock towards the weir. The traffic light on the bank showed red. There was nothing he could do to stop. What now? A first panicky thought.

A great green fish sprang out of the water, the colour of a tench, the size of a shark, terrifying him. 'Bastard.' Dickie belly-flopped over Jacko's stomach.

Under again, deafened, blinded.

His body jack-knifed. A rolling motion, left shoulder over right. He came up on his side, coughing, spitting, lungs burning with a fire that all the waters of the world couldn't put out.

Fatalistic thoughts now, acceptance. Oh, God. Make it quick. Get it over with.

He tried to pull his heavy head upright, failed. 'This . . .' A weird gurgling at his shoulder. A half-hooded head, a slimy green monster from the deep. '. . . time . . .' Gasp. '. . . bastard.'

Shoulders splashed up out of the water. Weights pressed down on the top of his head.

He somersaulted in such slow motion that time seemed to stand still. Endlessly still. Up again, face to face with him.

Dickie rose high out of the water. Jacko's unfocused eyes were not on him. A big bough from a tree was rushing towards them, skimming the surface, surfing, sodden papers and an old tyre crazily festooning its branches.

He didn't shout a warning. No breath, no time. And he wouldn't have even if he could have.

It caught Dickie on the back on the head: a dull, sickening thud, not a crack. Dickie pitched forward, face first. He vanished under the water. Gone.

A forked branch swept him up and towed him beyond the red buoys towards the safety barrage.

Everything was happening fast now.

Cracks.

Several.

One after the other.

All together.

Branches splintered against the booms. Shaking. Falling. Off his perch. From his tree. Against a cylinder. Spinning. Wildly. Like his head. Scrambling up. Spinning. Falling again. Cast aside.

A black chain appeared between two booms. He stuck out a hand. Contact. Fingers round it. Now one arm hooked it. A chance.

His legs were pulled horizontal. He looked along them. The weir was near, thunderously noisy. Closer was the island in front of the lock but still far too far away.

Fuck, he thought, matter-of-fact, without panic or rancour.

Why he hung on he never worked out. No point, really. Why add to the suffering? And suffer he did as his sleeve ripped, his arm skinned, his body stretched, the rope in a tug o' war, as the current pulled on his legs to claim him for the weir.

Numbness eased the pain. Soon his brain would numb, too. Then he could let go, accept defeat. His mind slowed down. Not long now, he comforted himself. Soon.

Tricia's wet face.

Where she came from, how she got there, he couldn't work out.

Hair, very dark, glued to her cheeks, she appeared from

behind the nearest boom. For a second he thought she was a sort of death-bed, death-bath dream.

Then he heard her. Just. She was taking deep breaths, shouting, screaming. 'Let go.'

No strength. Not a gramme. He let go. He felt his body being tugged by his trouser belt. His spinning head was jolted by a spinning boom.

At each gap between the booms she strung her arms out over the chain and faced him, her head disappearing time after time, under the waves, reappearing.

Spinning in her arms. Out again. On to the next boom. She crawled across him and beyond him, towing him to the next gap. In and out of her arms.

Only when they reached the steps up the island wall did he stay in her arms for a long, long time, hugging her, holding her for the first and last time.

Jacko, in a dry blue boiler suit, looked over the control panels out of the lock-keeper's cabin window down into the foot of the weir.

Every so often a great green fish would rise and fall back into the white foam.

They only managed a few private moments together in the packed King's Arms.

'I've something for you,' she said, digging into her shoulder bag, bringing a Colin Dexter paperback into view.

Simultaneously he fished a small box out of his pocket, gave her his present and took hers.

He rustled away yellow wrapping paper from two CD discs. 'Great Russian Classics,' one said. Among the pieces were Tchaikovsky's 1812 Overture and Prokofiev's 'Peter and the Wolf'. The other included Mozart's Serenades for Wind.

'I could tell you liked the Andante,' she said. 'It's gentle and tender.' A tender smile filled her face as she opened the box lid and looked down on a silver Imp on a tiny bed of cotton wool.

Their eyes came up and met. Hers were full of fondness. His, he hoped, weren't saying too much but he feared that they were. A bit – no, more – a part of him was dying.

Say something, he urged himself. Nothing flip like 'We'll always have Paris.' Nothing heavy like 'I only wish I didn't love you so much.' Nothing patronizing like 'I never made it with you, but I would never have made it without you.'

'In thirty years' time,' he said, 'if I live that long, I'll still be playing it and thinking of you and hoping that you are happy.'

Her wistful look. 'In another life, perhaps?'

'I hope so,' he said with as much hope in his voice and face and heart that a non-believer could muster.

Soon people pressed around them, separating them. Her chin up, unafraid, she drifted out of his life the way she had drifted in.

Just before closing time he looked around, over the heads of the crowd, but she had gone, sparing him the goodbye.